Savannah's Sentinel

Mountain Mastery Series

By
Avery Gale

© Copyright May 2017 by Avery Gale
ISBN 978-1-944472-39-9
All cover art and logo © Copyright 2017 by Avery Gale
All rights reserved.

Mountain Mastery® and Avery Gale® are registered trademarks
Published by Avery Gale Books

Thank you for respecting the hard work of this author.

This is a work of fiction. Names, places, characters and incidents either are the product of the author's imagination or are used fictitiously and any resemblance to any actual persons, living or dead, organizations, events or locales are entirely coincidental.

No part of this book may be reproduced, stored in a retrieval system, or transmitted by any means without the written permission of the author and publishing company.

WARNING: The unauthorized reproduction or distribution of this copyrighted work is illegal. Criminal copyright infringement, including infringement without monetary gain, is investigated by the FBI and is punishable by up to 5 years in federal prison and a fine of $250,000.

Chapter One

SILENTLY FUMING, LANDON Nixon leaned against the stone mantle that topped the fireplace in Nate and Taz Ledek's office. Listening to four men he liked (usually) and respected (always) patiently interview the petite blonde sitting with her back to him was snapping each of the steel cables that usually kept his iron-clad patience securely in place.

Savannah North was under the mistaken impression she'd scored a win when she'd maneuvered herself into a seat facing the other direction. She hadn't realized her error until a few seconds ago—when her gaze met his in the large mirror across the room. Landon could have told her there were very few places in the club where she'd be out of his view, but he wasn't feeling particularly charitable right now.

He'd never have agreed to be part of this mission if he'd known it meant pairing with her. Damn, the woman was the bane of his existence. She was in equal measures brilliant and impulsive, with a large layer of brash thrown in for good measure. Special Agent Savannah North had always been stunning, from her pale blonde hair to her Caribbean blue eyes. Their unique turquoise color pulled him in every time he looked at her. She personified temptation. But he'd never seen anything leading him to believe she was submissive, and that was a deal breaker for him.

Schooling his expression and hoping he could keep his personal feelings hidden from the men coordinating the rescue, Landon tried to push back his memories of the last time he and Savannah worked together. Jesus, Joseph, and sweet Mother Mary, she'd been so new to the Agency she hadn't had any business working the op, but his objections had fallen on deaf ears. His supervisor had insisted her previous work experience qualified her for the more advanced mission. *Since when did six months on the DC Metro Police Department count as experience for an international op?*

Letting his gaze roam around the room, Landon found it interesting that Nate and Taz, along with Kent and Kyle West, were all leaning back in their seats. Their body language clearly communicated their reluctance, despite the heartfelt pleading in Savannah's voice. *Fucking hell.* He might have personal issues with the woman her peers had quickly dubbed Ice Princess, but she was telling the truth. She had one small *tell* when it came to lying, and he hadn't seen it. If she'd so much as touched her hair he'd have outed her, but her hands never left her lap. At one time Landon had wondered if she would be capable of lying if she was pinned down. He'd managed—barely—to resist every subtle invitation she'd issued to find out.

Stepping forward, Landon directed his comment to the three men watching her and did his best to ignore Taz's intent gaze. The man's ability to sense the thoughts and feelings of others always seemed to peak at the most inopportune moments. "If she says the young woman is her goddaughter, then she is. Savannah isn't lying." Landon saw Kent West's lips twitch, but he'd suppressed his smile. Kyle, Kent's twin, showed no change in emotion—not that

Landon would have expected anything different. Kyle West's control had become legendary among soldiers in the Special Forces. He was just as measured and regardful in his responses leading the Prairie Winds team.

Nate Ledek was the only one who didn't try to hide his reaction. Landon and Nate had been friends for years, but they'd become particularly close since the Ledek brothers opened Mountain Mastery. The upscale fetish club was fast becoming one of the most popular kink clubs in the country.

Mountain Mastery had a different look and feel from the Wests' Prairie Winds Club, but they both followed the same strict guidelines. Vigorous pre-screening of members and stiff financial penalties for rules violations were just two of the reasons both clubs catered to elite clientele. Anything outside *safe, sane, and consensual* was strictly forbidden in both clubs. Violations of their stringent rules of confidentiality brought down hell-fire and brimstone on the perpetrator. Careers could be ruined with just a few keystrokes from Micah Drake or Phoenix Morgan, and neither man would hesitate if a member broke the trust of their fellow kinksters.

Nate's knowing smile spoke volumes about their trust. His friend knew Landon wouldn't vouch for Savannah unless he was certain. "Later, I'm going to want to hear more about why you are certain, but for now, I'm taking your word at face value." Returning his gaze to Savannah, Nate added, "Please continue. We'll need every detail you can give us in order to decide how we can best help."

Walking into Nate and Taz Ledek's office at Mountain Mastery had taken every bit of courage Savannah could muster. She'd spent nineteen hours flying to Montana from the other side of the damned globe. She'd been forced to rent a car when her Agency contact dropped the ball leaving her stranded on the fucking curb outside the airport. Then she'd driven straight from the airport to the club. Hunger and fatigue were beginning to take a toll, and she kept taking deep breaths, hoping the infusion of oxygen into her brain would buy her another couple of hours before she fell asleep on her feet.

Facing Landon Nixon had been the last thing she'd wanted to do, especially when she was feeling less than her best. But her brother's frantic phone call had pushed all her personal misgivings and anxiety to the back burner. She could deal with the man who sent her heartrate into the stratosphere and her desire rocketing out of control…the one man who'd made it clear he wasn't interested.

Giving herself a stern mental smackdown, she returned her focus to the task at hand. This didn't start out as an Agency sanctioned operation, but with her brother's connections, that would most certainly change. She could count on one hand the number of people at the Agency who were aware of her connection to the CEO of Intellicorp. Unfortunately, the anonymity she'd enjoyed was going to come to a screeching halt after this meeting.

She was a decade and a half younger than her brother, so most of his friends and business associates didn't even know she existed. He'd become a multi-millionaire before she'd even started school, and she'd always been grateful her parents had the foresight to enroll her using her grandmother's maiden name. Anytime Brit Fitzgerald intervened to help her over the years, he'd been careful to refer to her as a family friend. No one ever second guessed him, probably because super wealthy people didn't like being questioned...about anything.

Returning her attention to the men sitting around her, she fought the urge to squirm in her seat. Kyle and Kent West were damned intimidating, and adding Nate and Taz Ledek sent her anxiety into orbit. But it was Landon Nixon's presence that unnerved her the most. Just being in the same zip code with him was closer than she'd ever intended to be again.

When this was all over, Savannah was going to hug the stuffing out of her niece then rip her a new one for putting her in this position. Needing his help after he brushed her aside as if she'd been little more than a piece of lint was annoying as hell. Walking into the spacious office at Mountain Mastery and seeing him dressed in a white button down shirt and form-fitting jeans was not the reason her pulse pounded fast enough to make her light-headed. *And...I'm going to keep telling myself that until it's true.*

Taking a deep breath, Savannah refocused her attention on the reason she was here. The *only* reason she was here. There wasn't any question the top floor at the Agency only agreed to let her take time off because her brother wielded tremendous influence in Washington. DC was all about power and money, and Brit had both in abundance. And assuming her bosses didn't already know she was sitting across from the men who led the Prairie Winds team would be pure folly.

After a long, painful silence that was more about testing her than reflecting on Landon's surprising show of support, Kyle West was the first to speak. His grasp of the reins wouldn't surprise anyone who'd done their homework. It might not be his office, or his club, but Savannah doubted the former SEAL team leader allowed himself to take a back seat to anyone other than his brother. Their good cop, bad cop way of dealing with people was well known, and their mission success rate was phenomenal. The two men had recently expanded their team of contract operators and made Mountain Mastery their secondary base of operations.

Savannah wasn't sure how aware the Wests or Ledeks were about Landon Nixon's connection to the Agency. She needed to tread carefully until she could ascertain how much they knew about the man standing behind her. Damn, she'd been thrilled to find a chair facing away from his perceptive gaze. His deep blue-green eyes were too intense for her to ignore if she'd been forced to sit facing him.

"In our previous conversation, you referred to Ms. Fitzgerald as your goddaughter. How does the godmother of one of the wealthiest socialites in the country become a CIA operative?" Okay, that was a new take on the question. Her supervisor at the Agency had asked the same question, but in a notably different way. She always hesitated to reveal her connection to Brit, but if she wanted to get these men on-board with her plan, Savannah was going to have to lay it all on the line.

Looking up, her gaze locked with Landon's. His blue-green eyes watched her so intently her breath hitched. *Fuck a fudgesicle in February, how did I miss that mirror?* Taz snorted a poorly covered burst of laughter, and Savannah wondered for the first time if the stories she'd heard about him reading minds might have a thread of truth running through them.

Watching Landon push himself away from the mantle

he'd been leaning against, she held her breath when he shifted positions. The maddening man briefly disappeared from her view only to reappear a few feet to her right. He spoke to the others, but didn't take his eyes off her. "I think I can help clear this up. Savannah North, aka Savannah North Fitzgerald, is the younger sister of Brit Fitzgerald. I'd wager there only a handful of people in the Agency who know her real name."

"Well, then it seems her family has done a very good job of shielding her from the chaos that surrounds them since Micah didn't uncover this on his preliminary background check." Both amusement and frustration filled Kyle's voice. She gave him a shy smile, more out of gratitude for his charitable description of her family than for his attempt to hide his annoyance at being out of the loop. Calling the media circus that surrounded the Fitzgeralds "chaos" was a huge understatement.

Nodding in Kyle's direction, Savannah acknowledged, "From what I've heard about Micah Drake, he'd have found it on the second sweep. His computer skills are almost legendary in the intelligence community." Letting out a deep breath, she plunged ahead. "I'd wager he was looking for links to criminal organization or scorned business associates of Intellicorp. After all, who better to set up a kidnapping and then act as a negotiator than someone with an axe to grind, right? I can assure you that is not the case here. My niece and I are extremely close...more like sisters actually, since we're so near one another in age."

Savannah could feel Landon's eyes on her and fought the urge to wince under his narrow-eyed skepticism. He'd disliked her on sight, and it hadn't improved during the mission where he'd been forced to work with her. In fact, it had gotten worse...and she had only herself to blame. Why hadn't she kept her mouth shut? How had she convinced herself that his disdain was just a cover? Her vivid imagination had kicked into high gear, and she'd somehow managed to attribute her personal feelings to him. The delusion that he secretly wanted her naked and beneath him showed how young and naïve she'd been.

Realizing the room was deathly quiet, Savannah looked up and met Taz's knowing gaze. When his lips quirked up, she shook her head. "Please tell me the rumor about you being able to hear what people are thinking is just that...a rumor."

His smile was almost shy for a split second...then it turned positively sinister. "Well, it is a rumor that I can hear what *everyone* is thinking. But there are some people I can connect with—and you, Agent North, are one of the lucky ones I can hear perfectly."

Oh, yippy fucking skippy. Maybe I should head out now to buy a lottery ticket or two.

Chapter Two

LANDON LAMENTED THE fact this was going to end his low-profile status with the Agency. Nate had already been asking questions about his frequent absences. Sighing to himself, Landon knew his friend wouldn't have been mollified with lame-assed answers much longer anyway. Fucking hell, he'd never planned to be an operative. The whole thing started as a favor to a friend that fed his adrenaline addiction and then mushroomed out of control.

He'd be the first to admit his association with the Agency had been mutually beneficial. In fact, it had proven to be a financial windfall in many ways. Helping Uncle Sam and the government agencies fast-tracked his business applications, etc. Landon never asked for anything he wouldn't have gotten eventually, but he'd sure enjoyed getting his foot in the door on projects months before his competition on several occasions.

Landon's "sideline" also allowed him to keep himself out of the public eye. His business had grown exponentially, and he hadn't had to attend any of the usual corporate meet and greets he hated so much. His parents were the only people outside of the Agency who knew he occasionally worked ops. Saying they hadn't been thrilled was an understatement. As an only child, he was their sole heir. But more importantly, their hope for grandchildren fell entirely on his shoulders—a fact they mentioned with increasing frequency.

Taz's attention finally moved back to Savannah, and Landon breathed a sigh of relief. He suddenly had a lot more sympathy for Kodi. Taz and Nate had only been married a couple of months, but they'd been looking for the woman they considered "their one" for years. Her inability to shield her thoughts from them had led to more than one bare bottom spanking. Seeing her upended over any available flat surface was beginning to be a common occurrence for club regulars.

Savannah's voice drew his attention when he heard the first quivering in her words. For a couple of heartbeats, he was transported back to the only other time he'd heard her exhibit uncertainty. Turning down what she'd offered so sweetly that night had been one of the hardest things Landon had ever done. But everything about the timing had been wrong. She'd been too young, and they'd been ass deep in alligators on a sting. But his biggest issue had been her lack of sexual experience. If he'd fucked her the way he wanted to, she'd have probably run screaming into nearest convent and never been heard from again.

"My contact thought you could help me find a Dom to prepare me for the party."

Party? Is she fucking serious? Who the hell is her contact? Not even trying to hide his dismay, Landon rounded on her. "Party? You think these guys are snatching girls off the street and then throwing a soiree to introduce them to polite society?" If he hadn't been watching her closely, he might have missed her miniscule flinch, but she masked the reaction quickly. Her deliberately bland expression was as close to rolling her eyes as any Dom with his leathers would allow, and he wondered for a moment how she'd skated so close to the edge without plunging over and into the deep, dark waters of trouble.

"No. I'm simply using their term. They've issued an invitation to a Dom and his submissive to attend an upcoming *party*. Both the sexual dominant and his sex slave are fictional. They were recommended by an *insider*, an agent we've had undercover for months. The Agency has been working for two years to take down this group. It hasn't been my case, and I only heard about it recently."

Kyle leaned forward and frowned. "If they've had someone inside that long, why haven't agents already been trained? They should have had people ready to go before now." Landon understood Kyle's frustration. Protecting others was at the core of every man in the room.

"The agents who'd been preparing to attend have both left the Agency." Savannah didn't elaborate, but Landon suspected there was a lot more to the story. He wondered why two operatives who'd been training for weeks would suddenly back out of a mission.

He watched the Ledeks and Wests all exchange glances before looking at him. Savannah frowned at the men in front of her before turning her glare in his direction. "Be careful, Princess. Glaring in a room full of Doms is not a wise move." The words slipped out before he'd taken time to consider their consequences. Her eyes widened in surprise then dropped to the floor. Shock reverberated clear to his toes. *What the fuck?* Was there a submissive streak in Savannah North after all? How had he missed it?

When her gaze returned to his, the upward tilt of her chin told him the pampered Fitzgerald Princess was back in residence. "I'd prefer you didn't call me Princess."

"Why?" Simple and to the point. Landon wasn't going to let her attitude go unchallenged.

"While it may sound like an endearment when uttered by others, you and I both know that isn't what you're saying. Coming from you, it's a passive-aggressive verbal slap. The intent is to make me feel inferior as an agent because of my family's money." *Fucking hell.* The chuckles he heard from his friends told him he wasn't the only one who knew she was right, even if he was evidently the only one who didn't find it amusing.

"Point taken. I'll refrain from calling you Princess—for now." Landon gave her a small nod, but doubted she'd been fooled by his compliance. *Smart girl.* He'd already been briefed by Savannah's supervisor, but he wasn't ready to share that with her yet. The Agency wasn't officially signing off on her participation, but no one was foolish enough to hide it, either. If things went the way they were supposed to, he'd be able to call her anything he wanted to tomorrow, and there wouldn't be a thing she could do about it.

When Kent leaned forward, copying his brother's pose, Landon bit back his smile. The two men were textbook cases of mirror-image twins. He could only imagine the havoc they'd raised as kids. There'd been a set of identical twins in Landon's graduating class, and they'd caused the small school's faculty endless headaches by switching places whenever the mood struck. They'd grown up to be ministers, making Landon wonder what the world was coming to. If those two were now leading God's flock, it was terrifying to think what sort of trouble two former SEALs had caused in school.

Taz Ledek's roar of laughter brought Landon back to the present. Casting a withering stare at his friend had precisely the effect he would have predicted—none. "Don't give me that eat shit and die look, Nix. Your mind is bouncing all over the place today. What gives?"

What gives? I'll tell you what gives, you arrogant ass. Landon was usually able to block Taz's mind probing bull shit. But keeping his temper in check was robbing too much of his concentration to worry about what sort of hocus pocus the younger man used to eavesdrop.

Before he could spout off an appropriately rude response, Savannah spoke up. "I can probably answer that question. Landon isn't exactly what one would call the President of my Fan Club. I doubt he's thrilled to see me and even less so because he probably knows why I'm here." Landon felt his mouth drop open in shock. All four men burst out laughing, leaving both Landon and Savannah staring at them in shock.

KENT FINALLY RECOVERED enough to speak, but it hadn't been easy. Watching the bi-play between Landon and Savannah reminded him so much of Kyle and Tobi it was almost scary. The biggest difference? He didn't have a personal stake this time, so it was much more entertaining. When Tobi first came into their lives, Kent had been terrified Kyle was going to fuck up and scare her off. Thank God, she'd been much stronger than he'd given her credit.

"Sweetness, you remind me of another woman who completely misread a man's signals. Tobi was convinced Kyle's snarky attitude meant he didn't like her, but that wasn't the case at all. I suspect it isn't here, either, but that remains to be seen."

Savannah blinked at him in confusion, giving him another déjà vu moment. Damn. Petite, long blonde hair, gorgeous, and feisty—it was enough to make him wonder if Savannah was Tobi's long lost sister or cousin. Just thinking about his hot wife made his cock sit up and take notice. *Fuck, I'm glad we're headed home after this meeting. I can't wait to get her beneath me.*

Shaking off his wayward thoughts, Kent smiled. "I'm going to level with you, Savannah. We've already talked to your supervisor. He briefed us this morning." Landon saw Savannah's spine stiffen, but she didn't respond. *Wise decision, Princess.*

"Agent North, we've heard how the government wants this to play out. What we need to know is, how much training have you had as a submissive?" Typical Kyle. Do not pass go. Do not collect two hundred dollars—straight to the point.

Savannah's smile wasn't the reaction he'd been expecting. But it was her words that shocked the hell out of him. "I don't have any practical experience. At one time, I deluded myself that a man I was erroneously interested in was sexually dominant, but as it turned out, he was simply an arrogant ass. I'd done a lot of research prior to his rejection, but discovering he wasn't the super stud I'd built up in my mind pushed my interest in the lifestyle to the back burner."

Honest to God, Kent thought Landon's head was going to spin around on his shoulders. It took every bit of his self-control to stifle his laughter. Kyle's lips twitched, and Nate was suddenly engrossed in the contents of the file folder he'd been holding. But Taz was laughing like a loon, earning him a cheeky grin from Savannah and a death glare from Nix. Damn, she reminded him of Tobi. It was no wonder Landon looked ten seconds from stroking out.

Kyle leaned back in his chair with his arms crossed over

his chest, watching Savannah closely. Kent had been on the receiving end of that particular look his entire life. Whatever was coming next would be rife with verbal landmines.

"As my brother mentioned, we've already spoken with your supervisor and his superiors as well. The orders for this operation are coming from the highest levels. I've also talked with your brother, though I'll admit he didn't share your personal connection during our conversation." Kyle's voice was tight, and Kent knew he was editing his response for Savannah's sake. It wasn't her fault Brit Fitzgerald had failed to mention he was Savannah's brother. Kent could only imagine how well Kyle was coping with being kept out of the loop. They were both information obsessed when planning a mission—particularly when the operation was a hostage recovery—and having the target's father withhold information didn't set well. Brit Fitzgerald was going to pay dearly for the mistake.

NATE PICKED UP some of the silent by-play through his connection to Taz. But judging from the other man's hysterical laughter, Nate was certain he was missing a lot. His younger brother was a gifted empath who could usually sense what others were feeling and often would hear their thoughts as well. Unlike their grandmother, Taz hadn't developed much control over who he did or did not connect with, but she'd assured them that would come quickly now. For Nanna-son, everything good in their futures had always hinged on them finding their "one." Now that they'd found Kodi and made her their own, he and Taz had both noticed the connection between them was indeed becoming stronger. And Nate's own gifts were also strengthening, though he'd never match Taz's.

Focusing on Savannah, Nate asked, "Have you had any contact with the man since?" The question wasn't relevant to their discussion, but the expression on Nix's face was damned entertaining.

"No. I've counted myself fortunate...at least until recently." The last words were whispered so softly he might have missed them if he hadn't been looking directly at her.

Judging by Landon's body language, I'm not sure Agent North would be safe in his care tonight. He's wired way too tightly to begin now. Taz's words floated through Nate's mind, and he agreed. Amaryllis Fitzgerald deserved every chance they could give her, and that hinged on Landon and Savannah being properly prepared.

Savannah's niece had been taken right off the street one night as she left a club in New York. Thanks to a very astute witness, officials had gotten a good description of the two men who'd accosted the young woman. The college students who'd been seated at a nearby outdoor bistro had also memorized the license plate information of the black Towne Car the thugs pulled Amy into.

The information eventually led authorities to the Alvarez crime family. Unfortunately, they'd arrived at their private airfield too late to stop Amy's transport out of the country. Jose Alvarez's reputation for high-end human trafficking was well known, but so far, he'd evaded prosecution because his men were usually very careful. Their kidnappings were never random. Word on the street was the old man had recently handed over operations to his only son, and no one knew exactly what changes the younger man would make in the organization.

Amaryllis Fitzgerald fit their usual criteria in every way

except one; she had a family—a rich, well-connected family. Every man in the room knew the *real* reason Uncle Sam was allowing Savannah North to take this mission. Brit Fitzgerald might have a lot of influence, but that was secondary to the fact his sister was a dead ringer for her cousin. Both women were petite blondes with startlingly brilliant blue eyes the color of the south Caribbean Sea. They were slender, but physically fit, so they'd hold up longer to the rigors of sex slavery.

Cases like this one were a large part of the reason Nate and Taz agreed to partner with the Prairie Winds team. When a young woman from their small village was abducted a year ago, the entire community had been devastated. Sex trafficking was against everything Nate and his friends stood for—safe, sane, and consensual were more than letters behind the reception desks of clubs. Those three words were the guiding tenets of their lifestyle.

Chapter Three

LANDON WATCHED SAVANNAH with equal parts frustration and fascination. How the hell was he going to get through the next few weeks without strangling her? He'd known he hurt her feelings when he'd turned her down. Obviously, his attempt to save them both from the heartache he'd been certain would follow hadn't worked out the way he'd hoped. At the time, he'd assumed she was simply curious about the rumors continually swirling around him at the Agency. Since Landon wasn't a full-time agent and was only brought in for special cases, he'd always been something of an enigma.

Nate and Taz were doing the damned silent communication thing that drove everyone around them bat shit crazy, and for the first time, Landon knew they were talking about him. Dammit all to hell, he didn't need this complication in his life. He'd already decided to quit the Agency, it was time to start building his future. *Jesus, Joseph, and Mary, my parents' harping is starting to work.*

He'd heard the underlying pain beneath Savannah's bravado and hated that he'd caused it. The only consolation was knowing he'd done what he believed was right at the time. It was always easy to second guess decisions after more information became available. He didn't plan to fall into that trap.

Nate was intentionally pushing Savannah. He just hoped like hell his friend knew what he was doing. Despite her delicate physical appearance, The Fitzgerald Princess was as stubborn and tenacious as they came. She was also whip smart with a biting sense of humor Landon enjoyed—when he wasn't the target.

"So, there's nothing between you and this wanna-be Dom now?" Nate's eyes sparkled with mischief as he asked the question, and Landon had a sudden urge to remind the big man who'd won their last round in the ring. Taz's lips twitched, and Landon would bet the younger man knew exactly where Nate was leading her.

"No, nothing at all. I doubt it would have ever developed in to more than a brief, unsatisfying night of sex." There was that gloating expression again. Damn, he'd love to take her over his knee for that look alone. Savannah was about to get a lesson in D/s interaction she wasn't going to enjoy much. As an agent, Landon knew she'd been trained in a variety of interview techniques, but she had evidently failed the practicum. *First rule, Princess, answer the question and only the question. Don't give your interrogator any additional information to use against you later. Because he will.*

"That works, because you'll need to focus all of your attention on the Dom we're assigning to train you. He's already been approved by the Agency and your brother, so we won't entertain any protests about our decision." For the first time, Landon watched a flicker of doubt dance in her eyes. It wasn't there long, but he'd seen just a hint of insecurity. *Perfect.* He would capitalize on *that* when the time was right.

Kent grinned, and Kyle nodded before agreeing, "We're anxious to get back home, so we'll be heading out in a few minutes. We'll see you in two weeks. You and your Master will visit Prairie Winds on your way to Costa Rica. You'll get a last-minute briefing, and the team will assess your readiness for the mission."

Kent's smile disappeared as he leveled a look at Savannah. "Make no mistake, sweetness, we'll expect you to be fully trained as a sex slave when you arrive. Any flaws in your behavior will get you and your Master killed. You aren't going to be any help to your niece if you're fighting for your own life."

When Taz leaned forward and took her hand in his, Nate's eyes widened in surprise. Taz rarely touched people he'd just met, because it often established a connection that could take years to sever if things went south. "You're tired from traveling and need to rest before beginning your training. We've made arrangements for you to spend the rest of the day at the spa. Kodi will be here in a few minutes to walk you over and answer any questions you might have."

Her eyes were as round as saucers when Nate added, "I've texted the staff and had your overnight case delivered to our guest room upstairs. The rest of your luggage will be sent ahead to your new Master's home. He'll be expecting you to arrive first thing in the morning. He's already received your limit list, and we're asking you to use the club's safe word since you'll be playing here from time to time."

Landon could see her eyes were beginning to glaze over, whether from fatigue or the onslaught of information they were throwing her way, he wasn't sure. Likely it was a combination of the two, but it didn't matter—it was time to end this before he changed the plan and ordered her to strip here and now. He wanted her with him tonight, but he knew why they'd put the skids on that plan. Pushing away from the leather sofa where he'd been leaning, he nodded. "I suggest you aren't late—he's a hard ass about punctuality." Before she could ask any questions, a soft knock sounded at the door.

As he walked away, he heard Kyle speaking to Savannah behind him. "Here is a card with the phone numbers of the team members you'll be working with. Call if you need to, but let me caution you about jumping ship just because the sea gets bumpy. If we even suspect you can't handle this operation, we'll pull you. Sam and Jen McCall are available, though Sage, Jen's other husband and Sam's younger brother, is currently out of the country on a long term undercover job. They try to never all three leave the country at the same time for their young daughter's sake."

"We'll send them if we need to and pull Sage home. It'll compromise two different operations, but that's better than sending you into a dangerous situation you're not prepared for." Kent's voice took on a hard edge Landon hadn't heard before. Evidently, there was a hard ass beneath the man's easy-going façade after all.

Nate stood and offered her his hand as Kodi walked into the room. "What we're telling you is, when you're frustrated or start feeling rebellious, remember why you started." When she finally nodded in agreement, Nate introduced the two women and sent them on their way.

After the door closed behind them, Landon saw a rare smile move across Kyle West's usually stoic face. "Do you have cameras at your front entrance, Landon? I'd pay good money to see the look on her face when you open the door." Kyle's sense of humor didn't surface often, but it was wicked when it came out to play. Landon shook his head at the other man's inappropriate remark. "You've got your work cut out for you, man. She is going to be seven kinds of pissed." The others laughed as they nodded their heads as the meeting broke up. Fucking hell, they looked like a group of damned bobbleheads.

"She'll call you before lunch, mark my word. I'll be surprised if she makes it out of the front foyer before she's digging your card out of her pocket." Savannah's temper was going to light up like a drought fueled timber fire. She was a competent agent, though he didn't think the Agency had ever pushed her enough to find out how very capable she was. Savannah might think she'd escaped the boundaries her family wanted to erect for her, but her brother still orchestrated things from the background.

"I've told the spa technicians exactly what I expect. Don't give her the directions to my place until she's ready to walk out the door tomorrow morning." Nate and Taz both nodded, knowing she'd use her phone to research who owned the property. His dad had buried the information deep in several holding companies, but given enough time, she could eventually uncover the truth.

Nate patted him on the back as they all walked from the room. "Kodi won't spill the beans, either. She's had crystal clear instructions, and since she's already sporting a very tender bottom, she won't be anxious to earn another paddling for a while." Landon chuckled. He'd seen the fit she'd thrown last night when Nate and Taz told her they'd be buying her a new car. She'd politely declined their offer, assuring them she had the money to buy one when and if it became necessary. But all traces of *polite* flew out the window the minute she discovered they'd already disposed of her old car. She'd been upended over one of the stools in front of the bar before she'd finished her tirade. The hickory paddle they'd used resounded around the room with every swat.

Sighing to himself, Landon knew he needed some time to decompress before tomorrow morning, and he still wanted to meet with the household staff. His housekeeper, driver, and cook had been part of the lifestyle for years, but until now, Landon had never brought a submissive into his private living space. His private playroom was in the basement and included an attached bedroom and bathroom. There was a separate entrance, and all the doors leading to other parts of his home were secured with coded locking systems.

He'd never had a sex slave and wasn't thrilled with the idea. He'd called several friends around the world, seeking their input on the training regime he and Nate had put together. The next two weeks were going to be a challenge on multiple levels. Landon also wanted to talk to Senator Karl and Dr. Tally Tyson. He'd become their third not long after the disaster with Savannah two years ago, and he valued their friendship. The three of them had already discussed Landon's need to move on, but he wanted to discuss it with them personally. Club gossip would spread like wildfire, and he respected Karl and Tally too much to let their special relationship end that way.

SAVANNAH BREATHED A sigh of relief as soon as Kodi Ledek closed the door separating them from the testosterone soup in Nate and Taz's office. "Snails fuck faster than that meeting. I didn't think I'd ever get out of there." Kodi snickered as she led Savannah down a long hallway. "How long will it take us to drive to the spa? Do you want me to follow you? I'm starving and could use something to drink.

Do we have time to stop along the way?"

Kodi keyed in a code unlocking a heavy wooden door and motioned her through. "The spa is on-site. I'm sure they'll have something for you to eat, but we'll swing by the buffet table and see what's there on our way through the main room. It's very early, but we might find something you'll like. And I know where the bottles of water are kept behind the bar, so we'll grab a couple of those, also."

Savannah filled her plate as Kodi pointed out the best fare and then followed the other woman to the bar. The pretty brunette pulled bottles of water from a large cooler before heading to a door Savannah hoped led to the spa. "I loved your book. I'm going to get a paperback for you to sign. Damn, girl, that book is hot."

Kodi's cheeks flushed bright red despite her tanned skin tone. "Wow. Thanks so much. I don't get to talk to many readers face to face, so I'm really at a loss here. I have a couple of copies in my office. I'll sign one for you when we get back upstairs."

"I assume the former SEAL studs are Nate and Taz. Did they know they were erotic romance stars?" Savannah was pleased to hear Kodi's giggle. "Sorry, sometimes my filter doesn't work very well."

"Filter?"

"You know, the one that's supposed to edit brash personal questions before they fly out of my mouth? I think it gets clogged up by all the inappropriate things my brain cooks up, so the excess unfiltered comments make their way out the spillway." *Cripes, she's going to think I color way outside the lines if I keep talking like this. Nothing like advertising the fact you've escaped from the cracker factory, Savannah.*

"No worries, I still have that trouble at times, but I try to channel it into my characters now. It's easy to control the outcome when I'm the one writing it. Not so easy in my personal life. What was I thinking marrying two Doms? Probably should have my head examined." This time it was Savannah's turn to laugh.

"I can't even imagine. I've never been able to deal with any man for more than a week. The next few weeks are going to be hell on Earth." Grabbing Kodi's arm before she could open the door to the Mountain Mastery Spa, Savannah asked, "Do you know who they've chose to train me?"

Kodi's face flushed again as her eyes dropped to the floor, and for a few seconds, Savannah wondered if she would lie. "Yes, but I'm not allowed to tell you. What I can tell you is they've chosen a man I like and respect. He's tough, but he's fair." Savannah didn't say anything as she considered Kodi's words. Granted she didn't know her well, but she had worked with Kodi's brother, Koi. If she was as honest as he was, Savannah had nothing to worry about. "I'm sorry. I'd love to tell you, but I'm already sporting a sore bum for arguing with my Masters about a car."

Realizing she was still holding Kodi's arm, Savannah released her and nodded. "No problem. I understand. In my line of work, keeping secrets can save your life, so I get it." They stepped into the spa, and she wanted to cry with relief. The soothing music and refreshing scents calmed her like nothing else could. Working almost non-stop for the past several weeks had taken a toll on her body and spirit. A little pampering would surely go a long way to restore some peace in her soul. She could already feel a sense of calm moving through her.

Stepping up to the reception desk, Savannah casually perused the services list, trying to prioritize what she wanted most. She'd been so lost in thought she hadn't been listening to Kodi's conversation with the woman behind the desk until the pretty redhead gently pulled the list from her hand. "You're Savannah North, correct?"

"Yes. I was just trying to decide what I'd like to schedule. Which services have openings?"

Kodi shook her head and held up her hand. "Your Master has already taken care of all the arrangements." When Savannah stiffened, Kodi smiled. "It's not unusual. Mine have always done the same thing for me. I know it's hard to understand. There's a part of you that wants to push back every time they take over. But if you'll just roll with it, at least occasionally," Kodi's eyes danced with amusement and understanding, "you might enjoy the freedom it'll give you."

The receptionist gave her a knowing smile and added, "And, honey, you look beat. Is this really a fight you want to take up? Because better things are waiting behind that door, I promise you."

Savannah felt her shoulders sag in resignation. Dammit, her hands looked like she'd done a week's dishes in scalding water with lye soap. She hoped like hell her new pretend Master had lined up a manicure, because she might burst into tears of pure frustration if he hadn't. "Fine. But I'm going on record as saying if I don't get a massage and a manicure, I won't be responsible for my actions." The two women grinned and nodded. Savannah rolled her eyes at their enthusiasm and then laughed. *Roll with it, she says. Okay, let's do this.* Stuffing the last crumbs of her finger sandwich into her mouth, she groaned in satisfaction. "God in heaven, please tell me there's wine."

Chapter Four

Nate leaned against the brick wall with his arms crossed over this chest watching his bride and Savannah North bump into each other as they made their way out of the spa. Glancing to his side, he shook his head at the expression on his friend's face. Landon Nixon looked like he was about to pop a vessel. "Problem, Nix?" He didn't even try to keep the amusement out of his tone.

"They're sloshed." Landon's words were practically growled. "What if Kodi told her? She'll bolt."

And there it was, a crack in Landon Nixon's infamous iron-clad control. "I don't think so. My guess is they covered that topic on the way to the spa, so they wouldn't have gone back to it. Submissives are better at accepting secrets than we are. Dom's demand answers, but if their personality is naturally submissive, women can shrug off not knowing." It was actually something he admired about subs. He'd always been a bit in awe of their ability to live in the moment.

"I'm tempted to load her happy ass up and haul her home with me tonight."

Nate understood. A Dom's instinct was to shelter and protect when there was any perceived risk to the submissive in his care. And a beautiful, intoxicated woman would be at risk out on the street. But since she was only heading upstairs with Kodi, both teetering beauties would be under his watchful eye, so safety wasn't an issue.

"Probably not the best way to start. She needs to have some filters in place when she finds out you're the one training her. It's going to be a big enough of a challenge the way it is." Landon nodded, but Nate had the impression he wasn't entirely sold on the idea of waiting. "She'll be fine this evening. She needs rest, and the wine will help her sleep."

"I saw her flight schedule home. I'm not sure what her handler was thinking. He knew we needed to get started right away, but her itinerary was brutal. Sending her on a mission site on the tail of another job with almost twenty hours of travel time was an invitation to trouble." Nate had never seen his friend so "frazzled," as his mother used to say. He'd never fully understood what that meant until meeting Kodi. And damned if she couldn't *frazzle* him and Taz with nothing more than a sultry glance.

Shaking his head when Kodi couldn't get the private elevator to work, Nate pushed away from the wall. "I'm going to rescue our damsels in distress. It seems my lovely wife can't stand still long enough for the biometric reader to kick in." Telling the spa staff to let Kodi and Savannah have all the wine they wanted might have been a mistake. Every time the error message pinged, the two of them dissolved into a fit of giggle.

"How long until Phoenix calls about all the failed attempts to get into your living space?" Landon's wry tone was the first glimpse of the man's dry sense of humor, which was never far below the surface. Landon Nixon might look like the quintessential, carefree California surfer from the 1960's, but Nate knew the façade was smoke and mirrors.

He'd watched Landon play for years and was aware how committed he was to the lifestyle. Nate had often wondered if he'd end up with a full-time slave, something he nor Taz had ever been interested in. Landon was a serious player, but insisted he didn't want the responsibility of a slave. He was ordinarily an excellent teacher, but Nate had a feeling this was going to be different. Nate sensed there was history between these two, but now wasn't the time to push for answers. He hoped they could set aside whatever personal issues they had and work together. Amy Fitzgerald's life depended on it.

LANDON FOLLOWED NATE to the elevator. He hadn't intended to, but his feet must not have gotten the memo because they'd started moving all on their own. When Kodi turned and saw her Master approaching her entire face lit up. "Hi, Master Hottie Number One. I'm glad you're here. That palm tree thingy keeps moving."

Landon heard Nate's soft chuckle. "Do you mean the palm readers, Ayasha?" Nate's pet name for his submissive meant 'little one' and always make her melt against her enormous husband. How two men over six and a half feet tall ended up with such a petite wife was a mystery to him.

"Oh, yeah. Palm something or other. Anyway, it moves around and doesn't work. Can you help us get upstairs? We're all waxed and painted and trimmed and lotioned-up. It didn't hurt as much this time. My pain toes...totter...tollhouse...no, wait, that's cookies. What's the word for handling alcohol?"

Savannah laughed, "Damn, Kodi. You're a lightweight...even worse than me. The word is tolerance. And you were talking about pain, not alcohol. Although I think they both are applicable here."

Kodi spun around to stare at her new friend, her mouth gaping open in surprise. "Holy crap on a cactus. You drank as much as I did, and you are only weaving a little. What gives?"

Savannah looked around, but missed Landon standing to the side listening. "Well, I've probably had more practice. My parents drank wine with meals, so I'm pretty immune to it. But mix up a batch of margaritas and it's on, girl. I'll be dancing on the table before I've finished the first one. Remember that song about tequila making her clothes fall off? I'm pretty sure that song writer and I went to college together."

"Really? Or are you being fact...facility....faci....well, fuck it. Are you for real or is that just..." She didn't get to finish her sentence before Nate gave her a hard swat. "Hey, what the devil was that for? I didn't even find the word I wanted."

"I'll bet I know. I read some books about this stuff. Nate started looking all snarly when you said the f-word." She shifted her gaze up to Nate and grinned. "Ha! I'll bet you thought I was going to say it, too...and I didn't so you don't get to spank me." Landon rolled his eyes. She'd just thrown down a challenge Nate Ledek wasn't going to let slide. Hell, no Dom worth his leathers would walk away from that one.

Nate gave her two solid swats before she'd even realized he was moving. Her look of surprise would have been amusing if he wasn't itching to do it himself. "Hey! I didn't say the synonym for sex. No fair swatting me for no reason."

"I don't need a reason. You're in my care. I'm a Dom, and you are a submissive. I can swat you simply because I enjoy feeling your ass beneath my palm." Nate's no-nonsense tone and explanation obviously hadn't impressed her.

Savannah stomped her foot and glared up at the club owner. "Didn't your mama teach you that it is not nice to put your hands on a woman's ass until after you feed them?" The look on Nate's face was priceless, and Landon's snort of laughter gave him away. She spun so quickly she almost lost her balance, but he'd covered the short distance in record time and grasped her elbow to keep her from falling. "Dammit to donuts, it's not nice to lurk, you know. I'm gonna have Fiona send a copy of Emily Post's latest rules of polite company." Landon grinned at her use of air quotes. "She'll probably send a lifestyle coach, too. You don't want to get on Fiona Fitzgerald's etiquette hit list, trust me. Been there, done that."

"What the hell—o, is she talking about? Wow, my head is spinning from watching Master Landon move like The Flash. Good grief."

Landon shook his head at Kodi and grinned at Nate. "I assume you're staying upstairs with these two so they don't hurt themselves or burn the place down?"

"Taz and I planned to rotate this evening since we're expecting a full house. But I may change my mind about taking the first shift." Nate held the door of the elevator open and waited for both women to step in before turning his attention back to Landon. "I'll be back down in an hour. Don't warn Taz, or he'll stall." The last comment earned him a glare from both women, and Landon heard his friend's growl as the doors slid closed.

Walking back toward the bar, Landon couldn't help

but wonder how Savannah was going to react when he opened the door tomorrow morning. Part of him hoped she threw in the towel. But a larger need gnawed in his gut...the need to dominate her already bubbled deep inside him. The boiling cauldron of desire burned his patience to a crisp. Pulling one of the expensive imported bottles of beer from the cooler, Landon slipped back out from behind the bar. He wasn't working this evening, but he wasn't ready to go home, either.

"Hit the gym. That's what I do." Turning to look at Taz, Landon narrowed his eyes as frustration threatened to spill over.

"Kodi's right, you are a fucking ninja." Landon had worked with Kodi before her marriage, and she'd sworn the two club owners were as silent as ninja warriors. "You Special Forces guys always move like jungle cats. I'm starting to wonder if you take a special class or something."

"And you, my friend, are deliberately spewing crap as a distraction. Too late, I already felt all your frustration. Hell, I didn't need any special empathetic gifts to see your agitation. Helen Keller could have seen it."

"You're a real fucking comedian, you know that? You deserve your time upstairs. You need a drink limit for the spa. Your wife is sloshed."

"Damn. I need to get up there. Alcohol is truth serum for her. I'll be able to find out what she's getting me for my birthday." Taz's grin told Landon he didn't care jack about snooping on a birthday gift.

"Of course, you'd never dream of pushing a boundary or two with your inebriated wife."

"Nope, I'm a regular choir boy." Landon snorted a laugh and cursed when the beer burned the back of his throat.

"Choir boy my ass." Nate's voice sounded from Landon's other side. How the hell did they do that? Landon was a trained operative for Christ's sake. Being aware of his surroundings was often the difference between life and death. "I shudder to think about the lightning bolt powering up to strike you for that comment."

"Bite me, big brother. Why aren't you upstairs keeping our woman out of trouble?"

Nate rolled his eyes and snagged the beer Randy set on the bar for him. Ann, the bartender's Mistress, waved from the other end of the long bar. "I pointed them both toward their respective showers. If I'd stayed with Kodi, we wouldn't have come out of there for hours, and I didn't want to leave Savannah alone. I get the impression she is more worried about tomorrow than she's letting on."

"Well, get up there before they decide to reheat whatever Rosie left us to eat. We don't need another visit from the local firefighters. Jesus, Joseph, and Mary, the last time they were here when the club was open we like to never got them back out the door."

Landon laughed. "And from what I heard, none of their wives were any too pleased."

All it had taken was one man trying to talk his wife into letting him cuff her to the bed for the gossip to spread like wildfire. Of course, the truth was no match for the imaginations of pissed off wives. The men had only walked through the club's main room. Thank God they hadn't gotten a glimpse of the dungeon.

"I'm glad the mayor is a member. He was finally able to shut down all the chatter. I don't know what those women are reading or where they're getting it, but some of the kinky shit they were saying we'd exposed their darling husbands to was way over the top." Nate's voice was tight, and Landon knew he was still pissed. He'd spent the better part of three days answering calls from angry wives, and there are only so many ways to say, "Our rules of confidentiality prevent me from answering your questions" before it started sounding rude.

Landon grinned. "Did you notice you didn't hear a peep from the husbands of the two female firefighters? Hell, I'm betting they were too busy enjoying the perks to complain."

Taz nodded in agreement. "I told the mayor he might want to think about an all-female department." *Probably not a bad idea, considering how the whole disaster went down.* "He asked that Nate and I bar Kodi from the kitchen until he can make it happen." Taz's laughter was contagious, and Landon began to relax.

"I'm heading home. Give me a call when Savannah leaves here in the morning. I want to be sure I'm the one who opens the door. I'm afraid Lenore will spoil her rotten if I don't keep the two of them apart." His cook would have her lounging by the pool eating chocolate covered strawberries if he wasn't careful.

Saying his goodbyes, Landon made his way to the parking lot. The hair on the back of his neck stood up, and he glanced around the darkened lot, but didn't see anything out of the ordinary. Just as he shifted the small sports car into gear, Landon looked up and froze. One of the windows on the top floor framed the silhouette of a woman shifting from one yoga pose to another. Every detail of her graceful movement was now burned into his memory. Her perfectly rounded breasts and peaked nipples, the well-defined arms artfully positioned to aid her balance, and long legs shaped by toned muscles. His hunger for her raged out of control.

Her movements were fluid with no wasted effort. He watched her hold poses many advanced students struggled with. He'd learned yoga when he was a teenager, a counselor at school had suggested it as a way to help him learn to control his temper. Fencing helped vent some of his physical aggression, but yoga soothed his soul.

Swallowing back the temptation to stay where he was and enjoy the show, Landon slammed the car back into gear and tore out of the lot like the hounds of hell were on his tail. He'd double check to make sure everything was in place and remind his staff of the rules he'd put into place. Checking in with Karl and Tally would take a little longer, but it was important. Then he'd spend a couple of hours in his home gym, because exhaustion was going to be his only hope for sleeping tonight after what he'd just seen.

Chapter Five

Koi Green limped across the mat and swiped the sweat from his brow with the back of his arm. He'd only done two sets of katas, and he was already weaving on his feet. Rehabbing his leg was taking much longer than he'd anticipated, and he was growing more frustrated by the day. "Fucking pussy, suck it up and do it again."

"I'm not sure who you're talking to, but I'm hoping it's not me."

Koi spun around so fast his leg cramped, and he couldn't hold back his grimace. The pretty brunette standing behind him smiled. It took a second for Koi to recognize her—he wasn't sure if it was fatigue or the fact he hadn't been expecting anyone, much less a woman from Mountain Mastery, to walk into the Prairie Winds Club gym.

"Brinn, what a pleasant surprise." He hoped his smile backed up his words, because his trouble radar was spinning wildly out of control.

To her credit, she dropped her gaze and seemed genuinely humbled by his response. "I know you probably aren't thrilled to see me. Between my horrible behavior toward Kodi and following you after we had dinner, I doubt I'm on your potential BFFs list."

"Potential what?" Christ, his sister used to assume he

knew all the latest slang acronyms—and he never had.

"Oh, sorry. Best friend forever. I just wanted to stop and check on you. The company I work for is starting a big project here, so I'll be in Texas for a few months. I asked Master Nate about suspending my membership while I'm here. He talked Kyle into letting me transfer here. I appreciated their cooperation. It's nice to be able to hang out with like-minded people."

Koi wasn't convinced Brinn was as committed to the lifestyle as she claimed, but he wasn't interested enough to argue with her. "I want to thank you for your help after the accident. If you hadn't been *curious* and followed me, I probably would have died."

She flushed a pretty pink, and for the first time, he noticed how young she looked. The night he'd met her at the club, she'd just come from work. Her professional clothing had given her an air of sophistication that was missing today. With her hair pulled back into a high ponytail and her bright colored flip-flips, she reminded him more of a college coed than an engineering professional. Her frayed jean shorts and skin-tight tee shirt highlighted a world class set of legs and rack. But the sad fact was she didn't flip any of his sexual switches.

"You're welcome. I wish I could explain away my behavior, but I can't. But I want you to know I'm trying very hard to make some changes in my life." Koi heard the door behind him slam open and the sound of boisterous voices before they suddenly fell silent. Brinn's eyes went wide before her checks flamed scarlet, and her gaze once again dropped to the floor. "Well, I'd better get going. I...well, I just wanted to say hi and to apologize. I hope we can still be friends."

"I'd like that, Brinn. I don't think anybody can ever

have too many friends." Koi meant what he'd said despite the fact he didn't have many female friends. He had plenty of women in his past, but he rarely played with the same woman more than a few times. And it was very unusual for their paths to cross once the sexual part of their relationship ended—he made sure of it.

"Agreed. You've been holding out on us, Green." Koi glanced to his side and grinned at the expression on Parker's face. He'd met the recently promoted Chief of Police when he first moved to one of the small cottages behind the Prairie Winds club several weeks ago. Parker might have been talking to Koi, but his eyes hadn't left Brinn. Standing several inches over six foot, with blonde hair and blue eyes, Parker Andrews didn't have any trouble attracting women. Koi also knew the Chief and the man standing to his left shared their women.

Kent had introduced Koi to Dan Deal during his first week in the rehabilitation hospital. After a near fatal car accident in Montana, Koi had been transferred to a facility not far from the Prairie Winds Club. Kent and Kyle had been trying to recruit him for their team of contract operatives, and he'd been on his way to meet with them when his handler at the CIA ran him off a mountain highway.

Koi found out later the man had been under investigation for months. The handler had been on the take for several years and wrongly assumed Koi was the one who'd turned him in. The asshole had made hundreds of thousands of dollars selling out his fellow operatives and compromising missions. Koi had been understandably angry when he first arrived in Texas, and Dan had helped him deal with those feelings. The psychologist had a successful practice locally and helped the Wests vet club members and screen potential team members. He'd become friends with both men over the past few months since they often worked out together in the gym at the same time. But neither of his new friends looked at him today—their gazes were locked on Brinn Peters.

After introducing the three of them, Koi chuckled at how quickly the two men ushered her to the other side of the room. He couldn't hear their conversation, but he didn't miss them handing her their business cards before she finally made her way out of the building.

Sweetie, you'd better think long and hard about hooking up with those two. You won't be able to hide anything, and they won't be fooled by any of your usual nonsense, either.

SAVANNAH RUBBED HER sweating palms down the sides of her skirt and looked back up at the biggest door she'd ever seen. The home itself was enormous and spread out over what looked like enough space to build a football field. She guessed the landscaped front yard covered five or more acres. It had taken her several minutes to make her way to the door. Savannah stood mesmerized by the fountains bubbling at the center of the circle drive.

Sighing again, she peered up at the mammoth structure. *Hopefully, he'll give me a map.* Just thinking about the man she'd be working with sent a shiver skittering up her spine. She'd tried to wheedle information from the Ledeks during breakfast, but all three of them remained tight-lipped. Their reluctance to tell her anything about the man who would train her for the mission added to her anxiety.

When she'd walked into the office at the Mountain

Mastery club yesterday, Savannah wondered if Landon Nixon would be her trainer. The way he'd looked down his perfect nose at her made it clear he'd rather be anywhere but in the same room with her. Savannah didn't understand her frustrating push-pull attraction to him, but he turned on her sexual arousal buttons and spiked her frustration at the same time.

Sucking in a deep breath, Savannah shoved all thoughts of Landon Nixon aside. Reminding herself why she was here, she sent up a silent prayer Amy would remain safe until the party her kidnappers were planning. *Party. Yeah, right. A thinly veiled excuse for a sex slave auction.* Reaching forward, Savannah took another deep breath and pressed the doorbell.

Footsteps sounded on the other side of the door followed by the loud clicking of the locks disengaging. Time slowed to a crawl as the heavy door opened. Savannah didn't realize she'd dropped her gaze until the first thing that came into view was a pair of bare feet topped by the frayed hem of well-worn jeans. She'd never considered men's feet particularly sexy, but his were long and sun-kissed tan, making her think of hours spent walking on the beach soaking up the sun and listening as relentless waves splashed over the shifting sand.

Her eyes slowly traveled north, noting the tears outlined by soft tufts where the threads unraveled naturally after repeated laundering. The man in front of her had long, slender legs leading to an impressive erection pressing against his zipper. She licked her lips before she could censor the movement. His narrow waist showcased tanned, deliciously bare skin exposed even more than would ordinarily be visible because he'd left the top snap of his jeans open to highlight a golden arrow of hair pointing south. Large hands bracketed his waist, and Savannah felt her face heat when she thought about them touching her intimately.

A well-defined six-pack attested to enough time in the gym to keep himself physically fit. And muscled biceps curved into broad shoulders. Her visual perusal paused at the base of his neck while she took a bracing breath. There was something familiar about his posture, and she closed her eyes and sent up a silent prayer that her instincts were misleading her. Surely the Universe wouldn't be that heartless.

"Princess, open your eyes and look at me." Landon Nixon's voice wrapped itself around her so tightly Savannah's breath hitched. The words had been softly spoken, but an underlying thread of steel ran through them, ensuring she recognized them as the command they'd been. Lifting her lashes, she was shocked to find him standing much closer than he'd been a few seconds ago. His ability to move silently didn't surprise her, but she was humbled to realize she hadn't sensed his approach.

Tilting her head back to meet his gaze, Savannah started to shake her head and step away, but his frown stopped her. "Your safe word is red. Use it and we're done. You go back to the pansy-assed missions the Agency sends your way, and your niece gets sold to some depraved piece of shit who'll use her until there's nothing left." He shifted to cross his arms over his chest. Standing this close, she could feel the heat from his body radiating against her skin.

"This will never work. You hate me." Even she could hear the note of disillusionment in her voice, so there was little chance he'd missed it. The admission made her stomach flip over, but it didn't matter since she didn't stand any chance of walking away from this encounter with her dignity intact.

Something akin to surprise flashed in his eyes for a heartbeat before it was gone. For the first time, she saw a chip in his cool façade. She'd surprised him, and he obviously didn't enjoy the feeling. "I don't hate you." Stepping back, he motioned her inside, and she took a reluctant step forward before her feet glued themselves to the floor of his polished stone porch. "It's true that I'm not sure you'll be able to submit convincingly enough to pull off this mission. But I don't hate you."

Savannah's heart sank. If she backed out, she might well be signing Amy's death warrant. She would let down every single member of her family and would likely never again see the woman she loved like a sister. Every minute she stood out here whining about Landon hating her was wasted. Chewing on her bottom lip, Savannah studied his expression and worked to push aside her personal issues with the man assigned to train her.

Suck it up, Savannah. Learn what you need to and leave everything personal outside this door.

LANDON STOOD PERFECTLY still while Savannah fought an internal battle he already knew she couldn't win. Her hot gaze moving from his feet upward had tested his control, and he hadn't even gotten her inside the damned house yet. This whole operation had disaster written all over it. No matter how badly he wanted to sink his aching cock into her, Savannah North was a weakness he couldn't afford.

He weathered her visual caress without growling at her

and considered it no small feat. She got to him in a big way. Fucking hell, the next three weeks were going to be torture. Two weeks of training followed by a week in Costa Rica would probably drive him out of his mind—unless he strangled her first. As soon as he'd ordered her to open her eyes and look at him, Landon had seen her body language switch from heated sexual awareness to ice cold denial. Hell, he'd almost been able to hear the bricks slapping together as she built the wall around her. *Not this time, Princess. You won't be able hide anything from me when we're through.*

When she finally stepped into his home's large entry, he regarded her as she studied her surroundings. Landon had been in her brother's home, so he knew she was no stranger to beautiful residences. But her look of appreciation seemed genuine, and her smile told him he'd surprised her.

"I'd be lying if I didn't say I'm impressed. Your home is beautiful and not at all what I expected."

For the first time since he'd met her, Landon felt like his smile was genuine. "Thank you—I think." He knew what she meant. He'd heard the same comment from friends and family since he'd remodeled his parent's home. The outside still blended into the mountain surroundings, but the inside had been completely transformed. He'd removed most of the walls, preferring to distinguish the different areas with furnishings. He also added several water features, including a miniature lazy river that meandered through the cavernous room adding much needed moisture to the dry mountain air.

The ceiling in the main room was three stories high, and the front wall was made entirely of glass. Morning light streamed through the windows highlighting the various trees and plants. "It looks like a botanical garden. It's lovely." Savannah wandered to the edge of the room, but hadn't gone any farther. He wondered if she'd instinctively sensed she needed permission or if she was staying close to the door to make a hasty exit.

"Thank you. I enjoy it. Montana is beautiful, but there is nothing like the rain forest to restore your soul."

She turned to him and smiled. "It's an amazing refuge. Your job is very stressful, and I'm sure this helps diffuse the tension. Although…no, never mind."

"Tell me. There can be no secrets between us. This operation is unlike any other, Princess. If you're holding back, trained sexual Dominants will see it. And if they get even an inkling that you're not who or what you are supposed to be, everyone's life is in danger." He paused until she nodded her understanding. "Now, what were you going to say?"

"Well, I thought maybe you were a member at the club to blow off steam. But this seems like it would be even better." She might have been talking to him, but her eyes were wandering around the open space. He could practically hear her mind cataloging as many details as possible. Landon had watched other women do the same thing. The difference? Savannah was absorbing the aesthetics, not calculating value. He hadn't considered the impact that difference would make—but it was huge.

He'd never spent much time with women who were his financial equal, in part because there weren't many available. Perhaps he should reevaluate his options. The sudden realization he was painting Savannah North with a different brush brought his thinking to a screeching halt. Pushing those thoughts aside, he recentered himself. They needed to get down to business.

"We only have a limited time to prepare, so we need to get started." When she didn't return her attention to him, Landon wanted to growl in frustration. "Face me, Savannah." His use of her given name and the sharp tone of his voice had the desired effect. She spun back to him, eyes wide in surprise.

"When I'm speaking to you, you will look at me unless otherwise directed. I need to be able to judge your reactions, and there is a lot of truth in the old adage about the eyes being the windows to the soul." She didn't respond, and he reminded himself she'd had no formal training because he wasn't going to count the books she'd claimed to have read. He'd read books that were filled with nonsense no real Dom would tolerate, so he was discounting her research until he had more information.

"Did you read the documentation in your room last night?" Landon already knew Nate and Taz had both double checked that she'd found and read everything he'd left for her. But he wanted to hear it for himself.

When she nodded, he raised a brow and waited. "Yes, Sir. I read everything, but I have a couple of questions."

"Ask now, before we go any further." Landon had anticipated this, hell, he'd have been worried if she didn't have any questions. The contract he'd drafted was extremely broad, and he couldn't imagine her signing it without a few modifications.

"I don't want to give up my cell phone. I'll agree to stash it while we're training, but I don't want to be completely cut off from the outside world for two weeks."

"I'll agree to give you an hour each day to catch up on messages. In exchange, you'll avoid all social media until we've returned from Costa Rica." He raised his hand when she started to protest. "I'm not implying you would share anything that would compromise the mission, but their tracking methods are very sophisticated, and it's not worth the risk."

He watched her expression soften as she came to the same conclusion. She finally grinned. "I rarely check my social media accounts anyway, but I'll cop to enjoying the videos on Tumblr."

Landon couldn't hold back his chuckle at her honesty. "I assure you you'll have no need for mini-pornos while we're together." *What the hell?* He needed to get his head back in the game.

Chapter Six

SAVANNAH WORKED HARD to ensure her expression didn't give away her surprise at Landon's comment. She certainly didn't plan to read more into it than she should...she'd already made the mistake of misreading his signals once. She wouldn't subject herself to that humiliation again. Voices sounded from the next room, breaking the uneasy silence. When she started to turn her head, strong fingers stopped her. The callouses on the tips of his fingers attested to a man who didn't spend all his time behind a desk, and she wondered how much more there was beneath his cool exterior.

"Eyes on me, Princess. My staff is not your concern. You have a single objective, pleasing your Master. When you are with me, it's my job to worry about who sees you, who touches you, and who speaks to you." Landon's gaze never left her face, he was studying her. But rather than feeling like some sort of science experiment, it gave her an odd sense of safety that she couldn't explain so she pushed it aside.

"Your eyes are so expressive—every thought, every emotion plays in them for all the world to see." His last words were spoken almost reverently, and she felt her body lean toward him. Stiffening her posture, Savannah reminded herself why she was here...and it wasn't to open her heart to another thrashing.

"Any other questions before we begin? If not, I'll make the change to the contract and reprint it later." He still held her chin firmly in his grasp, focusing her attention on him. Savannah drew in a deep breath. He smelled of soap and warm sunshine. She'd noticed the tips of his sun-bleached hair were still damp when she'd arrived, making her wonder if she'd arrived earlier than he'd expected. Since she'd slept very little last night, she hadn't considered how early it was until after she'd already driven through the security gate just off the highway. The gates swung open as she approached, and she'd laughed because it was obvious Nate or Taz had given him a heads-up she was on her way.

"Princess, you are going to have to learn to stay *present* or you're going to earn a lot of time over my knees."

Blinking him back into focus, Savannah wanted to groan. "Sorry. I didn't get much sleep, and fatigue makes it hard for me to concentrate sometimes."

He nodded once and then firmed his lips into a tight line. "Understood. I'll watch for that." She wasn't sure exactly what he meant, but didn't think this was the time to push the issue. "Do you have any more questions?"

Licking her lips, she considered all the questions that had been running through her mind since the meeting yesterday. His eyes dilated as they focused on the tip of her tongue tracing the curve of her lower lip. Her breath hitched at the fire she saw in his eyes. She'd never reacted to a man the way she did with Landon. He was her kryptonite…and she needed to remember that.

"I'll be able to ask questions later, right?"

He raised a brow as if he wasn't sure he'd heard her correctly. "Savannah, you are not a prisoner. The restrictions I've imposed are to help you focus while you're learning. It ensures the integrity of the mission. I'll always answer your questions, if they are asked respectfully. Keep in mind being respectful includes asking at the appropriate time, either before or after a scene. You'll be using the stoplight safe word system most clubs use because it's simple and I don't want you focused on anything but learning what you'll need to know." He studied her for several seconds before continuing. "If you don't have any more questions, we need to get started. You're overthinking this, and I want to get you out of your head."

"I'll get my things, and then I'll be ready to start." Her voice was more tentative than usual, but she hadn't run out the front door screaming...*yet*, so he was counting their first encounter as a *win*.

"Your bag has already been brought in, and your car is secured in the underground garage."

Savannah was only marginally surprised. Her brother was much the same way. *Bossy.* Luggage always magically appeared in her room, and her car seemed to move about the estate all on its own. His posture shifted just as she opened her mouth to speak. "Do you know my brother?" Not sure why she'd asked the question, Savannah hated the fact the words had tumbled out before she'd taken time to consider the consequences. The shift in his posture wasn't nearly as subtle. He'd gone on point in an instant, and that made her more than a little curious about why he was so defensive.

"I do. But that isn't relevant to what we're trying to accomplish, so I'm not going to discuss it now."

Not going to discuss it now? Well, then when? If he thinks I'll just walk away from this without bringing it up again, he is in for a big surprise.

"If you don't have any other questions, we'll get started. And this is your one and only reminder. Once we start, all the rules are mine to make. Your body and your attention are mine to command. You are mine to protect, and I'll often do so in ways you may not agree with, but make no mistake, everything I do is with your well-being and the mission in mind. Think of me as your private sentinel." He waited for her to respond, and when she didn't, he frowned. "Once we are better acquainted, you'll know when I expect a response. And the only acceptable responses are 'yes, Sir' and 'yes, Master.' Remember, the rules are different for sex slaves. They don't have the option to deny their Master anything. It's all or nothing."

On a cognitive level, Savannah knew he was telling her the truth, but the whole scenario boggled her mind. How could anyone willingly surrender all their decisions to another person? She'd fought too hard to get out from under her family's thumb to walk into another situation where she had to ask permission before doing anything. Reminding herself that she was only training for a mission helped re-center her thoughts, and she finally nodded. "Yes, Sir."

LANDON COULD ALMOST write the script of what Savannah was thinking. The fire inside her would take a lifetime to tame. Not that he thought it should be done—it would be a travesty to contain such wild sprit. How she'd come out of her family with her zest for life unscathed was a mystery to him. He hadn't been lying when he said he'd met her brother. But knowing and respecting were not entirely the same. Landon wondered if she'd learned the real reason her big brother Brit was no longer married to Amaryllis's mother. He seriously doubted the twisted bastard had shared the details of his sexual perversions with his family, but only time would tell. Landon had been at the D.C. club the night Brit had burned his wife with hot wax. Personally, he'd never believed the incident had been accidental.

Watching Savannah try to wrap her head around voluntary sexual slavery was almost funny. Her eyes narrowed as she mulled over what he'd said. She didn't doubt what he'd said, but she didn't understand it, either. Not a problem for him, because he'd never understood why any man would want a partner he had to lead around by the hand. He liked obedient subs, but he also liked his women smart and driven. Where would be the challenge in having a sub who never challenged him?

Training Savannah without tarnishing her interest in the lifestyle wasn't going to be easy. He wanted her to come out of this thing ready to pursue a D/s relationship with a Dom who could give her everything she needed. As that thought passed through his mind, Landon felt something in his gut twist, and it felt too much like jealousy for his comfort. How could he be jealous of a woman who didn't belong to him?

There had only been two reasons he'd agreed to this train her for the rescue rather than relegating the task to someone else. First, she needed to understand exactly what it meant to have him as a Dom. It might have been possible for her to switch from the Dom who'd trained her to him, but it would be difficult. Their covers stated she'd been his slave for over a year, so any hesitance on her part would be a red flag during the party. *Party, my ass. Wish we could call it what it is—a fucking auction.*

The second reason was far more selfish, and he was

trying to shove it to the back of his mind. He'd pushed her away before because he'd known she wasn't ready for what he'd demand from her. But the thought of another Dom touching her, teaching her, and guiding her had set off an explosion of denial. At the end of their time together, it would be his imprint of the lifestyle she carried with her into any subsequent relationship, and he was more pleased by that than he should be.

He knew she was curious, but the nature of this mission was far darker than what he thought she was prepared for. Landon planned to train her, but he wanted to leave as much of her free-spirit in place as he could. The silence surrounding them was broken by voices coming from the kitchen. Savannah's muscles tensed beneath his fingers, but her gaze never left his. "Good girl. I aware that conflicts with your previous training, but the men holding your niece are expecting a well-trained slave, not an operative."

"May I ask a question? Well, make that two questions."

He grinned at her quick thinking. "Yes, though I reserve the right to not answer. I won't ever lie to you, Princess, but I won't always answer, either."

"Who else is here? Do they live here full-time? Am I allowed to speak to your staff? How many people work in the house? Do you have security staff, also?"

When she finally took a breath, he chuckled. "That's more than two questions, but since they all seem to center on one topic, I'll answer. There are three people here full-time with others who come and go as needed. The three who are here twenty-four seven have been apprised about who you are here and why you're here. They can be trusted, Princess. Anything they see or hear will never leave my home. Remember, above all, it's the Dominant's job to cherish and protect his submissive.

"Your safety and well-being are my responsibility, and I take that seriously—even if we're training professionally rather than personally." Her eyes widened as her pupils dilated with desire, and suddenly, the moment felt much more intimate than it should. Stepping back, he noted the flush covering her chest. *Do you realize how revealing that pretty, low-cut blouse is to a man trained to read every sexual signal?*

"Unless you're told otherwise, you'll strip as soon as you enter the house." Her eyes went as wide as any cartoon character he'd ever seen, but he didn't pause as he led her back to the entry. "You'll remove your shoes first and set them on the bottom rail of this table." He gave her a pointed look before moving his gaze to her sparkly sandals. She quickly unbuckled the dainty footwear and set them carefully on the mahogany shelf. "Then you'll remove your clothing. Fold it neatly and place it on the top. One of the staff will return everything to your closet."

When she didn't move, he waited a few seconds before arching his brow. This time her eyes darted around the room, and he saw unease bordering on fear reflected in the bright blue pools. "Eyes on me, Princess. Ninety percent of your training is going to center on trust. I know you don't trust me yet, but you will. Until then, try to remember why you are here. We both want to get Amy back. Trust me to get you ready to go to Costa Rica and bring her home. Any hesitation to strip on command would immediately raise alarms and would require me to punish you. They'd expect a severe and public reprimand, and I'd have to comply or we'd both be exposed as frauds."

He tried to steel himself against the tears he saw shining in her eyes. Landon knew he should feel ashamed for emotionally blackmailing her into compliance, but it was his only leverage at this point. Eventually, she wouldn't want to disappoint him, but there was too much tainted history between them for her to care about that, yet. It would be a few days before he'd be able to replace that memory with something more pleasant, but by the end of the week, things would be much easier for her.

Landon studied the play of emotions in her expression and wished he could read her thoughts. He'd often wondered what it would be like to be able to hear what someone was thinking and had asked Taz Ledek more than once to explain how it worked. Both Ledek brothers were empaths, but Taz's skill eclipsed his older brother's. Taz swore the gift was more curse than blessing, but Landon wasn't convinced.

Savannah inhaled a deep breath and moved her fingers to the buttons on her blouse. Her movements were clumsy as she rushed. "I'm going to enjoy watching you unwrap what's mine. Slow, graceful movements are the hallmark of a well-trained submissive or slave. Your yoga skills are going to serve you well during the next three weeks, Princess." She stilled and lifted her gaze to his. He smiled. "Your silhouette show last night was something to behold. I was tempted to sit in the parking lot and watch." Instead he'd come home and taken an ice-cold shower before calling Dean and Tally.

Every inch of bare skin she revealed sent another surge of blood to his cock. Jesus, the woman was killing him. Once she'd focused and slowed her movements, they'd become perfectly fluid. Savannah was doing a sultry dance of seduction that made him want to push her up against the wall and fuck her senseless. The irony was that he didn't think she was doing it intentionally. "You're beautiful, Princess—just as I knew you would be. Ivory skin that looks as smooth as silk. I can't wait to explore every inch."

She blushed, and he chuckled. "Sweetheart, if that makes you blush, you are going to be crimson for days." She'd folded her clothing piece by piece, stacking it perfectly on the table. When she leaned down to retrieve her lacy panties from the floor, he held out his hand. "You won't need these—or any other panties while we're together."

"I can't..." She stopped speaking when he frowned. *Good girl, you're learning.* He wouldn't allow her to wear anything at all for the first several days. It was important for her to be comfortable nude.

"I want unfettered access to you, Princess. If I want to do this," he reached around her and cupped her ass in his hand, "I don't want to have anything between my hand and your ass." She'd jerked, but he shook his head. "Remember, you are mine to play with, and I assure you any reaction other than acceptance and compliance will be noticed by the slavers." When she bit her lip, he shook his head and used his fingers to pull it free. "We've only just started, Savannah. I'm not scolding you—yet. I'm simply pointing out things I want you to be cognizant of, things that will scream newbie to anyone with an experienced eye."

"Yes, Sir."

"Good, girl." He was pleased when she took the hand he held out. "Come. I'll give you a tour." He took a step, but her feet were firmly planted in place. Landon had expected this reaction when he'd outlined what he wanted to accomplish with this initial meeting. But she'd done so well it was easy to forget every step was new for her. "Is there a problem, Princess?"

He held her hand tightly in his own when she tried to pull back. Fidgeting, she seemed to be choosing her words carefully. He gave her a moment to think before repeating the question. "Can you give me a minute to...well, work this through in my mind? It was really hard for me to take my clothes off in front of you. And now...now other people might see me. People I've never met will see me and that's even more terrifying."

Savannah's honesty surprised and impressed him. He hadn't expected her to level with him, and her admission pleased him more than he could say. Landon hadn't planned to explain until after she'd met his staff, but her willingness to be forthright deserved a reward. "Princess, I'm more pleased than you know with your candor. I aware our history isn't the best, and I'm honored you trusted me enough to be so transparent. All three of the people you're going to meet are Mountain Mastery members—they all gave me permission to share that information with you. They are not going to judge you, and nothing you or I do will shock them."

She didn't say anything, and he gave her a minute to mull over his words before continuing. "I'm going to push you, Savannah. Don't ever doubt that. We have a short time to prepare, and the timeline alone necessitates an accelerated training schedule. But even if we had an eternity to prepare, I'd still push you because that's what Dom's do. They find your boundaries and they challenge you to expand them."

He pulled her into his arms and knew instantly he'd made a mistake. She melted against him as his arms surrounded her. Damn, she felt perfect molded against him like a second skin. And when her arms wrapped around him, it took every bit of his control not to tip her lips up to meet his. Her skin was chilled beneath his fingertips, and he berated himself for not adjusting the air conditioning.

Barefoot, the top of her head tucked under his chin. So petite. So fucking perfect.

"I wish we'd been able to review a limits list together and negotiate our scenes. But this isn't that sort of arrangement." When she stiffened in his arms, Landon felt a pang of guilt, but what he'd said was true even if it stung her pride. He's seen the one the club owners insisted she complete, but they all felt that had been more about finding out how much she already knew about the lifestyle. Real sex slaves surrendered their ability to say no. It was an aspect of Dominance and submission Landon didn't expect Savannah to understand—hell, he had trouble making sense of it himself.

"Maybe it will help if I tell you what *my* limits are." Pulling back enough to retain his hold on her, while putting space between them so he could look into her eyes, he smiled. "I'm not a sadist, though there are some who might disagree with that statement. I'm not into anything that involves bodily fluids or needles. And I won't ever intentionally humiliate you. That's not to say I won't embarrass you as a punishment, but even that will be rare."

He saw the uncertainty in her eyes and smiled. "Let me give you an example of embarrassment as a correction for misbehavior. A couple of weeks ago, one of the Masters at the club had given his sub several warnings to stop staring at the stage where a scene was being set up. He knew the scene was going to upset her, and he was trying to shield her. She's terrified of fire, and the scene was a fire play demonstration."

Savannah's eyes widened in surprise and he saw a hint of fear in them, but she didn't interrupt him. "The sub needed a lesson in trust, and after years of listening to the wrong people, she is convinced her ass is too big. It isn't.

She is lovely, but the voices from her past have always been louder than the ones in her present."

"What did he do to her?"

"Upended her over a bar stool, exposing her pretty curves to the world. He put up a sign encouraging everyone passing by to smooth their palms over her curves and whisper words of appreciation. A couple of the Doms who have participated in scenes with them gave her several swats to remind her how much they enjoyed their time with her. She was embarrassed, but it was a lesson she won't forget." Landon had certainly enjoyed seeing his handprint bloom bright red over Chloe's ass cheeks.

"Okay. Well, that doesn't seem so bad. Embarrassment I can handle…probably. But humiliation will make me shut down, just so you know." Her voice had gotten quieter the longer she continued to speak, telling him she'd been revealing more than intended. This was a side of Savannah he hadn't anticipated. She was surprising him at every turn. He certainly hadn't expected her candor.

Stepping back and taking her hand once again, Landon used his hand to indicate the way he planned to go. He needed to get her back on track or she'd derail their entire morning. "Now, all that being said, and keeping our deadline in mind, let's get going."

Chapter Seven

SAVANNAH SHIVERED AS Landon led her through the house. He'd asked her if she was cold, and she assured him she wasn't...the temperature wasn't causing the sudden trembling. Her imagination was in overdrive, and knowing each room he showed her brought them one step closer to his staff was both terrifying and exhilarating. Landon's home was amazing. His nod to the outdoors didn't stop in the living room. The indoor pool area reminded her of walking in the rain forest.

Landon must have noted the look of longing on her face when they walked by the rock-lined hot tub. "Later. You'll probably appreciate a soothing soak after we've finished today. Although, as I've said, I believe your yoga training is going to serve you well. How long have you been practicing?"

"I started when I first went to boarding school. One of my teachers thought it would help my homesickness." She was surprised when he stopped walking and turned to face her.

"How old were you?" His expression could only be described as fierce—something she'd said had obviously pissed him off, but she wasn't sure what would have caused such an intense reaction.

"Ten. When Brit's business took off, Mom and Dad

thought I'd be better off at St. Regis. He was attracting a lot of attention, and they didn't want my safety compromised by his success." Actually, they'd wanted to enjoy all the media attention surrounding her brother rather than dealing with a precocious ten-year-old. She'd seen through their excuse, but no amount of pleading had changed her fate.

The homesickness had been completely debilitating the first few months. She hadn't been able to eat and had finally been admitted to the infirmary because she'd lost so much weight. When her family had been "too busy" for her to return at Christmas, she'd been devastated. They'd sent thousands of dollars in gifts and a letter explaining why they couldn't "host her" for the holidays. Her mother had also cautioned her against speaking negatively about her family, explaining why it was important to protect their reputation.

Savannah was pulled from her musing when Landon used his thumb to brush a tear from her cheek. Damn, why was she crying about this now? Shaking her head, she smiled but knew he wasn't fooled. "Sorry. It's all water under the bridge."

"If you were mine I wouldn't allow you to continue to hide from your feelings. I suspect you're tamping down a lot of pain. As your friend, I'm going to encourage you to exorcise it before it eats you alive." His voice was carefully modulated, but she was certain there was a note of warning in his words. Were they friends? Until this moment, she would have said no, but something between them was shifting. Savannah wasn't sure where their relationship was headed, but the anger she'd held on to since his rejection didn't seem as important anymore.

"Come on, Princess, I think it's time I gave you something else to think about."

Oh, boy.

LANDON MADE A silent promise to himself to find out what Savannah's family had been tending to that was more important than their daughter. He'd read her file, and she'd been forthright about living away from home, but he suspected the reason had little to do with her safety. In his experience, when there was a decade or more between children, the second one wasn't always as welcome as the parents might want the world to believe. He'd seen friends of his parents devastated when they'd learned they were going to be parents again just as they'd begun to enjoy more freedom.

The sadness in her eyes as she fell into her memories made his heart squeeze. He needed to set aside the personal aspect of her training or he'd end up being another in what he suspected was a long line of people who'd let Savannah down.

For the first portion of his tour through the house, she'd tried to cover herself when he looked at her. Each time, he'd patiently moved her hands back to her sides and continued talking. There would be plenty of reprimands in her future, and he didn't want to use punishments until it was necessary. Something told him she was going to learn quickly, but the walls they hit were going to be made of stone and mortar.

Leading Savannah toward the kitchen, he felt her hand stiffen in his. He didn't stop because giving her any additional time to *think* would be a mistake. Lenore Watts had been cooking for his family for almost twenty years. He'd never met a woman who could eat as much as Lenore. But despite her ravenous appetite, she stayed slender thanks to an exercise program that would put most Olympians' to shame.

His housekeeper, Ellen Mason, was another long-time employee. She'd moved to Montana years ago with her husband and had become a widow their first winter in the Treasure State. Deputy Sheriff Mack Mason had gone off the road one night while on patrol and frozen to death before his car was discovered the next day. One of the hazards of living in the mountains was the spotty satellite reception. Even though the local dispatcher knew he wasn't responding to her calls, the tracking device on his patrol car wasn't discoverable from the bottom of the ravine.

Landon wasn't worried about Savannah's reaction to either Lenore or Ellen. Both women were gregarious and would make her feel at home despite her nudity. It was his driver, James Carter, who would present a challenge. At six foot, Carter wasn't particularly tall, but his broad shoulders and heavily muscled frame made him intimidating as hell. Calling him a driver was a running joke, because his duties were far broader than simply driving Landon around. Although they'd been acquainted for years, Carter had only recently joined Landon's staff.

Just as he'd predicted, Lenore and Ellen made fast friends with Savannah. They had her eating fruit and chatting within minutes. He stood back and watched their interaction, hoping to gain some additional insight into the woman beneath the agent mask. Their short conversation about her family reminded Landon how little background information he'd really been given about Savannah North.

Sure, he'd read the Agency's profile, but he had a feeling that was a carefully crafted persona. Whether she'd molded it or her parents had imposed it on her, he wasn't certain, but in the end, it didn't matter.

Carter stepped into the room and stopped a few feet behind Savannah and gave Lenore and Ellen a warning glare ensuring neither of them would give away his presence. The flash fire from the explosion that ended his career as a Special Forces operative scarred him in many ways. Carter was still working with a physical therapist twice a week to regain mobility in his left shoulder. But it was the badly scarred skin on the left side of his face that caused him the most grief. If Landon had to guess, he'd say Carter wanted to observe Savannah for a few minutes before she looked at him and clammed up the way so many people did.

"These are delicious. Oh, my God in heaven, they practically melt in your mouth. I'll be able to roll faster than I can walk if I stay here very long. Every single one of these calories will go right to my ass. Some friends you're going to be. Extra yoga for me tonight or my caboose will look like the Titanic." Landon smiled at her comments, but held back a response when he saw Carter's arched brow.

"I don't know, it looks pretty spectacular to me." Carter could turn his southern drawl off at will, but he'd given her the full version.

Savannah spun around so quickly she nearly toppled over. He instinctively reached to steady her, but Carter had been closer—and quicker. "Hell's bells and sea shells. You scared the sugar out of me." She took a step back and appeared to completely forget her nudity. Her gaze moved over Carter's face, but her express showed interest rather than revulsion. "BLEVE?" Carter's eyes widened in surprise before he nodded.

"I'm impressed. Beautiful and smart, that's a killer combination. It's nice to meet you Savannah. I'm Carter." Hell, Landon was impressed, too. He'd be willing to bet fewer than a handful of agents in the CIA who would have correctly identified Carter's burns. Knowing they'd come from a boiling liquid expanding vapor explosion was fucking remarkable.

She reached up, but paused with the tips of her fingers hovering close but not touching his skin…waiting for Carter's permission. He gave her a quick nod, and Landon could tell by the way Carter's lips twitched her touch had been feather light. He'd once told Landon that contrary to what most people thought, the surface of his skin had very little sensation.

"Have you tried essential oils? I have a friend who is really into them. She pestered me forever about a scar I had on my back. I finally gave in and let her mix up some magic potion and rub it into the scar every day for a couple of weeks, and it looks a thousand times better now. And it doesn't hurt when I do my yoga stretches, either. I'll put you in touch with her if you'd be willing to try it. Can't hurt, might help."

Savannah seemed to suddenly realize where she was and what she wasn't wearing. She flushed a brilliant shade of red and shook her head. "Fuck-a-dilly circus. I can't believe I'm standing here stark naked talking to a man I don't even know about hooking him up with my friend to get oiled."

For the first time since before the explosion, Carter leaned his head back and roared with laughter. Lenore and Ellen were both chuckling so hard they had tears streaming down their faces, and Landon wondered how the hell he'd managed to lose complete and total control of the situation. "Princess, you've surprised me yet again. I'm going to want to hear where—and *why* you learned about BLEVE explosions. But for the moment, I'd like to formally introduce you to my driver and head of security, James Carter. There are cameras all over the house, but he and I are the only ones who will have access to the feeds for the next two weeks."

Awareness dawned in her pretty blue eyes before a deep pink blush spread over her cheeks. When she started to cover herself with her hands, he frowned. "Don't even think about it." She gulped and looked at the floor so quickly Landon sucked in a quick breath. Hell, how had he missed the subtle signals of her hidden submissive side? Holding out his hand in a clear signal for her to return to him, he watched as she padded the few steps back to where he stood.

"Look at me, Princess." When her eyes met his, he was shocked to see her pupils dilated with desire. "Did you eat breakfast?" When she shook her head, he glared. "Shaking your head is not an answer, Savannah."

He hid his amusement when her eyes flickered with annoyance. Landon had seen that same expression on Tally's face and knew Savannah had barely managed to keep from rolling her eyes. Acting as Senator Karl Tyson and his wife, Dr. Tally Tyson's, third had taught Landon a lot about dealing with unruly subs. Now that he thought about it, Tally and Savannah had a lot in common, which went a long way to explain his attraction to the beauty standing in front of him. He'd originally thought to introduce the two women, but for some reason, that didn't seem like a good idea now.

"No, Sir. I was too nervous to eat." That explained why

she'd all but inhaled the pastries Lenore had given her.

"Lenore, could you make our lovely guest something to hold her over until lunch? High protein would be preferable since she's going to be practicing positions the rest of the morning. We'll be in the sunroom." Without waiting for the cook's response, he held out his hand to Savannah. "Come. We have work to do."

Chapter Eight

SAVANNAH'S LEGS TREMBLED with exhaustion. She sent up a silent prayer of thanks for her years of yoga training, because without it, she would've collapsed hours ago. Kneeling once again when Landon glanced at the floor, she hissed when a muscle spasm seized in her upper thigh. "Princess?" Tears stung the backs of her eyes, but she held her position. "Look at me, Savannah." When she lifted her face, his eyes went wide as he cursed. "Dammit, I gave you a fucking safe word for a reason."

Lifting her into his arms, he effortlessly scooped her up from the floor. He moved quickly to the stairs, and she hoped he was heading to the hot tub and not giving up on her training. She let herself relax into his hold and laid her ear against his chest. The steady thumping of his heart had almost lulled her to sleep before she felt herself being lowered into the hot water. Cupping her head between his hands, he held her until she opened her eyes. "I'll be right back. Keep those pretty eyes open until I'm holding you again, Princess."

Nodding, she watched him step back and strip. He reached behind her, and she heard a series of beeps before the water began circulating rapidly around her. The lights in the room flickered off, and those under the water's edge shimmered as the bubbles moved furiously through the swirling tub. The soothing effects of the jets pounding her spent muscles pulled her closer and closer to sleep until she felt the water around her raise. When she was finally able to lift her lashes, she realized Landon Nixon was standing in front of her. His erect cock almost at eye level proudly pressed against his taut abdomen.

Good heavens, the man would give a Greek God a run for his money. He'd shed his shirt late that afternoon as he'd paced the warm sunroom. She'd known he'd turned up the heat to ensure her comfort on the cool tile floor. His muttered curses about his father failing to heat the floor of what had evidently been his mother's favorite room in the house amused her. From what Savannah had seen, this the only room in his home that didn't appear to have been remodeled. It was an interesting contrast to the rest of the house. The soft pastel colors and floral pattern of the furnishing were starkly different from the rich, deep colors in the other rooms. Leaving the room intact spoke volumes about his love and respect for his mother.

Realizing he'd spoken, she could only blink up at him. Her brain was just too tired to track anything. "Christ, woman, you have to learn your limits. I was pushing to see what it would take for you to use your safe word. How am I supposed to trust you to use it during a scene if you won't even tell me when you are about to implode from fatigue?"

Too tired to respond, she dropped her chin to her chest and pulled in a calming breath. He picked her up and took her place before settling her on his lap. His hard cock pressed between her hip and his firm body. Her eyelids dropped, shutting out the world as she relaxed against him. Any other time, she'd have been mortified to be sitting on a naked man's lap, but right now, she was too tired to care.

"So brave and strong. Now we just need to get you to a

point where you'll believe me when I say it's okay to say *enough*." His words sounded nice, but a part of her doubted she'd ever be able to draw that line. She'd spent her entire life trying to prove she was worthy of her parents' love and respect. She couldn't imagine ever feeling secure enough to quit before she'd completed a task.

"Can't quit. Not good enough yet." She hadn't meant to speak out loud, and his frustrated sigh made her wish she'd been more careful.

"We're going to work on your self-esteem, baby." Landon's sweet words made their way through the fog of her exhaustion and knocked down another piece of the wall she'd built around her heart. *Drat him, he's going to crash through if I'm not careful.*

MARCO ALVAREZ STARED at the shivering blonde. She was naked and shaking as the fan beside him drifted over her with each pass. Fear filled her pretty blue eyes, but her chin was tilted up as she tried in vain to hold on to her dignity. *That won't last long if I decide you aren't as delectable as you appear, pretty girl. You'll fetch a high price if I can continue to hide your identity from the buyers.*

Recognizing her immediately upon his arrival, Marco had begun searching on-line for any mention of the Fitzgerald heiress's abduction. There had only been one brief mention buried deep in the web, telling him her family was waiting for a ransom demand. *Let them wait.*

Victor, his second-in-command, stood by the door leering at her, but she hadn't taken her eyes off Marco. *Smart girl, keep your eyes on the most venomous snake in the room.* He let several minutes pass, but she retained both her posture and her strength during the long silence. Her gaze never wavered from his. The bruise circling her upper arm and deep purple marks on her left breast spoke volumes about Victor's treatment—he'd been asked to escort her to his boss' office and had apparently taken a few liberties along the way.

"You are bruised." His unasked question was answered when her eyes flickered to the side.

Victor straightened and cleared his throat. "She was uncooperative walking down the hallway."

"Do you usually guide women by their breasts, Victor?" The man had the decency to appear chagrined, and Marco made a note to fine the man a week's wages for damaging the merchandise. The hefty penalty would keep Victor and the others in line. Dealing in high end sex slave auctions meant the slaves needed to appear perfect. The buyers he catered to didn't purchase damaged good or seconds—they weren't exactly *bargain shoppers*. "I'll be deducting a week's wages as a reminder, Victor. No one is to avail themselves of our guests. Leave us. I'll summon one of the others to walk Amaryllis back to her suite."

Marco's menacing tone sent a shudder through Victor, who gave a quick nod and backed out of the door. When Marco turned his attention back to the woman, she watched him carefully, but some of the tension seemed to have drained from her posture. "I'm sorry he hurt you. He rarely strays beyond the boundaries I've set for him." She didn't respond, but the small lift in her aristocratic brow told him she wasn't convinced. There was something about her that intrigued him. For the first time in his career, he considered keeping this woman for himself.

Her long blonde hair was the color of sun-bleached

straw, the wavy strands curling around her baby pink nipples. She wasn't tall, but her legs were long and well-toned. The bright polish on her fingers and toes let him know she'd taken advantage of the manicure kit he'd sent to her room. He'd watched her pace the length of the room on the closed-circuit cameras and wanted to give her something else to do before she wore herself out.

"Have you sent the ransom demand yet?" Her question was unexpected, but he carefully schooled his expression, masking his surprise. *How interesting. If she thinks her father isn't paying the ransom...* He might be able to make this scenario work in his favor. If he could convince her that her father refused to pay a ransom to free her, she might well seek solace in his arms. After all, it would be easy to convince her he wasn't the one who'd ordered her abduction—since it hadn't been ordered at all. The two men who'd made the mistake would be on perimeter patrol for the next fifty years to make amends for the error.

Letting his eyes move over her, Marco didn't try to hide his growing desire. It would have been impossible even if he'd wanted to since his erection was clearly visible under his dress slacks. He opened his mouth to tell her the truth—that there had not been any ransom demands made. "No, I'm afraid there has been no response from your family. I'm doing my best to shield you from those above me, but they are not known for their patience." There wasn't anyone above him in the organization now that his father had handed over control of the family business. His recently retired father was still more involved than he needed to be, but his emphasis was quickly switching to more personal matters. He'd begun pressuring Marco to find a woman to provide him with grandchildren, so perhaps... Marco suspected the old man would happily forego the money Amaryllis would bring on the auction if his son would settle down and begin filling the halls with the pitter patter of little people.

Marco walked to the other side of the room, his steps silent on the expensive Persian rug. He loved the bamboo floors in his office and made sure his staff kept them polished to perfection. But he'd learned soon after moving into this office, the sound of his designer dress shoes walking over the surface was so distracting he could barely focus. As soon as his father turned the everyday operation of their organization over to him, Marco had ordered a specially designed rug to cushion the sound. Its irregular shape made it easy for him to walk around the office without the distracting clatter he'd found so annoying.

When he stepped back out from behind the hidden door to his private lavatory, he noted the beautiful woman standing in his office hadn't moved. She was facing away from him, and he slowed his pace to enjoy the view. The woman had a world class ass, and all he could think about in that moment was sinking his throbbing cock deep into her and not coming up for air until neither of them could walk.

Amaryllis Fitzgerald would certainly bring in a hefty sum, but something about her made him hesitate. None of the feelers he'd put out were turning up any significant internet chatter about the young woman's disappearance. It was likely her father knew she was missing, and if he was thinking along the same line as his daughter, the man was probably worried about involving the press.

The media was notorious for getting victims killed. Reporters loved blasting news of kidnappings from the gated driveways of the rich and famous. As soon as the broadcasts aired, thugs got nervous and cut their losses.

Marco had seen it happen again and again. Brit Fitzgerald didn't become one of the richest men in America by being stupid. He was watching and waiting. Marco's tech staff reported they'd set-up "trip wire alerts" all over the web for anyone researching Ms. Fitzgerald's disappearance. They'd assured him they hadn't set off any of the alarms themselves, and he hoped like hell they realized they were betting all their lives on it.

Stepping in front of her, he draped the robe he was carrying around her shoulders. After helping her slip her arms in, Marco pulled it together in the front and tied the sash. "It's a pity to cover such loveliness. But I'd like to talk to you, and to be honest, I'm more than a little distracted when I look at you. All I can think about is touching you, and I don't want to do anything to frighten you." Taking her hand, he led her to the sofa and seated her before uncovering the food he'd had delivered before her arrival. "Let's eat and talk."

He noted her hesitation, but she finally nibbled on anything she saw him eating. *Smart girl, don't sample anything you haven't seen your host eat.* He wasn't above drugging a woman, but he'd meant it when he said he wanted to talk to her. Five minutes into their conversation, Marco had already determined her fate. Now to convince her to stay with the man who had—up until a half hour ago—been determined to sell her into sexual slavery. He'd never needed to charm his sexual partners—in his world, money was the only conversation women understood. Smiling to himself, Marco decided he was up to the challenge.

Chapter Nine

SAVANNAH ROLLED OVER and stared at the ceiling of Landon's enormous bedroom. She'd been training with him for almost a week. His hands had touched her in places only her gynecologist had seen, but he still hadn't fucked her. She wasn't sure why he wanted her sleeping in his bed if he wasn't going to…cutting off her wayward thoughts, Savannah shook her head. "You are not going down that path. You already knew he didn't want you. Why assume things would be different now? Keep your head in the game, and for fuck's sake, stop talking to yourself."

Rolling out of the large bed, Savannah moved to the indoor spa Landon called a bathroom. After taking care of her personal business, she read the note on the marble counter.

> *Don't bother with a shower this morning. Go to the pool area after eating the breakfast Lenore has prepared for you. Follow Carter's instructions; then swim thirty laps. My meetings will be over before you've finished.*
> *Master Landon.*

The change in routine surprised her, and she wondered what Carter would have her do before she went to the pool. Stepping into the kitchen a few minutes later, Savannah froze in the doorway when she noticed Carter wasn't alone. He was leaning back in his chair watching her…his gaze moving over her like a heated caress. The man sitting across from him turned to face her, and she sucked in a breath at the sight of U.S. Senator Karl Tyson.

She took a quick step back, but before she could turn to run, Carter's voice cracked around her like a whip. "Stop." Savannah went completely still, frozen in place. Blinking as fast as she could to hold back tears of humiliation, she kept her eyes on the floor. She heard the murmur of voices, but couldn't make out what they were saying over the blood pounding in her ears.

When the toes of black leather loafers came into her view, Savannah tensed. "Eyes on me, sweetness." The voice didn't belong to Carter, and it took every ounce of discipline she could muster to raise her chin until their eyes met. His were soft and kind, but still keen with the look of an uncompromising Dom. "Better. I understand your reluctance to walk into the room. Under any other circumstances, our second meeting would play out much differently."

Her surprise must have shown because he grinned. "Yes, Savannah, I remember meeting you at the reception last year. Although I must say, I was surprised to learn you are Brit's sister. Who knew he was related to two beautiful women? Astonishing, really—as I've known him since we were both in college." He cocked his head to the side and frowned. "Why weren't you at his wedding?"

Savannah felt her eyes widen in surprise…no make that shock. She probably shouldn't have been impressed—after all, she'd heard the man standing in front of her was brilliant. Gossip on the Hill credited him with a memory for details that shamed most legislators. The smile she tried to pass-off must not have reached her eyes because she saw his jaw tighten. "I was at prep-school, and my parents didn't want to expose me to the media circus that surrounded the festivities." In truth, they hadn't wanted the world introduced to their socially inept, braces-wearing, geeky daughter.

He didn't respond for long seconds, but the tensing of the muscles around his jaw told her he sensed he'd been given the "pc version." God knew she was well-versed in PCBS. Her parents had trained her to spout politically correct bull shit from a young age. Hell, protecting the secrets of the CIA was nothing compared to those she kept for her family.

"I hope someday you trust me enough to be completely honest."

She froze. Would he pull her off the mission for not confiding her family secrets? She was well aware of his various committee seats. Senator Tyson had more than enough influence to get her removed from this assignment.

His answering smile was warm, understanding flooding his eyes. "Sweetness, I understand that you don't have any reason to believe me. And any reassurance I could give you now would be hollow. Trust must be earned, and friendships aren't formed overnight. Perhaps someday you and I will share both." She'd seen pictures of Landon Nixon and Senator Tyson together so she assumed they were friends. It was the only reason she could think of that he'd seem sincere about being her friend.

"Thank you. I should probably get downstairs to the pool. It was nice seeing you again, Senator."

When she started to step away again, Carter's hand encircled her upper arm. *When did he move? Fuck-a-doodle.* If

I keep letting people sneak up on me, I'm going to have to go back through training. "You haven't eaten. And I have a surprise for you before you go downstairs." Her eyes quickly scanned the table where he'd been sitting, but whatever he had for her wasn't setting out. Carter chuckled as he led her back to the glass-topped table. "You didn't think I'd leave it out for you to fret about while you were eating, did you?"

He pulled out a chair and motioned for her to sit. A soft towel covered the upholstered top, just as it had every other time she'd used one of Landon's dining chairs. She wondered, yet again, if the towel was to protect her or the furniture...she was betting on the later. After he'd pushed her chair in, he gave her legs a pointed glare before turning his attention to Lenore. Savannah rolled her eyes, but moved her legs apart and hooked her ankles around the legs of the chair.

"Did you just roll your eyes, little one?" Karl Tyson's words held a hint of amusement beneath the question, but she hadn't missed the thread of steel laced through them. He'd left little doubt he was a Dom.

Carter's attention spun back to her, his brow furrowed. He watched her as she took a big gulp of her orange juice. When she started to take another, he shook his head. "Answer Master Karl's question, kitten."

"Yes, Sir." Her gaze skittered between the two men, trying to determine how angry they were. Rolling her eyes had gotten her in trouble her entire life. It was like the damned things had minds of their own. "I wasn't trying to be disrespectful. I was embarrassed, and that was my way to feel more in control."

Karl Tyson leaned back in his chair and crossed his arms over his chest. He didn't say anything for a few seconds, but finally nodded. "Carter, I suggest you only add two swats to the ones she's already earned for trying to skip breakfast earlier."

What? She hadn't tried to escape…well, not really. She'd only taken a step or two back because she'd noticed Carter wasn't alone. His eyes glittered with devilment, and Savannah let out the breath she'd been holding when she realized he wasn't really angry with her.

"That works for me. I know she was told to eat breakfast before swimming, so I'm befuddled by her reluctance to enter the room."

Okay, now they were just fucking with her.

"Befuddled? Really? Befuddled? I don't think I've heard a grown man under the age of eighty use that word. Holy shi—ingles. I'll bet if I watch close enough I'll see your hair go gray right in front of my eyes." The look on both men's faces made her laugh out loud. Damn it felt good to laugh. "Oh my, you have no idea how much I enjoyed that. I haven't laughed since before I heard about Amy." She took a big bite of the omelet in front of her and moaned in pure appreciation. "I swear I'm kidnapping Lenore when I leave."

Lenore's voice sounded from the pantry, "I'll start packing. Landon is gone so often he probably won't realize I'm missing for months."

"Not true."

Savannah's head swiveled so quickly to the doorway it was a wonder she hadn't sprained something. Landon leaned against the doorframe, one leg bent at the knee and crossed over the other ankle, his muscular arms crossed over his chest. Holy hell, the man was hot. His gaze moved over her, and Savannah couldn't hold back the shudder of awareness that vibrated from her core.

Senator Tyson chuckled as he rose to his feet. "Christ, the air is practically crackling between the two of you." He leaned close to whisper in her ear, "You're perfect for him. He may not realize it yet, but it's true." As he walked by Landon, she heard him say, "Seal this deal, my friend. Windows of opportunity don't stay open forever."

Landon's gaze never left her, and she felt her cheeks heat furiously. "You know your way out. Give your lovely wife my best. I'll call you later, and we'll finish the discussion we started earlier."

Karl shook his head and continued walking. "We'll talk tomorrow night. Your sweet sub has a punishment coming, so I think you're going to be busy for a while."

Savannah's cheeks were flaming hot, and she couldn't believe Senator Tyson had just thrown her very bare ass under the bus. "That's just wrong. He's a public servant. Didn't he take some sort of oath to protect citizens? I'm a citizen. Figures that he's friends with my brother." She probably sounded petulant, but she didn't care. In her experience, her brother's friends were usually well-polished jerks.

"He and your brother aren't friends. They have mutual interests and mutual friends. But *they* aren't friends." Landon hadn't moved, but his casual pose didn't fool her. He was coiled tight and as lethal as any agent in the business. She wasn't afraid for her life, but she was certainly worried about the punishment Karl and Carter felt she'd earned. There wasn't a chance in hell Landon was going to cut her a break and look weak in front of other Doms. Oh yeah, this wasn't going to work out well for her at all!

LANDON FINALLY GAVE up trying to concentrate on the phone conference he'd been participating in when he saw Savannah try to back out of the kitchen. He'd cut the call short and watched the security feed until she'd rolled her eyes while Carter had been turned away. It was a classic Tally-move, and he'd be certain Karl wouldn't have missed it. Both Carter and Karl had seen him move into position, but he'd been out of Savannah's peripheral vision.

He'd been Karl and Tally Tyson's third for almost two years and thought of Karl as a brother. But seeing the lust in Karl's eyes when he'd looked at Savannah ignited something inside him. He'd never felt possessive of any woman, and he'd damned well never experienced jealousy—but that didn't mean he hadn't recognized both feelings when they'd swamped him. The minute Karl mentioned her punishment, Landon had launched to his feet, moving to the kitchen before he'd taken time to consider his actions.

The amusement in Karl's eyes told Landon his friend wasn't fooled by his nonchalance. The man knew him too well to miss his barely restrained need to pull her into the protective circle of his arms. Jesus, Joseph, and Mother Mary, this mission was going to steal his sanity if he didn't get a fucking grip. He'd sworn to himself he could keep her at arm's length, but each day presented a new level of hell.

"Finish your breakfast, Princess. You're going to need the energy today." His voice was rough despite the fact he hadn't spoken much above a whisper. Her nipples peaked in response, but she swallowed back whatever response had been on the tip of her tongue. He pushed away from the oak doorframe to stand across from her. It took a great amount of effort to hold back his smile when she realized why he was now standing directly in front of her. Who knew he was going to enjoy this glass topped table so much?

Savannah tried to inch her plate forward in a subtle effort to block his view of her bare pussy, but a slow shake of his head stilled her movement. "I want to look at you. And that's my privilege, Princess." He watched in amusement as a blush moved from her chest to her cheeks. She probably cursed her fair complexion as much as he appreciated it. Most of the submissives he dealt with rarely blushed, and those who discovered how telling the response was tried to mask it by tanning. He'd happily slather Savannah in sunblock, because he planned to keep her bare and fair as long as she was *his*.

The shocking realization he considered Savannah his hit him like a blow to the chest. He silently cursed his mother—she'd threatened to call one of her Voodoo buddies to cast a spell on him. Hell, he'd thought it was another one of her less than subtle hints about grandchildren, but now he had to wonder. His maternal greatsomething or other grandmother had been a well-known and, by all accounts, much-feared Voodoo Priestess. He'd never been particularly impressed, but his grandmother and mother had carefully cultivated and worked hard to maintain their New Orleans contacts over the years. *Great, just fucking great. Now I'm worrying about hexes and spells. I'm going to be certifiable by the time we get Amaryllis Fitzgerald home.*

"Have you finished your breakfast, Savannah?" She had been moving the remnants of her omelet around on her plate for several minutes—it was a safe bet nerves were overshadowing her appetite. She nodded and pushed the plate away with shaking fingers. Ordinarily, he wouldn't allow her to avoid looking at him or to simply nod in answer, but he could see the lines of fear in her body language and wanted to get this over with as soon as possible. He was not looking forward to seeing Carter's handprints on her ass, but it couldn't be avoided.

"How many swats does she have coming?" He'd directed his question to Carter without ever taking his eyes off her.

"Six. Four for trying to avoid breakfast and two for rolling her eyes. She's getting off easy on the second offense, because she was very candid in her explanation and Master Karl took pity on her." Landon heard the amusement in Carter's voice, but he doubted Savannah had.

"I have to say, I'm surprised Master Karl was so charitable since rolling her eyes gets his pretty sub in enough trouble to keep her from sitting through staff meetings at the hospital at least once a month." He wasn't surprised when Savannah didn't react. He would have bet she'd have done her homework. And even though Mountain Mastery's membership list wasn't public information, there was very little the Agency couldn't find out if they wanted the information badly enough.

If he'd been the one administering her spanking, he'd have her over his knees. He liked the intimacy, and subs typically found it much more difficult to hold themselves emotionally distant when their bare ass was positioned perfectly over their Dom's lap. The increased vulnerability enhanced the connection, but she needed to bond with him, not Carter. It was unfortunate her first punishment wouldn't be at his hand, but he planned to manage the scene closely—and that was going to have to be good enough.

"Come." He walked around the table and held out his hand to her. There was only a brief hesitation before she placed her small hand in his much larger one. Lacing his fingers with hers, he could feel the fear she was working so hard to hide. It wouldn't do him any good to tell her that her imagination was far worse than the reality, so he didn't bother.

Carter followed them into Landon's office. When Savannah heard the distinctive snick of the door lock, he felt the wave of panic move over her a split second before she tried to pull her hand from his. Before he could turn her to face him, she'd launched into full-blown panic. Her breathing accelerated to the point she was a heartbeat away from hyper-ventilating, and her eyes were impossibly wide. Savannah's pupils so constricted he doubted she was even seeing clearly at this point. Her frantic glances to each side told him she was seconds from running. He heard Carter's "What the fuck?" behind him but didn't have time to respond.

"Savannah. Stop. Now." He hadn't shouted, but he'd infused his voice with every bit of dominance he could muster while banding her tightly against his chest. He knew she wasn't thinking clearly. In truth, he'd expected her to meltdown before now. The only part of this that surprised him was how totally out of proportion her response was.

She went completely still in his arms, but the rapid rise and fall of her chest told him her body had responded to his command but her head hadn't caught up yet. He kept her in his arms, rubbing his hand soothingly up and down her spine until he felt some of the tension drain from her muscles. "Tell me what triggered that response, Princess." Whatever happened, they needed to conquer it before they went to Costa Rica. Absent that, he'd need to be meticulous about avoiding it and have a plausible story as to why.

When she didn't immediately answer, he pulled back enough he could read her expression. Her eyes were still dilated with fear, but the wild look was beginning to fade to fatigue. Obviously, she was particularly vulnerable to adrenaline crash—another thing he needed to remember. Her gaze flickered to where Carter stood to the side before returning to Landon's, and he saw her biting her lower lip as she fought through her unease.

"Answer the question honestly, Savannah. I assure you, Carter is not going to be insulted by anything but a lie." Landon hoped like hell he hadn't just misled her.

Carter nodded as he stepped closer. "Kitten, I think you're letting your imagination run away with you. I am happy to help prepare you for the mission. But if something about my presence is causing a problem, I'll step aside because your safety and your niece's life are more important than my ego."

She gave him a weak smile, but he knew Carter appreciated the effort. "I don't want to hurt your feelings, but...well, I don't know you. And no one has ever hit me...except for training and that's not really the same." She'd stepped back far enough to twist her hands in front of her, and Landon stood quietly waiting for her to finish. He wasn't surprised she hadn't ever been spanked at home. But it was common for upper crust private schools to use corporal punishment, so he was shocked she hadn't gotten at least one paddling there. Evidently, he'd gotten his *and* her share, and he'd only lasted one year.

He watched her shoulders slump and hated the bright

sheen of unshed tears he saw in her eyes just before she dropped her chin. Landon gave Carter a quick hand signal encouraging him to do her punishment as a two-two-two series. She'd get two warm up swats, two punishment swats that might—emphasis on might—remind her to not roll her eyes, and then two erotic swats to show her spankings could also bring intense pleasure. Carter's dark eyes studied him intently for long moments before he shook his head.

Carter stepped forward, lifted Savannah's chin with his fingers, and smiled. God, she looked so forlorn Landon wanted to pull her into his arms and reassure her. Dammit, one small set-back didn't equal failure, although he was willing to bet that was exactly how she was viewing it. "You are a beautiful woman, Savannah, and I'd love nothing more than feeling that sweet ass heat under my hand. But you're pushing the clock on this thing, and you need to be focused on training with your Master. I'm going to ask him to administer the punishment you've earned."

When the first tears breached the lower lids of her pretty blue eyes and rolled slowly down her cheeks, Landon clenched his fists. Carter framed her face with his hands and brushed them away with his thumbs. His expression wasn't lustful—fuck, the gesture would have appeared almost brotherly if she hadn't been naked. But Landon knew Carter had been looking for a woman like Savannah for a long time, and it was impossible to deny his relief at the man voluntarily stepping back.

Savannah surprised them both when she wrapped her arms around Carter, giving him a quick hug. Seeing her small body contrasted beside Carter's much larger frame emphasized the D/s dynamic he knew Carter was searching for. Hell, she was practically a textbook example of the women his friend had always dated. Landon heard the growl of frustration rumble in his own chest followed by Carter's chuckle. "Kitten, I don't think your Master appreciates your affectionate nature as much as I do. Perhaps you should reconsider your loyalty to him when this is all over. I'm much more open-minded."

"Out. Now." Landon's snarled words didn't faze Carter in the least. The damned man gave him a knowing look as he made his way out the door. He and Carter had been friends for several years and the skeptical glare he'd given Landon was easy to interpret. The other man wasn't buying the story this was all about the mission.

Chapter Ten

SAVANNAH WAS CERTAIN there'd been some sort of silent communication between Landan and Carter, but she didn't understand exactly what had taken place. She'd already guessed Carter would be accompanying them to Costa Rica. She wasn't sure why they hadn't mentioned it yet, but she wasn't going to let them off the hook, either. *Dammit, they can just suck it up and tell me the truth.* It frustrated her to admit how much the secrecy bothered her. So much for considering her an equal partner in her training and the op.

Obviously, her sudden swell of frustration hadn't gone unnoticed. When her thoughts returned to the here and now, Landon studied her with a practiced eye. "Tell me." It was a simple enough command, but she wasn't in the mood to let him off so easily.

Raising one of her perfectly shaped brows in question, Savannah gave him a look she doubted any man on Earth would misread. *Not going to make this easy for you, jerk. You want the information, work for it.*

"Your defiance just doubled your punishment, Princess. Better answer before you are in way over your head." The muscles in his jaw twitched from being clenched so tightly, and his words were pinched out in frustration. *Too fucking bad.*

Stiffening her spine helped shore up her resolve, and Savannah lifted her chin. "I'm tired of being treated like a robot. I understand I'm supposed to be learning to play the role of a sex slave, but it's just that...a *role*. No actor needs to live their characters twenty-four-seven to play a part. I'm a trained operative. I'm smart, and I'm capable. What I'm *not* is a brainless twit you need to hide mission details from. We are supposed to be partners, and it appears we have entirely different perceptions of what that means."

Damn, it felt good to unload on him. She'd been holding in her anger and frustration since the moment she'd heard Amy had been kidnapped off the street. He'd called her defiant...well, the jerk had no idea just how damned defiant she could be. "What is it about me that make you think I'm nothing but an air-headed twit you need to shield from the real facts of the case? I understand the information will likely scare the shit out of me. I get it...I do! But dammit to dachshunds, I deserve to be included. I don't like this dance of deception you all are orchestrating...not even a little. I know you'd rather have someone else, but we have to make this work for Amy's sake. Can you put aside your personal disdain for me until we get her home? Then you can go back to avoiding me like the plague. I'll stay as far from you as possible...I swear. I'm not a glutton for punishment. You aren't exactly good for a girl's ego, you know."

Her heart hammered in her chest, and her breathing was so fast and shallow it was little more than panting. Fucking hell. She hated losing control, and that's exactly what she'd done. Landon didn't say anything for long moments. He just watched her. She could feel his eyes taking in every clue her body language was broadcasting and had never felt as naked as she did in his moment. His eyes flashed with something close to disbelief before he masked it quickly.

He's a jackass who didn't deserve your attention...he's a jackass who didn't deserve your attention...He's a... She kept repeating the mantra over and over to herself. It was the only thing keeping the tears burning the backs of her eyes from unleashing in a torrent. In Savannah's opinion, her biggest weakness was crying when she was pissed off, because it was like throwing gas on a fire. The whole thing was a vicious cycle...get pissed, cry, then get pissed off for crying, and cry more.

For the first time in years, Savannah was homesick. Not because she missed her family, but she missed the small gym. Her parents built it at the back of estate because they hadn't wanted it cluttering their stately home. The separate building nestled in the trees, barely visible from the main house. They'd subtly added a living unit, and she'd happily complied.

On days like today, she could be found with her hands wrapped and shoved into gloves, pounding the training bag hanging in the corner. Letting her anger vent through pure physical exertion was the only way to control the rage she felt whenever she was discounted because of her looks or simply because of the family she'd been born into. Why people couldn't seem to understand the perks came with huge burdens was a mystery to her.

It didn't matter that she was naked as the day she was born standing in front of the man whose face she saw in her dreams...it was her father's voice she heard in her head. *"To those whom much is given, much is expected, Savannah. Fitzgeralds don't cry, and they don't let their opponents see them sweat."*

Finally! Landon had started to worry the woman didn't have what he considered a snap-point. He could have broken her the first day. But he didn't want to *break* her. He simply wanted to see some of the fire burning behind those icy blue eyes. She'd been patient to a fault and so compliant he'd started to wonder if there was anything left of the woman he'd known two years ago. Breathing a sigh of relief, he was grateful the spirit he'd admired was still there.

"We're going to talk about what triggered your outburst, but one thing at a time. Come." He shackled her wrist with his hand and pulled her to the sofa. He sat down but left her standing just to his right. "What's your safe word, Princess?" It wasn't easy to hold back his smile when her eyes went impossibly wide, but he was satisfied when she repeated what she'd been told verbatim. "Good girl. Use it if you need to, but be sure it's because you cannot physically or emotionally endure any more. Using your safe word simply because you are uncomfortable means we'll be turning this case over to the McCalls."

Landon watched the muscles in her jaw tighten with resolve. Stubborn little sub. He gave her arm a quick pull, and she landed over his lap. Her squeak of surprise made him smile, and he was glad she hadn't yet noticed the mirror a few feet away. She'd see it soon enough, and he hoped by then she would be too lost in the pleasure to be embarrassed. Savannah was a beautiful woman, but her sexuality had barely been tapped. Her position was so erotically vulnerable he worried she'd retreat if she saw herself the way he did. It was time to get started. Keeping her off-center was his best hope for knocking down the walls she kept so carefully erected around her heart.

Sliding her forward until her ass was peaked and perfectly positioned for his hand, Landon stroked over the pale silk of her skin. "You have a world-class ass, Princess. High and tight with perfectly rounded cheeks. I can hardly wait to see what shade of pink your ivory skin blushes." Before she had a chance to tense, Landon landed the first swat.

She gasped, and he felt her hand wrap tightly around his ankle. "You have eleven more to go, Princess. We're going to start out slow. Several warm-up swats first."

"Wh...what? Warm-up? Slow?"

He landed two more stinging swats in quick succession. "Would you like to rephrase that before we begin again?"

"Again, sir?" She was definitely a quick study. He made no attempt to hold back his chuckle.

"Yes, we'll begin again. I prefer to give warm-up swats to start. It brings the blood to the surface and will help prevent bruising." Although, with her light complexion and the added slaps on her up-turned ass, there was a good chance she'd carry the evidence of her punishment for a couple of days. Unfortunate, but not unacceptable. It was important to maintain consistency in her training, so he reminded himself to begin as he intended to go.

"Since this is your first punishment, I'll narrate, so to speak. But the price of this consideration is that I won't allow you to speak again unless you're using your safe word." As he'd been speaking, he felt her relaxing over his knees. Savannah might not realize it, but on some level, she trusted him. He hated how much his rejection had hurt her, but he'd made the best decision he could at the time.

When he'd finished warming her up, Savannah's ass was already scarlet red and hot to his touch. He wasn't going to be able to increase the intensity of the swats by much or she'd carry the bruises for a damned week. Her breathing was ragged, but when he checked her reflection in the mirror, he didn't see any evidence of fear.

"Open your legs for me, Princess." Her reaction wasn't immediate, which earned her another quick slap to her already heated flesh. When her thighs parted, he could see the glistening evidence of her arousal. "Well, well. It looks like someone is enjoyed their warm-up." Hell, her responses so far were almost perfect. She'd barely made a sound since he'd warned her about talking out of turn, but her body was speaking for her—loud and clear. He slid his fingers through the slick folds of her sex and watched her entire body stiffen in response. Her soft gasp preceded a rush of her cream flowing over his fingers.

Landon fought the urge to push his fingers deep into her heat. God, he'd love to see how quickly he could finger fuck her to a screaming release. He positioned a thick finger at the entrance to her vagina and smiled when he felt the muscles flex as if they were trying to pull him inside. She was soaking wet and he wondered if she knew how thrilled he was with her response. "Such a greedy little slave. You've forgotten you still have two punishment swats coming before we discuss that orgasm your body is clamoring for."

Her moan of frustration changed to a shriek when he pulled his fingers back and slapped her with a solid swat. The heat would have been entirely different from the warm-ups she'd gotten, but she didn't make any attempt to move off his lap. "Tell me why you're being punished, Princess."

She gulped in air before telling him again about her reluctance to enter the room when she'd seen Senator Tyson sitting at the table and rolling her eyes when Carter insisted she open her legs while she ate. He knew she understood on a cognitive level why Carter wanted her exposed, but until she experienced what it felt like to fully submit, she wouldn't understand the real significance of the command. If she belonged to him, Savannah wouldn't think twice about entering a room bare—she'd be confident to the depths of her soul he'd never humiliate or endanger her. The confidence that level of trust gave a woman was intoxicating.

The second punishment slap was harsher, but she'd barely registered it, telling him how deep she was sliding into the headspace where nothing existed but pleasure. He was thrilled he'd been able to push her far enough the line between pain and pleasure was becoming so blurred she couldn't distinguish one from the other. It was a damned dangerous place if the sub had placed themselves in the wrong hands, because they often missed their body's cues warning them it was time to safe word out.

Sliding his fingers back into her sex, Landon was shocked to find her wetter than she'd been before. *Fucking perfect.* Savannah's kinks seemed to be in line with his own, which would make it much easier to pull off the charade in Costa Rica. But he was beginning to worry it was going to make it very difficult to let her go when it was all over.

"I don't think spanking is going to be much of a punishment for you, Princess. Next time, I'll have to remember to use something you don't enjoy so much if I want to correct your behavior." He felt her shudder, but he wasn't sure if it was in response to his words or the slow slide of his fingers through the swollen folds of her sex. Using her slick syrup as lube, he began massaging the outer ring of her anus. When she clenched her muscles, he gave her a slap in warning. "What do you think was in that box on the table, Princess? Cupcakes?"

"No, Sir. Cupcakes would have been set out for all to see. I assumed it was nipple clamps or a butt plug since the box had a Pink Cherry on the side." Damn, the woman didn't miss anything. Hell, even he hadn't noticed the symbol for one of his favorite on-line retailers.

Pulling the small plug from his pocket, he slid it between the wet lips of her pussy. Rotating the tip just inside her opening, he chuckled when she tried to thrust her hips back. "Don't be greedy, Princess. The first time I fuck you won't be with a piece of plastic." It wouldn't be in his damned office, either. He was already going to be haunted by the image over her spectacular ass draped over his lap. He wouldn't have a chance in hell of erasing the memory of fucking her here, and he did have to work here when this was all said and done. Dammit, his business was already suffering from inattention.

The decision to leave the Agency hadn't been sudden, but he knew it was time. This was his last mission. He'd promised to help the Wests and Ledeks if they found themselves in a pinch, but he preferred staying in the background to advise. Once the thrill was gone, it wasn't long before operatives became liabilities.

Landon had never intended to devote so much time or effort to what had started out as an adrenaline fix. But his natural affinity for the work brought increasing numbers of assignments over the years. Unfortunately, it also meant his dad had been forced to carry too much of the business burden during Landon's frequent absences. The small heart attack his dad had a couple months ago was the wake-up call Landon needed.

"You are doing so well, Princess. Relax that pretty ass and push back into the plug. It's small so you won't have any trouble taking it." He felt her draw in a deep breath and relax just as he began pushing the plug past the tight ring of muscles. "Push into it, pet. There you go. Perfect. We'll leave this one in until after lunch and then replace it with the next larger one."

She shuddered as he stroked his hand over the heated flesh covering her ass. "We're going to finish up your spanking." When she stiffened, he gave her a quick slap. "You're going to enjoy this part." He shifted her forward enough to put her clit in line with the fabric of his jeans. The well-worn denim would provide the perfect amount of friction. He wanted to be sure she'd be more than willing to submit to another over the knee spanking. Damned if he wasn't enjoying it nearly as much as she was going to. She was going to leave a wet spot on his jeans, and he planned to wear it like a badge of honor for the rest of the day. *Fuck, I may never wash this pair of Levi's again.*

Chapter Eleven

SAVANNAH FLOATED IN a quagmire of sensations so starkly different from each other she wasn't sure if her body was experiencing pleasure or pain. The first slaps of Landon's hand against the tender skin on her ass felt like fire raining down on her, but soon, the heat made its way to her sex, and everything changed in an instant. Her pussy flooded with moisture, and she lost herself in trying to make sense of everything she was feeling until Landon told her those were just warm-up swats. She'd almost panicked realizing the pain was going to get worse, but something had told her to ride it out.

Navigating the strange fog made her feel like she was trapped in some sort of unearthly purgatory where she was caught between torment and ecstasy. Nothing seemed as important as her body's need for release. Every slap brought more heat and increased need until she couldn't even comprehend Landon's words. She knew he was talking to her, but nothing made sense. Her body wasn't interacting with her brain to process the information, but he was whispering soft words of praise against her ear, so she wasn't going to expend the energy trying to figure it out.

She'd used butt plugs before, trying them for her own pleasure. Savannah relaxed, pressing back into the plug.

Knowing he'd use a larger plug after their lunch sent a fresh wave of moisture from her sex. Imagining him bending her over the table in front of his staff had her sending up a silent prayer for an early lunch. "You love this, don't you, Princess? You were made to be draped naked over your Master's knees, your bare pussy begging for his touch."

Landon's voice was fading in and out, the words a disconnected jumble as her body neared implosion. She could hear him talking, but the roar of blood in her ears was louder than anything he was saying. The only words she heard were "Come when you're ready." *Is he kidding?* She'd been ready since ten minutes after she walked in his front door.

He gave her a couple of light swats between soft caresses, but it was only enough to push her higher. She knew he could sense her need, and he hadn't seemed in any hurry to give her what she needed until his palm landed a heavy slap directly atop her aching sex. That one perfectly-placed heated caress was all it took. Wave after wave of the most intense pleasure she'd ever experienced crashed over her like a tsunami. The power may have surprised her, but the intensity devastated her.

Gasping for breath as the last tremors faded away, Savannah sagged over Landon's lap like a limp rag. She couldn't have moved if her life had depended on it. *Mortal danger? No problem I'll just lay here…naked over the lap of the man who rejected me, awaiting my fate and trying to find any remaining pieces of my dignity.*

She was shocked when he gently turned her over so she was cradled in his lap. He pushed the loose strands of her hair away from her face and kissed away the tears she hadn't even realized wet her cheeks. The trembling in her muscles didn't abate, and the longer the involuntary contractions continued the more exhausted she became. "Come on, Princess. We need to get you some juice and a blanket."

"Can't...don't think I can...later." Laughing, he pulled a soft blanket from the end of the sofa and tucked it around her before standing up with her in his arms. "No. Too heavy." Her words were slurred, but she knew he'd understood what she meant when he chuckled.

"I don't think so, Princess. You're a very petite woman. A very beautiful, petite woman. I enjoy feeling you so sweet and complaint in my arms." He set her on the walnut bar, but kept one hand on her as he reached into the glass-fronted refrigerator to pull out a small bottle of orange juice. Holding it up for her, he said, "Drink." She was grateful he was holding the bottle, because her hands were still shaking and she had worried she'd splatter juice all over them both. When she took a small sip, he shook his head. "No, drink it all. It will help the adrenaline crash. I'm going to have to be very careful with you in Costa Rica. Having you this incapacitated would be too dangerous. It's good for my Dom-ego, but not safe for the mission."

She nodded because she understood, but that didn't mean she didn't feel like she'd let him down. "Fuck." He picked her up again and made his way back to the sofa. Landon settled her on his lap, but turned her enough she was forced to look directly into his eyes. When she felt the hard length of his erection pressing against her thigh, Savannah gasped. He gave her a tight smile. "Yes, I'm hard. Hell, I'm about to burst. But I control my cock, not the other way around."

The sting of his rejection shouldn't have hurt...dammit, it wasn't like it was the first time. But she was still feeling the effects of an earth-shattering orgasm and the residual vulnerability. He grasped her chin and returned her focus to his face. "Don't think for a minute I don't want you, Princess. You are testing my control in ways no other woman ever has. But we're doing this on my timeline, not yours—and certainly not according to my cock's selfish demands."

Parting the blanket, Landon shook his head as he took in her body's obvious signs of arousal. "You never cease to surprise, Princess." She cocked her head to the side in unspoken question. He grinned. "I didn't think you had a submissive bone in your body, Savannah. Quite frankly, when this mission came up I wasn't convinced you'd submit to *any* man. And I certainly didn't expect you to trust me after the way I treated you two years ago."

When she started to shift from his lap, Landon tightened his arms around her. "No, Princess. You do not have permission to move. I want to make sure we're clear on a couple of things. First, I *will* fuck you." His blunt words should have turned her off. Instead, they sent a strange hint of desire coursing through her blood. "Don't think I've missed the resignation in your expression. You are still feeling the effects of the train wreck conversation twenty-four months ago, but telling you that your timing sucked didn't mean I didn't want you. Hell, it took everything I had to walk away from you. If you're honest with yourself, you'll admit you weren't ready for any of this."

Savannah drew in a deep breath and slowly nodded. "You're right. I've changed a lot in the past two years. I've done a lot of research into Dominance and submission since then. And I think you're probably right. It wouldn't have ended well."

"*Probably?* No, Princess. It would have ruined any

chance we had of ever working together again. Remember, the brain is a very complex organ. It stores every detail to memory, but only recalls those with the strongest emotions attached, so your memory of our conversation that night is undoubtedly very tainted by the bruising your ego took."

Dammit all to hell. She knew it had been easier to be angry than embarrassed. And she'd been mortified when he'd seen through her sophomoric attempts at seduction and gently explained why it was a bad idea. Her head understood, but her heart had gotten a heavily redacted memo.

"Second, I want you to explain what triggered your reaction to Carter." He held up his hand when she started to speak. "Not yet. I want you to carefully consider your answer because he's slated to travel with us to Costa Rica." When she gave him a look she was certain he wouldn't misinterpret, he raised a brow in question. "As a side point, staring at your Master as if he's dumber than a box of rocks isn't a good idea—ever."

"I've been wondering how long it would be before you told me he was going." She started to roll her eyes, but remembered her stinging backside and stopped herself.

"Good save, Princess. See? Negative reinforcement is an effective behavior modifier."

Freaking dandy.

"It only stood to reason that a man with enough money to have already purchased one sex slave and who is in the market for another would also have a full-time security detail. Your concession to Alvarez's protest would be to only bring one member of your personal protection team to the resort. The other members of your detail…our team…will be at a nearby hotel in case their boss needs additional help." Savannah wanted to laugh when he didn't respond. Seeing Landon Nixon speechless went a long way to soothing her bruised ego. It was always fun to throw a dart into people's perceptions of her as a dim-witted blonde and watching them burst like a balloon. Yes, very satisfying indeed.

LANDON COULDN'T DECIDE whether to throw his hands up in frustration or laugh at his own stupidity. *I swear the Universe hates me. Why else would it surround me with women who are similar in so many ways?* He'd long marveled at how much Tally reminded him of his mother. Both women were underestimated because of their appearance and because they'd married powerful men. Both were brilliant and deserved respect for their own accomplishments, yet people often discounted them, assuming their credentials or any recognition they earned was simply by virtue of the men they loved.

He couldn't begin to estimate how many times he'd seen his mother all but patted on the head by his father's business associates. Those same men soon learned Ariel Nixon was a force of nature and his father's most trusted advisor. Amazed he'd made the same mistake, Landon smiled at Savannah. "I'm impressed, even though I shouldn't be. You're a trained operative, and you've made reasonable assumptions based on training and experience. And you did it without reading the case file, which we'll review together over dinner."

"If you'll make a copy, I'd like to study it thoroughly. I don't want to miss any details." She'd never liked working through meals. It was one of the few etiquette lessons from her childhood Savannah's mother had actually made stick.

Landon shook his head and grinned. "No, I have plans for you this evening. We'll be going to the club to play." He watched her eyes widen and her cheeks flush the pretty pink shade he was beginning to recognize as arousal rather than embarrassment.

"Play? Oh, boy." When she started twisting her fingers together in her lap, he covered her hands with his own, stilling the nervous gesture.

"A little trepidation is a good thing, but fear isn't warranted, Princess. I want you to be comfortable in a group of like-minded people. A Master wouldn't allow his slave to be nervous in front of others. She would trust him to care for her in all ways. Her life is literally in his hands. Her entire focus is on him. That is the part I think will be the most challenging for you, because you are trained to be cognizant of your surroundings. And in this instance, it's going to require a lot of finesse on your part because you'll be playing the role of a trusting slave solely focused on pleasing her Master. But, as a member of the team, you'll need to stay alert for any potential dangers to yourself, your team, or Amaryllis."

Fucking hell, it was a wonder he hadn't been struck by lightning for lying. Well, he hadn't actually *lied* when he'd said he thought it would be a challenge, but it was damned well one of the biggest understatements he'd ever made. More accurately, he thought it was going to be closer to impossible to pull off. She'd had almost three years of training as an agent, but was only going to have two weeks to train as a slave. He'd already let some of his created back-story leak, knowing it would get back to Alvarez. But he still worried the man was going to realize Savannah was completely new to the lifestyle.

Nate and Taz were equally concerned and had helped him set up tonight's visit to the club. The Dungeon Monitors and a few of the club's most trusted members had been briefed and would be observing her carefully for any signs that would tip them off. The more eyes on her tonight the better. Their feedback would go a long way to help Landon see things he might easily miss while topping her.

Extra eyes-on had been the Ledek brothers' suggestion based on their own experience with sharing women. Landon had heard similar stories from others in polyamorous relationships, and he'd agreed any additional insight would be helpful. Setting Savannah on her feet, he stood and pulled the blanket from her. "It's like unwrapping a delectable gift. Come. I'll catch up on a few calls while you swim."

"I'll be fine. You should stay and work. I've wasted enough of your time this morning." Landon had a feeling she'd revealed more with those few words than she'd intended, but that was a conversation for later.

"I don't want you swimming alone, Savannah. It's a matter of safety. I suppose I could get one of the gardeners to lifeguard if you'd prefer." Damn, when did he start thinking a woman was sexy when she blushed? There wasn't a chance in hell he was going to let his landscaper ogle her. The sudden heated wave of possessiveness surprised him, but he carefully blanked his expression.

He paused at his desk before picking up the file folders he'd need to make his calls. "What's it going to be, Princess? Am I going to watch your lovely scarlet ass swim laps or would you rather show off those paddled cheeks to a stranger?"

"You. Please. Sir." She added each word as she remembered. It wasn't perfect, but he hadn't needed to remind her, so he was counting it as a win. Nodding, he shifted everything into one hand, leaving the other free to wrap around her small hand. As they entered the hall, she stopped and turned to him. "Am I...oh, umm... Permission to speak, Sir?"

"Well done, pet. What would you like to say?" If she belonged to him, there would be far fewer restrictions, particularly when it came to conversation. He'd always thought having a twenty-four-seven slave would be a pain in the ass, and it was. But he couldn't deny how much he enjoyed knowing Savannah was in the house. Even when he couldn't see her, he could feel her presence.

"Am I supposed to walk behind you?"

"No, pet. I want you beside me where I can keep you safe. If Alvarez or one of his many minions mentions it, that is exactly what I'm going to tell them. Each Master has his own way of doing things, and I would never have a slave or submissive trailing behind me." Reaching up, he stroked the pads of his fingers over the soft skin of her cheek. "Princess, I am going to rewrite a few of the rules, because there are some things I'm not willing to compromise on. I'm going to keep saying this until your heart hears it. My priority is seeing to your safety, and part of that protection is making sure you aren't damaged emotionally by this experience." And he was convinced that subjecting her to what she would feel was degrading treatment would hurt her.

Flashing her the smile Tally always swore made women's panties spontaneously combust, Landon leaned down and pressed a kiss to her forehead. "Besides, my mother would have a stroke if I made you walk behind me. You're going to love her, Princess. You are both smart and beautiful." Savannah wouldn't have missed the implication she'd be meeting his mother, but she didn't comment on what sounded a lot like the Freudian slip.

His dad had always told him, "When you find yourself in a hole, for God's sake, stop digging." Over the years, Landon had learned how valuable the advice was. And right now, it seemed priceless.

Chapter Twelve

MARCO LOOKED ACROSS the elegantly set table into eyes the most unique color he'd ever seen. Amaryllis had laughed when he'd called them blue-green. "They're teal. It's ironic because, in nature, there is no such thing as a teal amaryllis." Her lilting laughter filled the small, private space on the terrace. Tall hedges bordered two sides, and the brick wall of his home's exterior was directly behind him. Marco never sat with his back to anything other than a solid wall during a meal. He'd seen too many men taken by surprise, the error costing them their lives.

The dress he'd had delivered to her room molded to her delicate curves and shimmered as the soft candlelight danced across the fabric's surface. They'd eaten dinner together the past several evenings, and Marco was quickly falling under the young woman's spell. Each evening, she'd relaxed a bit more, opening herself up slowly like the beautiful flower she'd been named for. They'd talked about everything but the reason she'd been kidnapped off the street. He wasn't sure she fully understood what the future held for her if he decided against keeping her for himself.

He was delaying the difficult discussion he'd have to have with his father about pulling her out of the auction. It should be his decision, but like any other son who took over the family business, he knew his father would never fully retire.

"Did you see the rainbow over the mountain this afternoon?" Her soft voice brought him back to the moment. The innocent question contrasted with the concern reflected in her eyes.

"No, but I'm sorry I missed it. I always think of my late mother when I see rainbows. She was a woman of faith and taught me Bible stories when I was a child. Noah's ark and the flood always frightened me. But she reminded me to be patient. To wait for the story's end, because that's where the rainbow was."

"Because they mean hope. A promise from God to never flood the world again."

"Yes. I didn't understand the real reason the story was so significant to her—that she was fighting cancer. She held out hope until the end. She was convinced the doctors would find a way to cure her and she wouldn't have to leave me."

Marco hadn't realized his fingers were tightening around the stem of his wine glass until it snapped, piercing his skin. Amaryllis was out of her chair before he'd seen her move. She set the broken pieces aside, and gently blotted the blood from his fingers with a napkin. "I'm sorry you lost your mother so young. It had to be very difficult to let her go." The small puncture hadn't bled much, but she still held his hand between her much smaller ones. The loving touch was so foreign he held perfectly still for long moments, simply absorbing the joy of being nurtured. When was the last time anyone had taken care of him because they cared? Sure, he'd been given plenty of attention as a child. But his nannies had been paid to take care of him. This was something else entirely, and he wanted to soak up every moment.

Marco always enjoyed their conversations, but he hadn't made any sexual demands of her. Each night after dinner, he'd walked her through the beautiful gardens behind the resort then escorted her back to her room. At the door, he'd kissed her on the cheek before promising to see her again the next evening. He was planning to take her walking on the beach tonight. The moon would be full tomorrow night, but the light tonight was softer, and he wanted to see her fair skin luminescent in the moon light.

When she slowly pulled his hand to her lips and pressed a gentle kiss against his injured finger, Marco's control evaporated into a fine mist. Growling her name, he pulled her to him, slanting his lips over hers. The heated kiss spiraled out of control, and Marco wasn't sure he'd ever be able to let her go. Eventually, the need for air forced him to pull back. "I should apologize, *mi hermosa flor.*" She was most certainly a beautiful flower, but she wasn't his—*at least not yet.*

LANDON LISTENED AS Nate assured him everything was in place for Savannah's first scene at the club. He hadn't doubted his friends' ability to see to the details, but he wasn't leaving anything to chance, either. "Have you talked to Kyle today?" Nate's voice was filled with concern, and Landon wasn't surprised. He had his own concerns with the way things were shaping up.

"Yes. What's your take?"

"Fuck if I have a clue. I know the Agency thinks you're going to be dealing with a classic case of Stockholm Syndrome, but something about that doesn't seem right to me. Have you talked to Savannah? She's in a great position to assess the situation since she's had all the training and has the added advantage of knowing the victim personally."

"I agree she's in a unique position." He didn't intend to explain exactly how unique her position was at the moment. After fifteen laps, he'd pulled her from the pool and directed her to repeat her evening yoga routine on the private sun deck just outside the pool area. She was drenched in sunshine, but sheltered from everyone's view except his. As he watched Savannah perform her final stretches, he noted the fine muscle trembling he hadn't noticed when she started. The damned woman didn't seem to know when to quit. She would push her body past all reasonable limits if he didn't intercede. She'd told him a few days ago how much she regretted not having time to work out as often as she wanted to. He suspected working out was a way for her to cope with life's frustrations.

Savannah's agency file was a treasure trove of information about the family dynamics of the entire Fitzgerald family. The agent who'd done her background investigation made one note Landon found particularly interesting for a couple of reasons. Not long before she was set to move home, Savannah's parents built a large gym with an attached apartment at the back of their expansive property. The structure was still inside the secured perimeter, but wasn't visible from the main house. When questioned, most of their friends weren't even aware the smaller building was there.

Savannah graduated and moved directly into the detached structure. The gym was well-outfitted, but the investigator noted it was the small workout bag favored by boxers that Savannah utilized most often. After seeing her in action this morning, Landon was betting the petite bundle of dynamite currently wrapping up her yoga workout used the bag to vent all that pent up passion.

"Fucking hell, Nix. Tone down the broadcasting, would you?" Landon blinked several times, trying to refocus his attention on the conversation.

"God dammit, Taz, when did you join in?" Taz Ledek's empathetic gifts had always been stronger than Nate's, but unpredictable. After Kodi entered their lives, both men mentioned they'd gained some measure of control over their ability to sense what another person was feeling and often he could hear what they were thinking. Evidently, Taz's gifts now included seeing what someone was seeing. *Just fucking dandy.*

Landon shook his head and admonished his friend, "Watch it, man, or I'll tell Kodi you've become a peeping Tom."

"Fuck you, Nix. A year ago, I wouldn't have even bothered to tell you. I'd have just enjoyed the show." Landon laughed because he didn't doubt Taz was dead serious.

He heard Nate's soft chuckle at their banter. Then there was nothing but silence before Landon heard the elder Ledek brother sigh. "Is she the one, Nix? If so, maybe you should reconsider this mission." Landon started to deny his friend's observation, but it was pointless. Nate knew him better than anyone else did, and Taz was probably already more tuned in to Landon's feeling than he was himself.

"I'd be lying if I didn't say there is definitely something between us. Walking away from her two years ago was one of the hardest things I've ever done. Now? Hell, I'm not sure I'm strong enough to do it again." He smiled at

Savannah as she reentered the pool area and nodded when she cast a questioning glance at the pool. She dove cleanly into the flat water and began measured strokes toward the far end.

"I'm not pulling her out of the mission. It wouldn't be fair to her, and even with the new information, I don't want to risk leaving Amaryllis in Marco Alvarez's possession any longer than necessary." The man might be treating Savannah's niece like an honored guest, but he was notoriously unpredictable, and his father was one ruthless son of a bitch. Rumors were swirling that the older man had turned over the business to his son, but he was never far from Marco's side.

"Be prepared, because I can guarantee you Kyle West is going to ask these same questions. Kent will be much more subtle, but he's going to have the same concerns." Landon wasn't as well acquainted with the Wests as Taz was, but he'd spent enough time in Kyle's company to appreciate his forthright communication style. Landon wasn't fooled by their good cop, bad cop routine. Both men were ruthless operatives and shrewd businessmen. Their MOs were the only difference, and God only knew their methods of operation were polar opposites.

"Understood. I'll cross that bridge when I get to it." *And hopefully I'll have a clear sense of where things with Savannah are headed before then.*

SAVANNAH WAS ON her last lap when she realized Landon was standing at the end of the pool waiting. She was using the breaststroke as a cool down, and as a bonus, she got to enjoy looking at him. At some point, he'd changed into a pair of well-worn cutoff jeans complete with frayed hem and holes tempting her with a clear view of his long, tanned legs. For her, the teasing peeks were almost as sexy as nude...*almost.*

Her fingers had barely touched the edge when large hands slid under her arms, lifting her from the water. "Up you go, Princess." She felt her breath catch in surprise. When he lifted her higher than necessary, she wondered what he planned, but before she could ask, his tongue drew circles around first one nipple and then the other. "Damn, you are a delight, pet. All that physical strength wrapped in such a delightfully feminine package. I've got big plans for you this afternoon."

By the time he set her on her feet, her knees threatened to fold out from under her, and it didn't have a thing to do with all the exercise she'd gotten this morning. The heat from the tongue lashing he'd given her nipples arced directly to her sex, and Savannah groaned as it clenched around nothing but empty space. Unfulfilled need triggered her body's responses to bypass her brain. She arched her back, trying to push closer.

"So delicious and so eager. I think there is a very wanton woman buried deep inside, and I'm looking forward to setting her free." His words sparked something in the depths of Savannah's soul, a need to please she hadn't even known existed. She wanted nothing more than to hear his words of praise, feel the soothing touch of his calloused palm as it pressed gently at the base of her spine.

"You've earned a reward, my petite temptation. Come." Taking her hand, he led her into the large changing room. There were several stalls along one wall and a long marble counter topped with a well-lit mirror. "The showers and restrooms are through that door." He'd nodded to an open door at the other side of the room, but didn't let go of her hand so she could explore. Instead, he grasped her waist and lifted her up onto the counter. She gasped when her warm skin touched the cool marble, and he chuckled.

"Don't worry, pet. I'm going to make you forget all about that minor discomfort." Oh, she bet he could melt her into a puddle without breaking a sweat. "Turn around and face the mirror. There you go. Now open those lovely legs. I want to see what belongs to me." Seeing herself displayed so openly should have embarrassed her. But when her eyes met his in the mirror, the heat and desire she saw reflected in the blue-green depths took her breath away. She was pulled in so quickly all thoughts of embarrassment evaporated under his heated gaze.

"Place your palms on the counter. Keep your eyes open." Unclenching her hands, she realized nails had been biting into her palms. The cool marble soothed the sting. "We are both going to enjoy your reward, Princess. You get to fly, and I get to watch." Her body responded to the deeper pitch of his voice; the command dripped with sexual promise.

His dark tan fingers contrasted with her fair skin, emphasizing the difference in their sexual skill. Landon Nixon was much more experienced...so much more intense than any man she'd ever been with it was like comparing apples and oranges. Her previous lovers were all men, just as apples and oranges are both fruit, but that's where the similarities ended. Long, and thick, his fingers spread open the lips of her labia, exposing her entrance and giving her a naughty view of the jeweled plug he'd seated in her ass before her swim.

"Let's see what you like, shall we? There are hundreds of ways to pleasure a woman, and I'm going to enjoy exploring each and every one of them with you. Before we leave for Texas, I'll have uncovered all of your secrets and will know exactly how to send you soaring into the heights of heaven. I'll also know precisely when to pull back, leaving you desperate for release." His words alone were pushing her quickly toward orgasm. His heated chest warmed her bare back; his muscled arms encircled her, anchoring her against his much larger body. When he tightened his hold on her, the unmistakable edge of bondage ramped up her desire, and she saw the evidence of her arousal glistening in the light.

"Watch how my fingers tease your clit, drawing it farther and farther out from under its hood. The bundle of nerves concentrated there is only one of a woman's most sensitive spots. We're going to spend the afternoon in my playroom exploring your body's mysteries, my lovely pet. I suggest you eat a hearty lunch. You're going to need it."

Savannah felt herself sliding further and further under Landon's spell. A small part of her hoped it was the lifestyle and not the man, but the whispering voice of her soul assured her no other man would ever measure up to the one wrapped around her. The tips of his fingers slid easily through her cream. Hot, slick, and devilishly accurate in their teasing.

"See how the petals of your sex flower open as the blood flows into the delicate tissues, making them swell? The ancients had it right when they referred to a woman's sex as a rose. The deeper shades of red paint your sex as your body prepares itself for a man's possession. That's why you find deep red roses painted on the armor of knights. What man wouldn't want to remember the vision of such beauty waiting for him at home?"

Savannah felt the warning trembles in her muscles, her body racing away without waiting for her brain to catch up. "Please. I...Sir...please." The words stuttered out unbidden. She wasn't even sure what she was asking for.

"Although I do love hearing you ask so sweetly, we're working on my timeline, not yours, Princess. Your body is mine to play with and command. You do not have permission to come, pet." And he would play it like a finely tuned instrument. Savannah didn't doubt his ability to give her pleasure beyond anything she'd ever dared to imagine. What worried her was whether or not she was going to be able to walk away with her heart intact.

Landon plunged his middle finger into her empty sheath, curling it and pressing against her G-spot with accuracy born of more experience than a man should possess. She started shaking in his arms and was sure her heart was going to beat right out of her chest. The pounding was so fast and loud she was beginning for feel light headed when Landon's voice cut through her confusion. "Eyes on me, pet." She lifted her lashes and locked gazes with him. The intensity of his stare was so strong it was almost its own form of bondage.

He gave her an almost imperceptible nod she knew was an acknowledgement of her compliance. "Come for me, Princess." Her body responded before her mind registered his words. Every muscle seized, and she heard a scream bounce off the marble and tile surfaces. The burning in her throat told her she'd been the source of the shrill sound, but she hadn't even remembered opening her mouth. What she did remember was the explosion of light behind her eyelids and Landon's palm slapping her pulsing sex. "Open your eyes, Savannah. Don't you dare hide from me. Your pleasure belongs to me, and I want to see it."

Wave after wave of blinding pleasure assailed her, but she kept her eyes focused on his. Landon's sharp commands ramped up her response despite the fierce expression on his face. She was sure he wouldn't ever hurt her, but his intensity amplified her desire. When honey poured from her sex, Landon's nostrils flared, and she saw him shift his gaze down to her fully exposed pussy as he growled something unintelligible. She sagged in his arms and heard him whisper "Mine" just before her eyes closed and she let herself sink into the darkness.

Chapter Thirteen

LANDON REMAINED PERFECTLY still for long moments, willing his body to stand down. For the first torturous seconds, he'd been fighting to not embarrass himself like a hormone crazed teen. But then the urge to fuck Savannah on the damned dressing room counter had almost trumped the promise he made to ensure their first time together a sweet memory for her to cherish. It was entirely possible she'd walk away after they returned from Costa Rica, and he was determined to make certain it wasn't easy.

Watching her come undone under his hand had sealed her fate. She might not stay, but he didn't want it to be easy for her to go, either. Hell, she might never believe he was serious after his earlier rejection, but he would do everything possible to convince her.

When his body was once again under the big head's control, Landon lifted Savannah into his arms and moved her to the shower. Setting her on her feet, he steadied her until he was sure she'd roused enough to stand. Stripping off his jeans and tossing them aside, Landon started the water then led her under the warm spray.

"Let's get the chlorine out of your hair, Princess." He remembered Tally commenting how damaging pool chemicals were to her skin and hair, so he'd assumed Savannah would face the same challenge. It was remarkable how similar the two women were in many ways. He hoped they'd be friends, but feared his previous relationship with Karl and Tally would be a difficult hurdle for Savannah to overcome. Only time would tell.

"Stand still and let me help you." He was probably more pleased than he should be by the dazed look in her eyes. There was very little more satisfying for a sexual dominant than knowing he'd given the submissive in his care an orgasm strong enough to glaze over her eyes and render her temporarily helpless. But he would also need to remember to hold back once they left Montana. He wouldn't push her this far during their stopover at the Prairie Winds Club. They'd already be in mission-mode, and he wouldn't compromise her professional reputation.

"Oh dear God in heaven, that feels so good." He smiled at her softly moaned words as he massaged her scalp with strong fingers covered in citrus scented shampoo. She leaned her head back into his hold as he slid them through the silky strands.

"You have beautiful hair, Princess. It feels like wet silk in my hands. I'll condition it for you, and then I'm going to step back and watch you finish your shower. It's going to be a pleasure to see you run your hands over your body. Make sure that I enjoy the view." Her breathing hitched, and he saw her pulse begin pounding once again at the side of her slender neck.

By the time he'd finished rinsing her hair, his cock was so hard he thought it was going to split the tender skin stretching around it. *How in the hell am I ever going to survive watching her slide those dainty hands and pink-polished nails over her wet, naked body?* He sat on the shower's bench and stretched out his legs as he leaned back against the tiled wall. Crossing his ankles, he hoped the added pressure on his balls would be distracting enough to keep him from erupting like Mount Vesuvius.

The teasing look in her eyes as she lathered her body made him growl with frustration. "Be very careful, pet. You are playing with fire. I have plans for you, and they don't include fucking you blind against the shower wall." And that was exactly what was going to happen if she didn't stop taunting him. The seductress Savannah North kept carefully hidden from view was finally coming out to play. He hadn't seen any evidence of the temptress before she'd shown up on his doorstep, but now he wondered how the hell he'd missed it.

The corners of her mouth turned down for just a second before her expression smoothed once again. She was still protecting her heart—still perceived every delay as rejection. *I'm going to shatter all those defenses, baby. You've got some important lessons in trust coming, and I'm going to enjoy showing you how sweet surrender can be.*

He dried her and then pulled on his jeans. Laying a towel over the marble counter, he pressed a hand between her shoulders until she bent over. "Spread your legs, pet. I'm going to insert a larger plug." She shuddered but spread her legs wide enough he didn't have to adjust her position. "Good girl. Perfectly done. Now arch your back a little more. Yes, just like that. Perfect." He didn't waste any time removing the smaller plug and wrapping it in a towel. He'd deal with it later.

Pulling the lube from the warmer, he chuckled when her eyes widened in the mirror. "Yes, I was prepared, pet. Now, let's get that lovely ass of yours stretched out a bit more, shall we?" He saw the flash of uncertainty in her eyes and shook his head. "No, Princess, I won't be taking your lovely ass today. You're not ready." Circling her rear hole with the lubed plug, Landon moved it into position and flattened his hand between her shoulders to keep her in place. "Take a deep breath and let it out slowly. Yes. Now push out against the plug. Very good." He slid the larger plug in and back out several times, making a bit of progress with each stroke.

She groaned softly but didn't speak. Her breaths were little more than shallow panting, telling him she was aroused. Her ass cheeks were still a lovely shade of pink from her spanking, and he was anxious to see if she responded as well to a flogger. He'd need to be careful, her delicate skin would mark easily. There was so much he wanted to introduce her to. But it would take much longer than the small window they'd allotted for her training.

One step at a time, man. One step at a time.

THE SOFT FABRIC of Landon's tee-shirt felt strange against her skin after being nude since she'd arrived. She smoothed her hands slowly down her torso after he'd dropped the well-worn garment over her head. "It's so soft. And it smells like you." She heard the airy tone of her own voice and hoped he hadn't noticed the way it made her sound like a girl with a crush on her big brother's best friend. *Geez, Savannah. Get a fucking grip.*

They were almost to the kitchen, but he stopped and turned to her. "We're having lasagna for lunch. The pasta and sauce will both be extremely hot, and I don't want you to be accidently burned. I love seeing you bared to my view, but I must admit that I'm also enjoying seeing you in my shirt. I especially enjoy seeing your nipples drawn up so tight they look like pebbles pressing against the fabric. It reminds me I need to double check on your wardrobe."

"Wardrobe? For the trip? I brought the few things I could find before jumping on the plane. But I admit I didn't have time to get much. Come to think of it, where are my suitcases? I should probably review—" She stopped mid-sentence because he was frowning at her.

"First, your clothes have been hanging in the closet of the bedroom we are sharing since the day you arrived. Second, there is very little there I'd consider remotely suitable for our mission in Costa Rica. And finally, it is my honor and duty to provide your clothing for the trip. Masters provide for their submissives or, in this case, slaves. That's just the way it is." Landon sounded mildly affronted, but for the life of her, Savannah didn't understand why.

"Obviously, I've insulted you...although I don't know why. This is a job; I've been reminded of that time and again...so you aren't under any obligation to provide my clothing. I'm—" Her words were cut off when she found herself with her back against the wall.

Landon lifted her until they were eye to eye, then slid his right leg between hers so her quickly dampening pussy rested on his denim clad knee. "Stop talking, pet. One of my father's favorite bits of wisdom reminds people to stop digging when they find themselves in a hole, and you are definitely in a hole."

Holy shit, he's strung tight. Do not poke the bear, Savannah. Do not pass go. Do not collect two hundred dollars.

He was pissed, no doubt about that. She wasn't afraid of him, but she was confused by his anger. Her muddled state must have shown, because he shook his head, muttering under his breath. "Wretched mission."

Huh? What the hell did that mean?

The haze of frustration cleared from his eyes just before he lowered her to her feet. "Let's eat. We have a full slate of training this afternoon, and I'd like for you to rest a while before we go to the club tonight. There have also been some interesting developments in the case that we need to discuss."

"Developments? What's happened? When did you hear about these developments?" She suspected he'd heard the confusion in her voice, but she didn't care. She wanted to be treated like a partner, and that meant there wasn't any room for being left out of the loop.

"I got the call while you were swimming. There was no need to interrupt you since neither of us can do anything about it. As you are aware, we have an informant on the inside who's been willing to keep us updated on your niece."

"Please cut to the chase. You are scaring me to death. I understand that it's just a mission to everyone else, but Amy isn't just my niece. She's also my best friend. And I'm terrified for her. She must be frightened to death."

Landon pulled out a chair for her, and she noticed the soft towel covering the rough upholstery. Without missing a beat, she spread her knees wide and hooked her ankles around the chair legs. He nodded his approval and then moved to the seat directly across from her. Savannah felt her cheeks flush when she realized he had a bird's eye view of her exposed pussy through the clear glass table.

"What a wonderful view. Being able to see the swollen folds of your pussy is going to do wonders for my appetite." When she frowned at him, he surprised her by laughing out loud. "I swear I should paddle your ass for that glare, Princess. But I'm forced to admit I had it coming. Obviously, the news about Amy isn't bad, or I wouldn't be teasing you with it." His expression changed entirely, and she felt the ice walls around her heart begin to melt. *Dammit, I don't want to fall for him. It's a bad idea on every level.*

"According to our source, Marco Alvarez is treating Amaryllis like an honored guest. For all intents and purposes, he appears to be wooing her."

Savannah felt her mouth open, but thank God, none of the jumbled words in her mind tumbled out. She was certain she must look like a fish out of water, but she was too stunned to respond. A hundred possible scenarios had run through her head over the past week. But this? This had never even been close to her radar. "Holy shit. What does that mean? I don't even know how to process this, Landon…I mean, Sir."

He chuckled at her quick attempt to save herself from another spanking. "We're having a conversation as partners now, Princess. We both need to have a break from the protocol every now and then. And to be honest, I enjoy your company. I also respect what you're bringing to the table, pardon the pun, for this mission—the entire team is damned impressed with the progress you've made."

Damn her fair skin. She felt the flush flood her cheeks at his kind words. Gracefully accepting compliments had never been her strong suit because it happened so rarely. They'd certainly never come her way at home, and she'd had to fight for every ounce of respect she'd gotten at the Agency. Everyone always assumed she received the easy assignments because she was a lazy, rich girl, but being kept out of the action wasn't her idea. Hell, she hated being coddled and held back.

Hearing that she'd earned Landon's respect humbled

her. When she ducked her head, Landon's voice caught her attention. "Look at me, Savannah." When she lifted her chin, letting her eyes meet his, she saw nothing but banked desire and pride. "I know it hasn't been easy for you at the Agency. To be honest, I'm not sure why you've stayed. Once this mission is over, we'll be having a long conversation about where you see yourself in five years. I'm retiring and might have a few suggestions for you. You need to remember those weren't empty words. It wasn't a compliment for the sake of boosting your ego. I simply stated a fact."

She could hear the sincerity in his voice and pleased to see nothing in his eyes to indicate he was simply placating her. "I'm aware people blow smoke up your ass because of your brother. Hell, I've seen evidence of it in briefings and wondered what keeps you from becoming a first-rate bitch. You're going to learn the Prairie Winds Team won't sugarcoat it for you. It's one of the reasons I'll continue helping them after I retire from the Agency."

Her eyes burned as she blinked back tears.

"Princess, you're doing a great job with the training. I understand you've been thrown into the deep end of the pool, and you've impressed me more than I can say."

She nodded but was too overcome with emotion to speak.

Their lunch had been served, but Savannah wouldn't pick up her fork until her host took his first bite. He smiled at her. "Your manners are perfect, pet. My mother is going to love you. Now, eat, please. I dislike eating alone, especially when I have such lovely company."

This was the second time he'd mentioned that he thought his mother would like her. The first had given her the impression it had been a slip that embarrassed him. But this one had been deliberate and felt much more like a test. As if he'd been checking her reaction. Deciding against taking the bait, she simply smiled and savored her first bite of lasagna. *When in doubt, keep quiet.* Perhaps she'd learned more from her mother than she realized.

"As for what Alvarez's behavior means, no one is sure. What we do know is that she isn't being harmed, and that's the important thing. The team is running the information past a profiler, and if it turns up anything interesting, we should hear about it before we leave Texas. We need to have some idea what we're walking in to." She agreed, but at the moment, the only thing on her mind was gratitude. Hearing that Amy wasn't being mistreated, no matter what the reason, was a huge relief.

Pulling herself back from the emotional side of things, Savannah refocused on the table in front of her. The food was perfect, and she had to make herself push the basket of garlic bread out of reach. "Oh my stars and garters, I'm going to be able to roll faster than I can walk if I'm not careful."

"You're going to burn up all of those calories and then some this afternoon. Drink the rest of your water, pet. I want your bladder full when we begin." The horror must have shown on her face because he immediately grinned. "No, Princess, I have no desire to experience a golden shower. A full bladder will make it more difficult for you to hold off your orgasm and make it much more intense when it overwhelms you."

Terrific.

Chapter Fourteen

How do I get myself into these pickles? It hadn't taken Landon long to divest her of the shirt she'd worn during lunch and escort her to his playroom. And now she was tethered between two six-foot-tall posts and any carbohydrate induced brain-fog she'd experienced from the pasta had evaporated like a water dropped onto a hot iron. *Steam indeed. I already feel like a crispy critter, and he's only just started.*

"You are so right, Princess. I've just started." She could hear the amusement in his voice. The rat bastard could have been a gentleman and pretended he hadn't heard her musing aloud. *Whatever happened to social decorum?*

His hand fisted in her hair, tilting her face back until his blue-green eyes moved over her like a heated caress. Landon's gaze was so penetrating Savannah had once likened it to sex. Amy had laughed at her romantic musing, telling her she'd missed her calling. *I'd be a lousy romance author...I don't think drooling over and waxing poetic about Landon Nixon would pay well. I'd write the first chapter, come, and that would be the end of my writing career.*

"What was that, pet? What are you planning to write?" She tried giving him her best confused blonde face, but he simply laughed at her. "You don't actually expect that to work, do you? You are one of the most intelligent women I know. The ditzy blonde routine is far beneath you, pet."

"Fudge. I should have figured you'd be a hard ass...et." She heard the flogger he'd been using thump against the concrete floor a heartbeat before his hands cupped the underside of her breasts. Landon's thumbs and forefingers pinched her tightly drawn nipples with enough force to make her gasp. The pressure was just over the edge of pain. In the microsecond it took the pain to move to her sex, the sensation changed to mind-bending pleasure. "Oh, God. Please, oh yes, please."

"There's the look I've been waiting for. That sweet dazed confusion that tells me you don't understand why the pain feels so wickedly delicious. Your mind and body battle to make sense of the sensations. You can't process it, but you don't want it to end." The tips of his hair brushed against her jawline a second before she felt the soft caress of his lips over the pulse point at the side of her neck. "Your skin is hot beneath my kiss, and I feel your pulse pounding as your heart races. Powerful stuff, Princess. Desire is a pure aphrodisiac for a Master. Knowing I can elicit this response from you makes me want to put my stamp of ownership on you, pet. But a simple collar wouldn't be enough. If you were mine, the mark would be far more permanent."

Savannah was falling under his spell...she knew better, but her body wasn't listening to her head's words of caution. "You're thinking too much, my precious pet. I'm going to have to see if I can't push all those troubling thoughts out of your head. You are supposed to be focused on the pleasure only I can give you. The relief that is mine to provide when it pleases me." She wasn't sure where he was until the warmth of his breath moved over her bare sex. When had she closed her eyes?

She jerked against the bonds when the hot tip of his tongue slid through her wet folds. The cry from her lips was strangled, sounding more like that of an animal than her own voice. "More, please."

"Sweeter than a ripe peach and every bit as juicy. I'm going to taste every inch of you. And when you come, I'm going to savor every drop." Savannah felt her muscles begin to tremble before his devil-blessed mouth returned to her pussy. His tongue plunged deep inside her channel, and every thought she'd had splintered into a million pieces.

A soul shattering orgasm swamped Savannah so quickly she hadn't been able to hold back the scream burning her throat. Nothing existed but the fire of pleasure searing her body from the inside out. In the back of her mind, she heard Landon's growl of approval and relished the vibration that threw her back into the bottomless abyss of pleasure. Through the sparkling lights blinking furiously behind her eyelids, she saw nothing but midnight blue as she hurtled through the twinkling stars. When the light show faded, Savannah let herself slide silently into the darkness.

THE SOFTNESS BENEATH her was a cool contrast to the heat blanketing her from above. But Savannah couldn't seem to coax enough of her synapses to fire together to process the difference. *Just gonna roll with it. Enjoy the cloud and float along and hope the warm blanket keeps me from rolling off and plunging to Earth. Damn that would suck. Too far to land on my feet.* The warm blanket laughed, but for some reason that didn't seem at all odd. *I don't think blankets are supposed to*

laugh, but then again, who can be sure? I'll think about that later.

"Open your eyes, pet. I want you to see who your pleasure belongs to." The huskiness of Landon's voice cut through the fog. Savannah thought the monumental effort required to open her eyes should earn her some sort of Congressional medal. "Yes, pet. You have most assuredly earned a reward. But yours is intimately linked to my own." His eyes were so dark, the pupils so dilated only a narrow ring of blue encircled them.

There was a flash of an emotion she couldn't identify a split second before it was gone and nothing remained but desire. She'd barely had time to process what he'd said before she felt the hot tip of his cock slipping through the swollen folds of her labia. She'd never had sex without a barrier between her and her partner. And now? Now, she wasn't sure she'd ever be able to give up the incredible intimacy of being skin to skin.

When she tried to tilt her hips up, begging for more, Landon used his knees to spread her legs wider, robbing her of the leverage to move. He maintained the physical advantage long enough to whisper in her ear. "Don't. You're pleasure belongs to me. It's mine to give when I feel you are ready to receive it."

Say what? Holy Hannah, I'm going to die if I don't move.

"You're so fucking tight, pet. And scorching hot. Steam heated silk squeezing my cock. Testing my control. Pushing me harder than any woman ever has. *Mine.*" The words were electrifying...it didn't matter that she was certain they were spoken in the heat of the moment. He was far more experienced, and he was playing a role, but it was still hard to discount the intensity she felt in his words and actions.

When the head of his cock pressed against her cervix, Savannah didn't try to mask her body's reaction. Arching her back was pure instinct. Landon's chest pressed against her own, pinning her to the bed. That hint of bondage ratcheted up her desire and sent a flood of moisture to her sex. "Fuck. You just liquefied around me, pet. You love being bound for my pleasure, don't you?" Did she? How could she be submissive? She'd given up letting anyone else be in charge years ago. The one time she'd given in to her curiosity, she'd been shot down...by this man.

He must have seen the uncertainty she was feeling because his eyes softened. "It's not a sign of weakness to submit, Princess. The strongest women I know are the ones who find the greatest rewards when they hand over control to their Masters. That level of trust requires great strength. Let go. I'll always catch you." He'd sworn he would protect her, and she didn't doubt he'd give his life for hers on a mission. But this was different. This was a leap of emotional faith...not her personal area of expertise. *Indecision is a decision.* Her father's mantra replay in her mind, and for the first time, she truly understood what he meant.

Taking a deep breath, she nodded.

LANDON HAD NEVER been given a more precious gift. The competing emotions playing out in Savannah's turbulent blue-green eyes had been some of the longest moments of his life. She'd been balanced on the very edge of trust, unsure if it was safe to risk her heart again. But the moment she'd let go was so sweet he'd felt a wave of relief wash over him. Knowing she trusted him with her body was hot, but watching her surrender even a small portion of her heart was the most valuable gift she could have given him.

"Mine." The simple declaration made her pussy spasm around him, shredding his control. Pulling back then pounding forward, Landon set a relentless pace. He wouldn't come before she'd found another release—but it was going to be close. "Hands above your head, pet. Wrap your fingers around the spindles of the headboard. Don't let go or I'll stop." The movement pushed her breasts closer, and he couldn't ignore the invitation. Sucking first one tight bud and then the other into his mouth, he lashed each until Savannah squirmed beneath him. "If you let go of the spindles, I won't let you come, pet. But if you behave, I'll reward you. Would you like to come, Princess?"

"Yes. Oh, God. Yes, please...Sir." He'd have laughed at her quick-thinking save if he hadn't been gritting his teeth to stall the release burning its way up his spine.

"Come for me, Savannah." The command had barely left his lips when she screamed, and every muscle in her body tightened like a bow string. She swept him over the edge with her, and in a distant part of his mind, Landon heard his own guttural cry of pure sexual pleasure. He caught himself on his forearms before he crushed her beneath his much larger body, but he wasn't going to be able to move until his muscles regained some of their strength.

"I swear I'll move as soon as I can, pet. But to be honest, I'm not sure my legs would hold me yet. We're going to soak in the hot tub and then nap before our trip to the club tonight. I want you well-rested." She would cope with everything he had planned better if she wasn't fighting fatigue. The dark circles under her eyes had finally started to fade, and he didn't want to see them reappear.

When Savannah didn't respond, he moved back just as her eyelids slid closed. *Looks like resting isn't going to be an issue.*

Chapter Fifteen

LANDON WATCHED SAVANNAH'S gaze dart around the room. Her mouth had dropped open as she tried valiantly to not stare at the people surrounding her. When she'd balked at the outfit he'd given her to wear, Landon had informed her he was being generous. Now she could see just how true his claim had been.

They'd reviewed the rules on the way to the club, and she knew she wasn't supposed to be gawking. But there was just so much to see. *Face it...these people are definitely dressed to be noticed, so she probably thinks it would be rude to not accommodate them, right? As absurd as it is, it sounds like something she'd say.*

"Pet, you are going to find yourself over my knee before we've made it fully into the room if you don't drop those wandering eyes to the floor." He'd kept his tone even, and the warning was spoken quietly enough no one else would have heard the reprimand. She appeared grateful for his consideration. She'd read enough to know many Masters wouldn't be so accommodating.

"Sorry." He was certain the apology had slipped out before she could call it back. He smiled to himself. She didn't have permission to speak, either. Technically, she'd already made two mistakes, and they'd literally just stepped through the door. For a woman like Savannah, who took great pride in perfection, the glaring errors would be a huge annoyance.

Landon stepped in front of her, and his large hands cupped her shoulders. "Look at me, pet." When she tipped her face up to his, Savannah's eyes widened in surprise. Had she expected him to be angry? Hell, he'd agreed with the Wests and the Ledeks when they'd told him to expect this reaction—he'd have been astonished if she hadn't gazed around, her eyes overflowing with curiosity. "Don't apologize unless I tell you it's necessary. You are my sub, not a doormat. No one here is going to fault you for a few minor infractions. You're new to the lifestyle, and mistakes are bound to happen. One of the reasons we're here is to give you a chance to experience the environment."

What they weren't telling her was everything she was seeing had been carefully choreographed. This had been Taz and Kent's brainchild. The two men reasoned she should *see* as much as possible to prevent the wide-eyed wonder she'd just exhibited from becoming an issue during Marco Alvarez's party. He'd watched her take in the people surrounding them and almost laughed out loud as her expression morphed from apprehension to astonishment.

Their contact inside the Alvarez compound hadn't been able to provide much information about the auctions, so they'd decided to err on the side of the angels. Taz reminded them it would be better for Savannah to be at least somewhat desensitized to the debauchery she was likely to see. Landon's sources insisted the auctions were more like upscale cocktail parties with naked men and women serving drinks, but he'd hope for the best and prepare for the worst.

"You'll be given time to look around, but I want to get you settled first. There is no reason to insult our kinky friends." When she didn't respond, he pressed a kiss to the tip of her nose. "Remember, the only person expecting you to be perfect is *you*."

He heard a soft gasp and turned to see Tally grinning up at him. She was practically bouncing on the balls of her feet with excitement. If he didn't give her permission to speak, she'd blurt whatever it was out in a torrent, getting herself into trouble, so he took pity on her. "Spit it out, sweetheart. What has you so wound up this evening?"

She gave her Dom a quick glance, and at his nod, she burst out with, "You, Master Landon. I never thought I'd live long enough to hear you say you weren't expecting perfection from a sub." She turned her attention to Savannah and grinned. "I'm so glad to meet you. Any woman who can soften up Master Landon has won my admiration. I'm Tally, by the way."

Landon stepped to the side, shielding the two women's exchange from the room. He knew Savannah would easily slip into professional mode. She wasn't well-trained enough in club protocol to hold back. But she'd been schooled in the fine details of etiquette her entire life. He often forgot her parents' social standing because she was nothing like the debutantes he'd been forced to mingle with for years.

Savannah grasped Tally's extended hand and smiled. "The pleasure is mine, Tally. I'm Savannah, by the way. I'd appreciate any tips you can give me. It's always a challenge to fit into a new group."

Karl Tyson rolled his eyes heavenward. "Don't encourage her, sweetness. She'll spend the entire evening regaling you with stories." Shifting his attention to Landon, he added, "Let's get these two off to the side before we cause any more of a scene." The two of them hustled their chatty subs to a corner sitting area where they could visit and watch the room without causing too much disruption.

Once they settled the two women at their feet and admonished them to speak quietly, Karl asked, "What do you make of the fact Amy is being treated like a guest rather than a captive?" Karl's question had been little more than a whisper, but when he felt Savannah stiffen against the side of his leg, he knew she hadn't missed his friend's inquiry. Shifting so he could lay his hand at the base of her neck, Landon gave her a reassuring squeeze then left his hand in place as a reassurance.

"There have been rumors Marco's father is pressuring him to marry and have children. It seems the old man wants to ensure his son has an heir. Perhaps Marco is humoring him, or he may actually be smitten with her." *If she is anything like her aunt, it's easy to imagine Alvarez being completely captivated by her.* He was relieved when Savannah relaxed and seemed to get caught up in her conversation with Tally.

"I was expecting Kodi to greet us. Have you seen her?" Landon's question brought a chuckle from behind him.

Taz stepped into view and pointed toward the corner by the bar where Kodi stood facing the wall. Her short dress was tucked up into a scarf tied around her waist, exposing her very red ass to the room. "Our lovely wife thought her duties as hostess trumped my brother's instructions to wait upstairs until one of us brought her down. She decided to come down on her own, and big brother wasn't happy. Personally, I'd have rather fucked her on stage, but it wasn't my call."

"I'll just bet you would have. You know she still struggles to orgasm in public. Are you sure you aren't a sadist?" Karl had been teasing, but Landon noted Savannah had once again gone stock still. *Time to get her moving and give her something else to think about.*

"As much as I'd love to stay and chat about Taz's perversions, I think I'll show my lovely pet off a bit. The short dress she is wearing teased me all the way to the club. It's time to repay the favor." He'd seated her on a soft towel and made her spread her legs on the drive into the club, and the tantalizing scent of her sex had taunted him more with each passing mile. If he lived any farther up the mountain, he'd have had to pull over and push himself into her wet depths because the temptation had ramped up to the point there almost wasn't enough blood flowing to his brain to drive safely.

LANDON LOOKED ON as Savannah tried to stand without flashing the room. Much to his amusement, she didn't have much success. "Don't bother. I doubt Master Landon will allow you to stay covered long anyway." Tally's sweet giggle warmed his heart, but for some reason, it didn't make his cock throb the way it once had. However, Savannah's tight smile caught his eye. She was the consummate professional, and he didn't doubt for a minute she'd done her homework when she'd received the order to fly to Mountain Mastery. His previous relationship with the Tyson's wouldn't have escaped her attention.

Before he could step away, he felt Tally's hand on his forearm. "I'm sorry if I spoke out of turn. I didn't mean to upset Savannah...I like her. And even more, I like how happy you look with her."

He could see the sincerity in her eyes and hated the fact

she was worried. "Thanks, sweetness. Your friendship and support mean a lot to me. I'll make sure she understands." He was grateful Karl had stepped up and was distracting Savannah. Seeing his interaction with Tally would have only made matters worse.

Pressing his hand against the small of her back, Landon moved Savannah through the crowd. He didn't rush, giving her plenty of time to sneak peeks at anything catching her eye. Once they'd reached the bar, he settled her on a seat before moving around to help himself. Her eyes widened in surprise, and he grinned. "I have worked for Nate and Taz since they opened the club. It gave me a bird's eye view and kept me off the streets."

"When you weren't out saving the world or adding zeroes to your bank account?" He'd have been insulted if another woman had made the same comment, but with Savannah, everything was different. For one thing, she was just as guilty in both areas as he was.

"Says the woman who hasn't taken a break from saving the world in two years. And we won't even start on the bank account comment." He grinned at her and saw her shoulders tense. Savannah didn't like being reminded she came from a moneyed background, but he wasn't going to let her get the upper hand in the discussion.

Her frustration had started with Tally's comment, and he was determined to keep it from snowballing. There was no reason for her to be jealous of Tally. He suspected she was more annoyed by her own response than she'd been with Tally's familiarity. "Tally is a trusted friend, and I hope the two of you will become friends, also. She is feisty and smart as a whip...you have a lot in common." And adding Kodi to the mix would be more than any of their Doms could handle. She didn't respond, but he hadn't expected her to.

Handing her a small bottle of water, Landon shook his head when she only took a small sip. "Drink it all, Princess. You need to stay hydrated. I have big plans for you." When he waggled his eyebrows at her, she shook her head in mock disgust but drank the water down in a few fast gulps. He led her across the room and smiled when she stopped in front of the small stage where a sub was bound to a St. Andrew's cross. Pulling her against his chest, Landon wrapped his arms around her. One hand played with her unbound breasts, easily slipping into the low-cut front of her dress; the other slid beneath the sky-high hem with unerring accuracy.

When she gasped, he chuckled. "This is why I didn't allow you to wear the bra and panties you lobbied for."

"Going out without underwear is scandalous. I shudder to think what the women in polite society would think." She was using sarcasm as a defense, and he gave one erect nipple a sharp pinch as a reprimand.

"Remember your place, slave. You should be grateful you are wearing anything at all. I'm sure you have noticed many of your peers are wearing much less." When she squirmed against him, he growled in her ear, "Careful, pet. I'm already riding the edge of control. If you don't want me to bend you over and fuck you right here, you'd better stop teasing me."

He pushed his finger into her and smiled at the sudden rush of moisture in response to his threat to take her in the middle of the room. "Your words sound so perfectly proper, but your body craves sin." She tried to shake her head, but with the side of his face pressed against her cheek, the motion was muted. "Don't deny yourself because you've been programmed to pigeonhole sex,

Princess. If you think all those up-tight old biddies in your mother's social circle aren't getting their own kink on, think again."

Adding another finger, Landon began the slow push and retreat he was certain would frustrate her. Her folds were so slick her honey was dripping off his fingers. "Watch Master Rafe send her over with the next lash of his whip. He knows exactly how much she can take—how much she needs to reach sub-space."

"It looks so barbaric…so painful." He doubted Savannah realized she'd spoken aloud or that he could hear the longing in her voice.

"Pleasure and pain are two sides of the same coin, pet. He's led her to the place where the two become confused. Master Rafe isn't her Master, yet he can sense exactly what she needs. How do you think he does that, pet?" As an agent, Savannah was well-trained in reading body language; she knew all the signs Master Rafe was monitoring.

"She strains toward the lash, not away from it. I can see the steady stream of moisture trickling down the insides of her thighs. Her moans deepen after every stripe is laid, and her eyes are glazed with desire." Savannah was becoming entangled in the sexual snare of the scene, and Landon was going to capitalize on it.

"I want you to come when she does, pet. Give me your pleasure." He felt her shudder against him, and for a few seconds, he thought she might come before Rafe sent the little sub over the edge. As if his friend had heard him, Rafe dropped the whip and stepped up to the woman and spoke. The words had been loud enough for only her to hear and had obviously been the permission she'd been waiting for. Her scream bounced off the concrete and brick outer walls of the old warehouse the Ledeks had revamped into a top tier sex club. Savannah's soft moan as she trembled in his arms was the only outward sign she'd orgasmed in his arms, and he found himself pleased he hadn't had to share the moment with those surrounding them.

"Beautiful, Princess. Knowing you trusted me enough to shelter you during those vulnerable moments pleases me more than I can tell you. And seeing how this scene turned you on makes me want to push my aching cock deep into your heat and fuck you until we are both too spent to walk." Her knees folded out from under her, but he'd been ready. "I'll always catch you, Princess." He knew he'd used the same words earlier, but he planned to repeat them until she believed him.

Holding her was pure pleasure, but he wanted her to regain her footing so they could continue. Once she was steady again, he led her across the room. She paused briefly to watch a scene playing out in the medical room, but the shudder that moved through her didn't seem to have anything to do with arousal. "I can't imagine wanting to be that...umm, well, exposed. I have to psych myself up to go for my yearly physical."

"You're going to be bare very soon, and you'll be as exposed as your Master wants you to be." She might not think she wasn't an exhibitionist, but her body was telling him something else entirely. It was time to find out if he was right.

TOBI LEANED BACK against the lounger and closed her eyes. "Damn, I needed this today. I'm glad you suggested it." She and Gracie had both been working long hours drawing up the blueprints to relocate the forum shops at Mountain Mastery. As soon as Nate and Taz finished renovating one of the smaller buildings on their property, they planned to open a full-service day spa and to expand the number of venders they could host. She and Gracie would have to return to Montana at least one more time before the merchandise was moved in, but for the next couple of weeks, they were going to enjoy a slower pace.

"Montana is beautiful, but nothing beats Texas sunshine." Tobi glanced at Gracie and rolled her eyes. Even though her best friend wouldn't have been able to see the gesture behind the dark sunglasses she wore, Tobi hadn't been able to hold back her disbelief.

"Are you shitting me? It's ten o'clock in the morning, and it's already hot. By noon, we'll be hiding inside by the pool and cranking the air conditioning down to a setting equivalent to a Canadian winter just to keep the pool water from boiling." Tobi often swore her friend's Central American blood made her immune to heat.

"Your language is going to get you in trouble, Tobi. And I'm too tired to go down with the ship with you this time. You didn't see me complaining when it was cold this winter. Although I did keep peeking outside expecting to see a penguin parade marching up the driveway."

Tobi choked on the drink she'd just tipped up to her lips and waved her hand dramatically, trying to clear iced tea from her lungs. "Fudgesicles. I'm sure you did that on purpose…you're going to drown me someday pulling that stunt." She grabbed her towel and wiped the tea from her breasts and shook her head. *A lot of good it did me to slather on sunblock.* "I only saw you a couple of times all winter. You hid inside and only went outside when the temperature was over sixty…and you thought it was warm enough for a parka. And the one afternoon I ventured to your house to see you, I had to change into shorts and a tank top it was so hot in there."

"It wasn't that hot. You're exaggerating again."

"Your kids were roasting marshmallows over the furnace vents!" Tobi loved teasing Gracie, but truthfully, it wasn't much of a challenge.

"When are Landon and Savannah arriving?" Tobi wanted to laugh at her friend's lame attempt to change the subject.

"Late tomorrow evening. They'll be staying two or three days, and I need to check the cabin to make sure everything is ready for them. I'm still fuming about Kyle's lecture." After all this time, the man could still make her homicidal...amazing.

"It wasn't really a lecture. It was more of a plea."

"What the holy hell is that supposed to mean?"

"He simply asked you to set a good example for Savannah while they are here. She has to pretend to be Landon's sex slave when they go to Costa Rica, and well...you aren't always a textbook submissive." Tobi sat up, turned to her friend, and pushed her glasses up until they were balanced on top her head. "I can be good...usually...when I want to. When have I ever led a newbie astray?" Before the words finished tumbling out of her mouth, Tobi realized she'd made a mistake. *Don't ever ask a question you don't want to have answered.*

Gracie laughed. "Tobi, I want to rest and let the sunshine soak all the way to my bones. It would take too long to list all the times you've gotten me caught up in your schemes. Micah called me Ethel for weeks after your last 'scathingly brilliant idea.' Do you have any idea how hard it was for me to figure out why he was calling me by some other woman's name? I didn't grow up watching all those sit-coms. Jax finally took pity on me and told me to Google, 'Lucy and Ethel.' If I'm Ethel, that makes you Lucy, by the way."

Oh yeah, she knew. Kent had called her Lucy more often than she was willing to admit. "Whatever. I still find it insulting that he feels the need to point it out. He could try charm for once. I respond well to charm." Okay, so that wasn't entirely true. She tended to ignore Kyle's requests if they weren't issued in a stern voice because that was her clue he was serious. Kent was her charmer...he could sweet talk her into anything.

"Insulting or not, we've both been warned to be on our best subbie behavior. I'm sure we can handle it. But I'm voting for a margarita party in the afternoon before their club visit. There's a new place in town that has specials for ladies in the afternoon, and their lunches are supposed to be delicious. It's the one Lilly was telling us about last week." Tobi remembered her mother-in-law raving about a new upscale place in town. Surely Kent and Kyle would approve them going to a place their own mother recommended. Then again, she and Lilly tended to amplify each other's outrageousness.

"You're just hoping I'll be too juiced to be sassy."

"Yep."

"A fine lot you know. How has booze ever worked out in our favor before?"

Gracie's well-endowed chest heaved with a put-upon sigh. "Fudgesicles."

Chapter Sixteen

LANDON SHOOK HIS head, trying to refocus his attention. It seemed to be getting harder and harder to remember he was supposed to be training Savannah for their upcoming mission rather than giving in to his desire to claim her as his own. God, he'd love nothing more than to take her small hand and lead her as she explored her submission. Being the one to witness all those firsts was going to be a joy, but it was also a pleasure he needed to postpone. His first order of business was getting her ready for their upcoming trip to Costa Rica. Cursing under his breath, self-recrimination was front and center in his mind when he felt a brush of air signaling someone had stepped up beside him.

Letting Savannah observe a nearby scene, Landon looked to his left and barely held back his grimace when his eyes met Taz Ledek's. *Fucking perfect. Just what I need when I'm already ass deep in alligators—a fucking mind reader more meddlesome than my Aunt Nancy.*

Taz's bark of laughter brought a startled gasp from Savannah and a curse from Landon. His friend reached out and wrapped his large hand around her upper arm, and Landon wanted to slap it away. "Sorry, Savannah, I didn't mean to startle you." Landon felt a wave of relief when the other man released his hold on her. She smiled and returned her attention to the couple in front of her.

Landon almost groaned when Taz turned his insightful gaze back to him. "Are you sure you don't want to make any changes?" Landon cocked a brow at his friend, aware he'd been deliberately vague. Taz left it up to him to interpret whether he was asking about the plan for tonight or the plan for the two of them to rescue Amaryllis Fitzgerald. He wouldn't pull the plug on Savannah's commitment to bring her niece home safely, but he had considered moving their scene to a less public part of the club. *Damn.*

This time Taz's laughter was much more subdued. "It's not that bad, you know. The trick is admitting you've fallen. After that, it's easier to accept the changes in your thinking."

"You're a real pain in the ass sometimes. You know that, right?"

"He should. I tell him all the damned time." Nate's amused voice came from his other side, and Landon shook his head at his teasing tone. The change in Nate Ledek since Kodi entered his life was nothing short of remarkable. The former SEAL had always played strictly by the book and was as driven as any Wall Street tycoon Landon had ever met. But love had smoothed many of those razor sharp edges, leaving a much more affable person in its wake.

Taz snorted a laugh that he tried unsuccessfully to cover with a cough. "Why don't you just tell him you think he's turning into a pussy? *I* tell him that, and he still walks around with his head in the clouds."

"Fuck you, Taz. Just because our lovely wife is angry with me and batting her pretty lashes at you tonight doesn't mean it will last. I'll be her favorite again in no time." Nate might have sounded flippant, but Landon could hear the remorse in his voice. Evidently, he hadn't enjoyed his sub's punishment any more than she had.

"You keep offering, brother, and I keep turning you down. When are you going to figure out that invitation is just wrong on every level?"

Landon shook his head. Leave it to Taz to focus on the first rather the last part of his brother's response. "Could you two cut the Laurel and Hardy routine for a minute? Fucking hell, Kodi deserves a medal for not murdering the two of you in your sleep." Landon appreciated their attempt to calm his internal storm.

Taz shrugged and grinned. "Fine. But I still think you should tell him he's a pussy. Our lovely wife usually leads him around by his balls."

Nate waved his hand in Kodi's direction and growled, "See that paddled ass? Those aren't your handprints, brother. She was out of line, and I dealt with it." Nate might have been talking tough, but the look on his face said he was feeling more than a little guilty about punishing Kodi. Landon shook his head and chuckled. He missed working at the club and feared it was going to be awhile before he got the chance again. His time at Mountain Mastery had never been about the money. He'd taken the job as a favor to his friends and as an outlet for his kink.

Lowering his voice to keep Savannah from hearing, he asked, "Will it be a problem to move to the smaller stage upstairs? I'd like to start with a smaller audience." What he'd really like would be to put Savannah back in the car and take her home. He'd fuck her until they were both too spent to care about where they were.

"No problem, man. And just for the record, I understand your reluctance to expose her to the general club membership. We'll be careful who we send up." Landon was relieved his friends would screen the audience, something in the back of his mind was niggling with concern about doing a scene in front of the entire membership. Since they still weren't certain why Amy Fitzgerald had been targeted, there was a lingering worry about spotters working in clubs to find unattached subs. He wasn't sure how much Savannah knew about her niece's personal life, but it seemed Amaryllis had been dabbling in the lifestyle prior to her abduction.

Before Landon could summon Savannah back to his side, she turned, and he was struck by the heat in her eyes. Looking over her shoulder, he saw one of the club's more popular Doms flogging a sub who hadn't belonged to the club long. The woman was trembling under the Dom's lash, and even though her skin glowed crimson with raised welts, they would fade before the next morning. The tenderness would remain for a few days, reminding her of her submission, but all outside appearances would be gone before she returned to her law practice tomorrow morning.

"I need to use the restroom."

Savannah's voice brought him back from his observations, and he smiled. *Oh no, Princess, I know exactly what you're planning. There will be no self-pleasuring on my watch.*

"Use the private bath behind the office." Taz's grin confirmed what Landon had suspected. The woman he was *training* intended to take the edge off before their scene, but she was in for a big surprise.

Landon let her take the lead up the stairs, the scent of her arousal wafting over him. He pushed his hand up the inside of her toned thigh and chuckled when her steps faltered. "Careful, pet. I'd hate to see all this heat wasted by a trip to the emergency room." She muttered something unintelligible. He hadn't heard the words, but he'd certainly understood her tone. *Feeling a little bit edgy, pet?*

By the time they reached the door of the Ledeks' private bathroom, Savannah was practically dancing in place. When he stepped into the room with her, she turned and stared at him, her eyes wide with surprise. "What are you doing? You can't follow me into the bathroom."

He cocked a brow, and he let a sinister grin curve up the corners of his mouth. "Actually, I can. And if you're brave enough to be honest with yourself, I think you'll know exactly why I'm here. Your body is broadcasting your need, Princess. Slaves do not come without their Master's permission—ever! Your pleasure belongs to me." Landon would have laughed out loud if he hadn't been absolutely certain it would piss her off, and her anger would give her an out he wasn't willing to provide. *No, pet, we're going to meet this challenge head-on.* The only emotion he didn't see play out over her pretty face was denial. He held her gaze until she dropped her eyes to the floor, her face blazing with embarrassment. *Busted!*

SAVANNAH WAS SURE her blood pressure was peaking near stroke level by the time she walked from the opulent bathroom attached to Nate and Taz Ledek's office. She'd been so aroused after watching the scene downstairs all she could think about was relieving the throbbing in her sex. Instead, she'd been unceremoniously marched upstairs to pee while Landon Nixon stood nearby, grinning at her like the cat who'd swallowed the damned canary. Rat bastard that he was, he'd refused to turn away and allow her even the barest minimum privacy.

He wasn't even trying to hide his amusement. *Jerk! I'll show him, I won't come during our scene. He'll look like a fool in front of his little Dom play-group, and I'll find relief later when he isn't around.* It sounded like a great plan…and she'd make it work, too, even if it killed her.

DAMMIT, HE WAS going to kill her. He'd walked her directly to a secluded area on the second floor and ordered her to strip before she'd taken her last step onto the small stage. When she'd blinked at him in surprise, he'd growled at her and ripped her dress right down the centerline. It fell in tatters at her feet, leaving her too stunned to respond, but she once her brain kicked back into gear, things had taken a sharp turn for the worse. Yeah, asking him if he'd lost his fucking mind hadn't been her brightest moment.

He'd moved her against a St. Andrew's cross, pressing the palm of his hand against the small of her back until the cool surface met her warm skin. She gasped as goose bumps raced over her skin. There was no way to hide her reaction, and it seemed pointless to try since he'd just watched her take care of personal business…*the rat bastard*.

Landon wrapped the leather buckles around her wrists before bending and doing the same to her ankles. She'd been grumbling under her breath about his God-complex when he'd smacked her behind with enough force to make her question his parents' marital status at the time of his birth.

"I assure you my parents were married longer than

nine months before I was born." When she glared at him, he moved so fast she'd barely registered his shift in position before the other side of her ass felt like fire had just exploded over the surface.

"Holy frosted fairies that hurts." She heard snickers behind her, but couldn't turn her head far enough to see who was standing nearby.

"That's why it's called punishment, pet. What's your safe word?" He listened and nodded when she recited what was now becoming a tiresome recitation. *I wonder if he'll ever get the message that I've mastered this particular point?* She must have muttered under her breath again because he stepped in front of her and glared. "You'd do well to keep quiet unless I give you permission to speak. I don't want to gag you. We haven't reached that level of trust, yet."

Gag me? Now I know his last marble is rolling silently out of sight. This time it was a man's husky chuckle that vibrated through her, but she recognized it as belonging to Taz Ledek and wanted to groan in frustration. Not only was her mouth going to get her in trouble, now she wasn't even going to be able to think without it being splashed on the Dom News Network.

Taz's hearty laugh filled the small space just before he stepped into her view. "I promise I won't share what I'm hearing unless it involves your safety. Anything else is an invasion of your privacy." When she looked at him skeptically, he grinned. "I didn't say I wouldn't hang around for the entertainment."

Nice man, but he obviously ate too much paste as a kid.

NATE WAS BARELY holding back his laughter as he stood in the back of the crowd watching Landon set up the scene. Savannah needed to count her lucky stars her Master couldn't hear what she was thinking. Even Taz was struggling to keep his expression neutral. His brother had always been the more gifted of them, but Nate's gift was growing stronger since his marriage to Kodi. His grandmother had assured him it would happen, but he'd never taken her seriously. Now it seemed he owed Nanna-son an apology.

Savannah North was perfect for his friend. The young agent was smart as a whip and her mind worked at warpspeed. Kyle West was fast-tracking her background investigation and fully intended to lure her away from Uncle Sam once she and Landon returned from Costa Rica. When Nate had questioned the wisdom of hiring a husband and wife team, Kent and Kyle had both reminded him about how well it worked with the McCalls.

Ken had laughed as he'd explained, "Landon has already said he wants a lesser role, so he'll be training and then offering strategic advice on missions. I don't think there will be much actual field work in his future."

"And if he and Savannah end up together? Do you think he'll be on-board with her going on ops without him?" Nate already knew the answer, but asked the question anyway.

This time it was Kyle whose laughter came over the line. "That's theirs to figure out. Sam and Sage seem to have found a system that is mutually beneficial."

"And Jen lets them think they're in charge, so it works out well all the way around." Kent's added comment was likely truer than the McCall brothers wanted to admit.

Taz stepped up on the other side of Kodi and pulled

her out from under Nate's arm and into his own. "Come here, baby." Nate wanted to roll his eyes at Taz's attempt to soothe her heated ass. *Just an excuse to cop a feel…you're a jerk.* He knew Taz had heard him when his younger brother flashed him a wide grin over the top of Kodi's head. They settled her between them and turned their attention back to the scene unfolding in front of them.

When she started shifting her weight from foot to foot, he looked down ready to admonish her for not standing still. The command to stop moving died on his lips after he realized she couldn't see what was going on, and they'd promised her a front row seat when she'd expressed her desire to support Savannah. Because of their height, both he and Taz forgot their petite wife didn't share their ability to see over the heads of everyone else in the room.

"What's the matter, Ayasha?" Nate had pinned the nickname on her from the moment they'd met. Referring to her as "little one" in the language of his Native American ancestors was more than appropriate considering the difference in their sizes.

He smiled at her disgruntled expression. "Not all of us are giants. I promised to be front and center to support Savannah, and I'm failing miserably. I didn't greet her when they arrived, and now she'll think I'm not even here. We talked on the phone last night, and I swore I'd be here for her." Her eyes went glassy with unshed tears, and he could feel the distress radiating from her. "Tally is my only friend here, and I was hoping to add Savannah to our group, but I'm blowing it."

Nate felt a stab of guilt because he knew how isolated Kodi felt. As a bestselling romance author, she spent most of her day sequestered in her office upstairs writing. She was just finishing up a three-book series, final two books following her debut novel that had taken the romance market by storm. She'd been working for them prior to their marriage, but they'd wanted her spare time for themselves so they'd asked her to write full-time, freeing up her evenings to spend with them.

Kodi still helped out in the club when they were short-handed, but her contact with the outside world was limited by her circumstances. Of course, if he and Taz had their way, she'd be busy with a baby sooner rather than later.

Grabbing her hand, Nate led her around the crowd to a spot where she'd be able to see. He pulled her against his chest and felt his cock respond. Leaning down, he whispered against her ear, "Ayasha, you would tempt a saint—and Goddess knows I'm no saint. Hold still or you will not be here long enough for Savannah to notice you." As if his words alone conjured her attention, Savannah turned her head and locked gazes with Kodi. Nate could feel his sweet wife trying to telegraph her support, and the relief in Savannah's eyes was easy to read. He'd been in the lifestyle so long Nate often forgot how vulnerable newbie submissives felt during their first public scenes. *Great Goddess, if we'd sent her out on the op without getting these first scenes under her belt, it would have spelled disaster for sure.*

Chapter Seventeen

Savannah leaned back in the soft leather seat aboard the Wests' private jet and tried to not wince. Damn, it had been two days since her scene at Mountain Mastery, and her backside was still tender. Glaring at Landon's smug look, she turned and focused her attention on the small buildings of the local airport.

"What's the matter, Princess? Still being reminded why smarting off to your Master is a bad idea?" She was determined to ignore his taunting question, but he wasn't having it. "Not answering isn't going to work out well for you, pet." This time his voice held more warning than the teasing tone she'd heard in it earlier.

"Yes, Sir. I'm still quite uncomfortable." That was all he was getting from her. *If he is expecting more, he is going to be sorely disappointed...pun intended.*

His soft laughter ignited her desire and annoyed her in equal measure. Damn, he could be the most aggravating man on the planet when he wanted to be. After he'd used the world's biggest paddle on her, Landon had flogged her until she'd come screaming his name. She wasn't sure what bothered her most, the spanking in front of people she was just beginning to think of as her friends or the fact she hadn't been able to hold back her orgasm. Savannah was still seething about her lack of self-control.

"Tell me why you are so angry, pet. And let me caution you against lying. The only thing that will get you in trouble faster than lying is putting yourself in danger unnecessarily." *Good thing you added that last qualifier since putting myself in danger is a very large part of my professional life.* "Lying to yourself won't be tolerated, either, and I'm mentioning it again because I suspect you're angrier with yourself than you are with me. I'm just not sure why."

Savannah didn't answer for so long she wondered if perhaps she could get away with ignoring him altogether. "It's not a huge space, pet. I'm not going to forget you are nearby or that I'm becoming impatient waiting for your answer. Stop trying to figure out how to frame your answer and just respond truthfully." It wasn't that she didn't want to answer his question or that she was trying to skirt the truth. Her struggle was an internal battle as she fought to *understand* the answer.

Taking a deep breath, she decided it was best to just to plunge in with both feet. *What's the worst that can happen? He'll laugh at my naiveté? Certainly, wouldn't be the first time that happened.* She knew better than to accept such an oversimplified answer. The truth was much more unsettling. Over the past ten days, she'd not only forgiven him for the humiliating rejection two years ago, she'd started falling in love with him. Dammit all to hell, she'd promised herself she'd protect her heart. And worst of all, she realized vanilla sex would never be enough for her now. *Oh yeah, all those pansies in suits with their five hundred dollar haircuts and two hundred dollar manicures my family keeps trying to shove my way are going to be falling all over themselves to hook up with a woman who gets off on being flogged.*

She looked up and met his gaze, hoping he wouldn't see what she was about to share was only a small part of the truth. "I'd promised myself I wasn't going to come. I have no self-control around you, and to be honest, that just pisses me off." She wasn't sure what she'd expected, but his careful consideration wasn't even on her list of possibilities. "It's like you have more control over my body than I do. How can that be possible? I don't understand it, and I feel powerless to change it."

"And you don't like it." She didn't miss the fact he'd made it a statement rather than a question. "Do you dislike it because I can bring out responses you're trying to withhold or because you don't appreciate my intimate knowledge of your body?" He reached forward and fastened her seat belt, his eyes never leaving hers. The jet vibrated beneath her feet as it readied for take-off.

Dammit, his scrutiny made her feel like a bug under a microscope. She hadn't considered some of her frustration might stem from the fact she knew exactly how he'd come to know his way around a woman's body. *Fuck me! I'm not jealous. I can't be; he's not mine.*

"Savannah, listen carefully. I'm your Master, and as such, it's my job to read every signal your body is giving me. You've studied enough body language to understand it's only the basics that are universal. After that you need to know the person—does the color of her eyes deepen when she's happy? Do her pupils fully dilate when she is aroused? Do they constrict when she thinks I'm not aware of the fact she is holding back?" She felt the flush of guilt staining her cheeks.

She shook her head in frustration and dropped her gaze to her hands. He reached forward and unfastened the belt. Landon wrapped his hand around her wrist, and with one quick pull she landed with a sequel of surprise on his lap. Savannah looked outside and was surprised to see they had already taken off. Landon used his fingers to turn her face back to his. "Do you really think you can fool the man who knows your body better than you do, Princess? I'd be a miserable failure as a Dom if I wasn't intimately acquainted with every square inch of you. Hell, I'd have to surrender my Dom card if I couldn't make you come when you didn't want to."

Shaking her head, Savannah couldn't hold back her smile. He'd used humor to make his point rather than scolding her, and she appreciated that more than she could say. "Thank you for understanding I wouldn't have dealt well with being reprimanded today." Her emotions were still too raw from the intense scene they'd shared. And the icing on the cake was not sleeping last night. She'd tossed and turned until Landon had pulled her against his chest, wrapped his arms tightly around her, and threatened to put her over his knee if she didn't lay still.

"If you'll talk to me when something troubles you, I think you'll find I'm a very understanding man." She would have rolled her eyes if they hadn't been so close to drifting shut. He stood up effortlessly with her in his arms and headed to the back of the plane. Savannah had flown in private jets her entire life, so she knew exactly where he was going, but once she laid her head against his shoulder, darkness surrounded her, and she never felt him settle her on the plush bed.

LANDON HAD KNOWN she was holding back during their scene, and he'd suspected it was just her stubborn pride so he'd pushed her over anyway. He hadn't talked to her or coaxed her; he'd simply dominated. For the purposes of this operation, her body did not belong to her—it was his to command. His to play with when and how it pleased him. And it had certainly pleased him to watch her fight the explosive chemistry between them.

Nate and Taz had both sent him messages late last night suggesting he plan a similar scene with Savannah as part of the new Dom training they were starting next week. Both men also sent several suggestions on how he could piss her off in advance—great friends, those two. After settling his sleeping slave into the jet's bedroom, he sat down with his laptop and tried to catch up on some of the work that had been pushed to the back burner.

He wondered how his dad managed to juggle a wife and son while building the business from the ground up. Landon was finding it difficult to keep up, and he didn't have the same family obligations. Leaning his head back against the seat, he realized he hadn't spoken to his dad in almost a week. Dammit, after his father's heart attack, Landon had promised himself he'd never let an entire week go by without calling them. Grabbing his phone, he dialed his dad's number. He grimaced when his dad answered. "Landon, is everything alright?" God, was he so self-serving that his dad assumed something must be wrong for him to call?

"Everything is fine, Dad. I just wanted to touch base and see how things are going with you." *And to ask you how you managed to have it all when I can't seem to accomplish half what you did.*

Thankfully, his dad didn't miss a beat, launching into a story about an encounter he and a friend had with an alligator on a local golf course. Landon laughed as his dad recounted their attempts to play through the area where the female had evidently stashed her babies. They chatted for several minutes before he heard what sounded like a door closing. His dad said, "What's weighing so heavy on your mind, Landon? Spit it out, son. It's not like you to be so evasive."

Chuckling to himself, he couldn't help but wonder why he'd thought he could fool the man who'd raised him. Nobody fooled Ashton Nixon for long. "How did you do it? You never missed a game or school event, yet you built the business from the ground up. I was the luckiest kid in the world, and your marriage is the envy of everyone I know. I can't keep up, and I don't have a family to divide my time."

"True, and that's something your mother and I worry about. If you had a wife and children, you might stop and smell the roses occasionally. I might have built the business, but it was little more than a solid foundation when I turned it over to you. Most of the significant growth has occurred since you came on board, and it's really taken off since you assumed the helm." His father's praise sent a bolt of pride through him. Hearing his dad acknowledge how hard he was working made him smile.

When Landon didn't comment, he heard his dad sigh. "You've excelled in two entirely different careers, and you're not even forty. Hell, you've exceeded every expectation your mother and I ever had for you—save two." Landon didn't have to ask. He knew full well his parents were itchy for him to marry and give them grandchildren. When he didn't say anything, his dad asked, "What's her name?"

Swiping his hand over his face, Landon shook his head. How did his dad always recognize what was at the heart of things. He didn't want to jinx any future he and Savannah might have by talking about things too soon. "Who?" Even as he asked the question, Landon heard how lame it sounded.

"Damn, son, that's just plain insulting. You've never worried about how I juggled a family and my business obligations. There's only one thing that can make a man that introspective—and it's not some woman you're dating casually or topping at the club." Fucking hell, why did he think he could maneuver his way around his dad? It had never worked in the past—the man was one of the most intuitive people Landon had ever met.

"Savannah. Her name is Savannah, and we're working together now, but...well, I'm hoping..." He didn't get to finish the thought because he could see the woman in question through the open bedroom door. She swung her feet over the edge of the bed, but she didn't appear to be fully awake. He smiled at her slightly dazed expression. Damn, she was cute when she was confused. As the fog began to clear, she looked up and smiled. Landon felt like someone had just kicked him in the chest, and he knew his dad heard his soft gasp.

"Go to her, Landon. Never let an opportunity to touch your woman pass by. Touch her every time she walks by you and any time you are in the same room. The smallest touch often means the most. I'll give your mother your love." And then he was gone.

Landon set his phone aside and thought back on his childhood. His dad had always been very tactile. Landon didn't remember ever seeing him walk by his mom without touching her in some way. Some of those touches had been overtly sexual and embarrassing as hell for a young boy, but most had been small bits of tenderness that had probably gone largely unnoticed by everyone but his mother.

He was on his feet and moving toward her before his mind registered the desire his heart already felt. Without a word, he urged her to lift her arms over her head and slid her soft tee-shirt off and tossed it aside. He hadn't let her wear panties or a bra, and now he was grateful, because her soft pink nipples were already peaked, their color darkening with arousal. Running his palms down her sides, he savored the feel of her soft skin. "You're so beautiful, Princess. Your skin reminds me of soft moonlight, just enough pink to lend a subtle tint to the white…perfect."

When he saw the denial in her eyes, he shook his head. He'd heard the same complaint from Tally—in a world where tan skin is revered, those with lighter skin tones often felt ostracized because they didn't fit the beach babe mold. Personally, he loved the fact they cared enough to protect themselves from the aging damage of the sun. He reached for the button of her slacks and smiled when nothing but bare skin came into view as the zipper slid down.

"If we lived in Texas, I'd make your tailor sew weights in the hems of your dresses so you could wear them everywhere we went. I'd throw away all your panties and enjoy unfettered access to the slick folds of your pussy whenever the urge struck. Parties, restaurants—anytime I wanted to touch you, I could. There'd be no need to worry the wild Texas winds might flash what belonged to me to everyone nearby. You'll discover I'm very particular when it comes to who sees what's mine—I'm unashamed of how possessive I feel." He stopped before he added *with you*, but the surprise he saw in her eyes told him the words weren't necessary.

He skimmed his hands over every smooth inch of exposed skin and sighed as the intoxicating scent of her arousal assailed his senses. Savannah's instinctive responses fueled his desire in ways he'd never anticipated. When he'd first met her, he'd questioned whether she'd be well-suited for the lifestyle he knew he'd never be able to give up. He regretted that it had taken the kidnapping of an innocent woman to make him realize his error, but he wasn't going to let this opportunity slip through his fingers.

Chapter Eighteen

SAVANNAH WONDERED WHO Landon had been speaking with on the phone when the soft murmur of his voice woke her. Had that conversation fueled the change she sensed in him? Whoever he'd been talking to seemed to have unlocked a floodgate of emotion she hadn't seen before, and it gave her hope the attraction she felt wasn't as one-sided as she'd feared. His much larger body blanketed her own, every square inch warmed by his heat. She'd been so lost in her thoughts she hadn't noticed him shedding his own clothing until the sensuous feel of bare skin sliding over bare skin alerted her.

The bed kept her from feeling the full impact of the vibrations of flight, but the soft motion of mild turbulence added to the sensation of floating. *This has to be what it's like to make love on a cloud.* "I'd love nothing more than making love to you in the clouds, Princess. You'd blend in perfectly with the angels." The tip of his cock teased her entrance, sending a lightning bolt of heat up her spine as desire swamped her.

Her body stopped obeying her brain, and he growled his approval against her ear. "That's it, pet. Let go. I'll always catch you." One thrust and he was seated deep inside her. The sensitive tissues were so swollen in anticipation she felt every ripple and vein of his cock. She sucked in a quick breath when the heated tip of his penis pressed against her cervix. He filled her in more than just a physical sense. Her mind could shut off when he took control of her body, and the sense of peace was like being transported to a different plane of existence. Would she always react so strongly to his possession?

"So good...oh, God, the burning stretch always takes me by surprise." Speaking her thoughts aloud left her feeling vulnerable, but she hadn't been able to hold the words back.

"I live to surprise you, pet." He slid out before pushing in again at a pace he knew set her on fire. "Your walls are already rippling around me, a thousand tiny fingers caressing and taunting me. God help me when you discover how much power your body wields." The lower timbre of his voice lulled her into an almost dreamlike state where nothing existed but the two of them.

Her body was shaking with desire, and Savannah worried she wasn't going to be able to hold back her release. She sent up a silent prayer he'd say the magic words before it was too late. "You're drenching me, Princess." He moved so he could look down where their bodies were joined, and she could have sworn she heard him growl with satisfaction. "Seeing your honey glistening on my cock tests my control and makes me want to ravage you instead of savoring the moment."

"Yes. Ravaging sounds good to me. Let's go with *that* plan." Her voice sounded raspy with an edge of desperation she was certain he hadn't missed. When he leaned back even farther, changing the angle of penetration, the stiff ridge of his corona pushed against her G-spot with every stroke, and she began shaking with the need to come. "Oh. My. God. I can't stop it. Please let me come.

It's too much…too good." She was dangerously close to release and knew, in a few seconds, it was going to be impossible to stop the runaway train of her orgasm.

"Come for me, pet. Take the pleasure and then return it to me. I'll be right behind you—next time." Savannah didn't have time to consider Landon's last words before her muscles contracted and her scream filled the small bedroom of the jet. Somewhere in the back of her mind, she hoped the crew didn't barge in worried she needed help. But the concern was fleeting as lights exploded behind her eyelids in a brilliant display of fireworks worthy of every Independence Day celebration she'd ever watched. She'd never seen colors as vivid as the ones bursting against the black background in her mind's eye.

Landon slammed his mouth over hers in a kiss so heated she felt the sizzle all the way to the tips of her toes. *Probably would have been a good idea to do that a few seconds earlier and save the crew from the audio assault of my screaming.*

His tongue explored her mouth slowly, the contrast between that simple seduction starkly different from the raging storm of her orgasm. The discrepancy was too much, and she plunged over the edge into a deep ravine of another release before she'd recovered from the first. "Yes, Princess. Perfect. Your pussy is gripping me so tight I'm not sure I can last." *Last? What? He's not there yet? I had to fall for Super-fucking-Man, didn't I? Mr. Endurance is going to kill me. Death by orgasm. Is there a box for that on death certificates?*

AMARYLLIS STOOD AT the foot of the most enormous four-poster bed she'd ever seen, watching as Marco moved around the room lighting candles. She'd wondered if he was ever going to make love to her. He'd charmed her during their dinners every evening, and she'd loved their long walks through the lush gardens inside the tall walls of what he referred to as the compound. Marco had even driven her out of the secured estate so they could walk along the beach. They'd met other couples, and it was only later that she realized how easy it would have been for her to call out for help. *Why hadn't she?*

"What are you thinking about, *mi pequeño la flor?*" She loved it when he called her his little flower; the transition from her given name made it easier for her to forget the circumstance that brought them together.

"I was enjoying seeing you move so purposefully around the room. With each new candle set to flame, the light dancing around the room changed subtly." She hadn't been anxious to admit how much she wanted him to take her. After all, she was still technically his prisoner.

He raised his hand to her cheek, but she no longer flinched at the gesture. Smoothing the pads of his fingers over her heated flesh, he smiled. "You think I don't know when you are trying to deceive me? I assure you I do. Now, tell me the truth, so we can move on to more pleasant things." For the first time, she heard something in his voice that sent a small shiver of warning skimming over her senses. He must have noticed her reaction, because he shook his head and smiled. "You have no reason to fear me, Amaryllis. I mean you no harm. But I don't want there to be any secrets between us, either."

"I'm sorry, Marco. I was embarrassed by what I was thinking." He didn't respond. He just continued to watch her so closely she wondered if he wasn't trying to read her mind. "I just, well, I wondered what's wrong with me.

How can I want you so much when I'm your prisoner?" She'd spit the words out in a heated rush, afraid if she stopped she'd never regain the courage to speak them.

To her surprise, he smiled at her indulgently. "Do you feel like a prisoner, *mi pequeño la flor?*"

She shook her head. "No, I don't. And that's another thing I don't understand. How can I be…"

"Falling for me when you don't feel as though you should?" He held his arms open, and she walked into his embrace. "Would it help if I told you I'm falling for you, also? That I know my father is going to be equal parts furious and thrilled?" She wasn't sure what his last words meant, but to be honest, she hadn't heard much after he'd admitted their attraction wasn't one-sided.

"I want to make love to you, *mi pequeño la flor*. I want to hold you in my arms and push myself so deep into your soft depths neither of us remembers we were ever two separate souls." Amaryllis felt the last of her hesitance shatter into a million pieces as she listened to his sweet words. "Tell me this is what you want, also. Otherwise, I'll escort you back to your suite. I am willing to wait until you are ready, *mi amor.*"

Hearing him call her his love made her heart sing. How had she managed to find love under such unusual circumstances? Would he ever allow her to contact her family? She wanted to let them know she was okay. Perhaps he'd allow her to visit them soon. What would happen if he tired of her?

Sighing at the weight of all the questions battering her mind, she focused on the way her body hummed in anticipation and pushed all the troubling doubts from her mind. "I want you to make love to me, Marco. I've waited to hear that you wanted me as much as I did you."

A look of surprise spread over his face. "I've done you a great disservice if you doubted my desire for you, *mi pequeño la flor*. It's a mistake I plan to fix immediately." He stepped back and crossed his arms over his chest. "Remove your clothing slowly. Show me the sensual woman I sense lurks below the surface. I want to see the side no other man is allowed to see—the side reserved for me alone."

Was she naïve to be enraptured by his possessive tone? Perhaps, but her body was trembling. She was vibrating—sexual desire pushing every other thought to the back of her mind. He was a Dom, no question, and she was self-aware enough to know how her body craved dominance.

Lifting the dress he'd given her to wear over her head, she laid the silky garment in his outstretched hand. He nodded his approval before tossing it aside. Amy watched his eyes flare with heat as his gaze moved over her bare body. She hadn't been allowed to wear undergarments on any of their dates, and she knew he'd seen her bare over the surveillance cameras in her suite.

She'd been stripped and forced to shower in what reminded her of the reception areas in the prison movies on late night television. Amaryllis had held her tears as two members of his female staff stood by watching. She'd been denied clothing before being led down a dimly lit concrete hallway where they'd met a security guard. His rapid-fire Spanish caused both of her female escorts to suck in surprised breaths before they turned and ushered her quickly in the other direction.

Amy had cursed herself for not taking the last semester of Conversational Spanish her advisor had recommended. Maybe she would have been able to track the women's hushed conversation if she'd sucked it up and taken the upper-level class. Their pace had slowed so she was no longer forced to race-walk to keep up, and she noticed an immediate change in their demeanor. The guard used a card to access the elevator, and Amy remembered her surprise when they'd stepped into the gilded lift. When she'd shivered in the air-conditioned space, the guard smiled and assured her she would be in her suite soon. It wasn't until the door slid open that she realized he'd spoken to her in perfect English.

"Come back to me, *mi pequeño la flor*." Marco's voice shook her out of her musings, and she impulsively wrapped her arms around him and squeezed. He went stock still for just an instant before encircling her in his embrace. "To what do I owe this sweet outburst?" The warmth of his breath fanned over the shell of her ear, and she sighed.

"I was thinking back on the day I arrived. You saved me that day, didn't you? I'm always amazed when fate intervenes and changes my course." She pulled back and was grateful when he allowed the separation by loosening his hold enough she could gaze up into his eyes. "Thank you, Marco."

She saw a flash of emotion in his eyes that looked like guilt, but before she could blink, it was gone. "I walked into the estate's security control center and found myself captivated by your beauty and courage. In that moment, you became mine. I just had to convince you it was true." He closed the distance between his lips and hers, kissing her with coaxing strokes of his tongue until she opened to him. The sensual glide of his warmth seeped to the depths of her soul and stoked the fires of her arousal.

MARCO FELT THE moment Amaryllis surrendered and fought the urge to shout in triumph. His mouth made love to hers, and he let his hands skim over her naked flesh. The high definition surveillance cameras in her suite didn't do justice to the brilliance of her fair complexion. She glowed with good health even though he knew she'd lost weight since she'd arrived. He'd see to it she regained those pounds and filled out all the lush curves beneath his fingertips. Capturing her moan when he gently pinched her peaked nipples sent a surge of heat to his cock. It was time to claim the only woman he'd ever cared enough about to seduce.

Chapter Nineteen

SAVANNAH WOKE UP with a start, but for several seconds had no idea where she was. Looking around, some of her surroundings started to emerge from the fog clouding her mind. The front door rattled against its frame, and she heard a woman calling her name. "Fuck a duck, that must have been what woke me up. Prairie Winds. That's it. I remember now. We got here last night."

"Come on. Come on. When I'm up, everybody's up."

Savannah wondered about the woman on the other side of the door. She'd done her homework and knew Tobi West wasn't a big woman, but whoever was pounding on the door had to be enormous. "Hold on. Hold on. I'm coming. Damn, give a girl a break."

"Don't answer the door naked, either. We'll probably see each other's pink bits soon enough."

"Yeah, let Chatty Cathy in before she breaks the sound barrier and brings Doms running from every corner of the damned place. That rarely ends well, and we have plans that include us being able to sit down." Savannah was scrambling to find something to wear. She'd been halfway to the door before she'd realized she was naked. *I guess Landon was right, I did get used to being without clothes. And isn't that just Jim-fucking-dandy. I'll probably end up being arrested for indecent exposure on my next op…okay, make that the one after next. Pretty sure I'm going to be naked a lot once we get to Costa Rica.*

She was breathless when she opened the door to find two beautiful, blonde pixies standing on the small porch of the cottage. The closer of the two stuck her hand out, and Savannah grasped it numbly as she introduced herself. "Hi, I'm Tobi West. Guess I should have said that before you opened the door. Fuddle, we better not tell anyone you opened the door without checking the peep hole."

"Who says I didn't?" Both women flashed mischievous smiles Savannah took as approving of her sassy response.

The second woman was even smaller than the first, but every bit as stunning. She stepped forward and offered her hand. "Hi, I'm Jen McCall. I'm in charge of the Texas Tornado over there." She used her thumb to indicate Tobi.

"Hey!" Tobi glared at Jen, but it didn't seem to have any impact; because Jen winked at Savannah as soon as Tobi turned her back.

"I'm Savannah North. It's nice to meet you...I think. Let me go freshen up a bit, and if you'll tell me what's on tap today, I'll try to find something appropriate to wear." She was already moving toward the bedroom when she heard Jen laugh.

"Don't be long. I can't promise how long I can keep Tobi the Snoop from barging in and chattering at you while you're dressing. And I'm hungry."

"You're always hungry. Honest to Pete, I think you have a tape worm with a pet tape worm. Nobody should be able to eat that much and not gain weight."

"Nursing burns up a lot of calories, sister. You need to have another baby. You've gotten senile and forgotten about nursing. Tobi had a birthday last week, but don't say anything, because now she's forgetting things like her phone and where she parked her car. That's why I'm her keeper today."

"You are *not* my keeper. Kent was just kidding. And besides, think about it...do you really want that responsibility?"

Savannah nearly jabbed herself in the eye with her eyeliner pencil she was laughing so hard at the banter taking place on the other side of the door. She'd never had a real friend other than Amy, and even then, they'd never enjoyed this kind of easy camaraderie.

Calling out to them while she slipped on her shoes, Savannah asked, "Where did you say we are going? And please tell me it isn't far and they have coffee." If she didn't get her morning jolt of caffeine, things could get ugly.

"Not far. We'll be there in no time. We have a crazy woman for a driver." Tobi's voice rang with amusement while she could hear Jen grumbling in the background. If anyone asked Savannah, the "crazy woman" title was up for grabs. "We're meeting the others there, and yes, they have coffee, but their mimosas are to die for. And Vitamin C is good for you."

Savannah was having trouble focusing on what she was supposed to be doing as evidenced by the fact she was wearing two different shoes. It seemed Tobi West was every bit as distracting as her reputation implied. She quickly swapped out one shoe and was almost out the door when Tobi added, "But as soon as the clock strikes two, we can start on margaritas."

Two? Savannah almost tripped over her own feet when she glanced at the small bedside clock. She'd never slept until after noon in her entire life. Savannah was going to kill Landon for letting her sleep when he left. And where in the hell was he anyway?

Reemerging from the bedroom, she looked around for a note and found it on the small bar separating the kitchen from the living space.

Princess,

Tobi West and Jen McCall will stop by at one o'clock to pick you up. You'll be spending the day with the girls, and I'll see you this evening. We'll eat dinner in before going to the club.

Enjoy and behave.

Landon

Behave? Was he serious? The expression on her face must have given her away, because she heard Jen snicker beside her. "I saw the note. Don't be offended by the *behave* comment. That's more about us than it is about you. Tobi's rep is terrible."

Tobi nudged her then grinned like a Cheshire cat. "He must have really worn you out. Gotta love that. But it was nice of him to let you sleep since all the guys met at the gym at the friggin' ass crack of dawn for training. How are you still getting out of hand to hand, Miley?" Tobi's grin told Savannah there was a story behind the question.

Jen pointed down at her large breasts and grinned. "None of the guys want to risk touching the girls and watching Sam and Sage come apart at the seams. I may nurse Suzie until she's in junior high."

"You aren't still nursing. You haven't been near a breast pump in months. I can't believe they are still falling for that."

Savannah realized she was standing with her mouth gaping open, staring at the two women in confusion. Looking at Jen, she said, "Wait, I thought you said your name was Jen?"

When she grinned, Savannah wanted to laugh out loud. Here was a woman who enjoyed life to the fullest. "It is. The team nicknamed me Miley because they think I'm a wrecking ball. They claim I'm reckless, but that's not it...I'm just fearless, and it scares them." Tobi's eye-roll made Savannah want to ask more, but the moment was lost when the shrill ring of a cell phone sounded.

Tobi smiled when she pulled the bright pink device from her pocket. "Hi, Mom. Yes, we're leaving now."

Her conversation faded to the background as they moved out the door, and Jen motioned Savannah into the front seat. "Might as well sit up here. She'll be on the phone with Lilly until we walk in the door. They are thick as thieves and about as much trouble."

"Her mother?"

"Oh no, Lilly West is her mother-in-law slash partner-in-crime." Savannah's eyes widened in surprise. "You'll see soon enough. I'm not kidding when I say they are both trouble magnets. Things tend to blow up when they are together...and I mean *literally* blow up."

For the first time, Savannah wondered if she'd made a mistake getting in the large SUV. Before they could drive past the enormous main structure she assumed was the club, a hulking man stepped out of the shadows, stopping at the edge of the concrete drive.

"Fuck-a-duck. Heads up, Tobi. We're being tanked."

Tanked? This whole thing just keeps getting stranger by the minute.

"Oh, for the love of God. No, Mom, I wasn't talking to you. Looks like your sons are sending a supervisor along."

The man in question was easily six and a half feet tall. Savannah whispered, "He's huge" as the car slowed to a stop.

"He played for the NFL, but repeated concussions meant he had to choose between his career and being able to form complete sentences. *He chose wisely.*" The shift in Jen's voice as she said the last words made Savannah burst out in giggles. Obviously, she'd found another Indiana Jones fan.

"What's up, Buttercup?" Jen's flippant greeting made the man smile.

"I'm your driver for the day, Miss Jen." She couldn't see his eyes hidden behind his dark aviators, but Savannah was sure the corners of his mouth had twitched in amusement.

"As you can see, I'm doing really well. I'm pretty sure I can handle it. Don't you have something else you'd rather be doing? Something more entertaining than watching us drink and gossip about our men?"

Savannah almost felt sorry for the poor man.

"My bosses were very clear. I'm to drive you and stick to you like glue until you are safely back under their watchful eyes." Tobi was muttering what sounded like colorful ways to castrate her husbands, but Jen seemed undeterred.

"If I cut through all that PCBS, I get...you are going to shadow us like white on rice and report back to the team every time one of us goes to the bathroom. Is that about right?"

This time he didn't even try to hide his laughter. "Yeah, I'd say that about covers it. And they told me whoever gave me the most grief had to buy my lunch, so guess that's you, Miss Miley." He reached inside and unlocked and opened the door so quickly Savannah had barely registered the movement before she saw him hold his hand out to Jen.

Scrambling to exit the SUV, Savannah moved quickly. "I don't know where we're going, so Jen, you should ride shotgun. I'll get in the back with Tobi." She and Jen both circled the vehicle as the man shook his head and ducked inside.

"Might not be politically correct, but when I was a kid, we called that a Chinese fire drill." Jen's laughter filled the small space as Tobi reached forward and swatted the top of her friend's head.

"Good grief. Doesn't your mouth have a filter?" Tobi's comment brought howling laughter from Jen and the man they'd introduced as Tank, and Savannah found herself looking around for the *Pranked* crew. They had to be hidden *somewhere* nearby.

Chapter Twenty

L ANDON WATCHED AS Regi, the Wests' part-time office manager, walked in the room carrying a sheaf of papers. Handing the stack to Kyle, she smiled and announced, "I'm heading out. Hopefully, I can catch a ride with Tobi and crew before they leave."

"Tank's already driving them into town. If you don't want to drive, one of us can take you in. Your men can collect your car later." Landon knew Regi had been with Kent and Kyle since they'd first started the club, but she seemed genuinely shocked by her boss's comment.

"You made Tank drive them in?" When Kyle nodded without looking up, she switched her glare to Kent, who was suddenly busy studying a piece of lint on his slacks. "What did he do to *you*?" Kyle glanced up, trying to feign a puzzled expression. Regi rolled her eyes and sighed dramatically. "Oh, please. Don't even try that *whatever do you mean* bull with me. I know you too well, Kyle West. You sent the big fluffy lion to guard a bunch of killer sheep. Cold, Kyle, very cold."

After she'd stalked from the office, Kent shifted his attention to his brother and smiled. "I warned you. Our women all love Tank, and they're going to feel sorry for him. We're going to be the ones who end up looking like asses. He's going to be treated like a prince despite the fact they'll know he's reporting back every move they make." When Kyle shrugged, Kent switched his attention to Landon.

"Learn from my brother's mistakes. Don't put a teddy bear in charge of a pack of wolves." Landon frowned and wondered if perhaps he should have declined their invitation for Savannah to spend the day with some of the other women from the Prairie Winds Club.

"Surely it's not *that* bad." Landon hoped he'd sounded more condescending than wishful, but wasn't sure he'd succeeded.

His comment caused Kyle's head to jerk up, and he grinned. "You have no fucking clue. And what my besotted brother doesn't know is that I've also given Parker Andrews a heads-up. He's a club member, as well as the newly appointed Chief of Police. He'll check in and have dispatch alert him to any trouble at the Posh."

Kent must have noticed Landon's concern, because he laughed. "Posh is the name of the fancy bar and restaurant where the girls are holding court this afternoon. The only reason he agreed to this outing is because he thinks the more dignified atmosphere will discourage them from getting into trouble. I think he's wrong, and we've got a grand riding on whether or not the afternoon ends with us being summoned to break up a ruckus."

"Ruckus? Paying?" *Jesus, Joseph, and Mary.* What on Earth had he done sending Savannah with these women?

"Yes. Bail, damages, or fines. Any of the three means my idiot brother matches my donation to a local after-school program later this month. The kids want to go to summer camp, and I think it's a slam dunk at this point, because what *my brother* doesn't *know* is that Mom is meeting the girls there."

Kyle West was a blur of motion as he stood and slammed the papers down on his desk. "God dammit, I should have known today was going to be a cluster. Come on, let's get to the range. I need to shoot something." He stomped from the room, but not before Landon heard him mutter, "They'd better not blow anything up this time."

Fuck me.

SAVANNAH LEANED BACK in her seat, watching the antics of the women surrounding her. She wondered if she should heed the warning voice in her head telling to get out before all hell broke loose or stay as a witness. Just as Jen and Tobi had predicted, she'd fallen in love with Lilly West. The dark-haired beauty was still model gorgeous, making Savannah wonder what she'd looked like as a young woman.

Leaning closer to the woman who'd been introduced as Merilee, she asked, "Was Lilly a model?"

Merilee grinned and nodded before launching in to a list of products and ads that had featured the older woman over the years. All Savannah could do was stare at her in shock. Merilee pointed to her temple and laughed. "Eidetic memory. Great for recalling insane amounts of data, but not very good at helping me understand the basic concepts of social chit-chat sometimes. Sorry about that. The short answer is yes. Before she married Dean and Dell, she did quite a lot of modeling and won several beauty pageants. But we love her because she is fiercely loyal and talks like a pissed off sailor when she gets rattled."

"What on Earth could possibly rattle her? She seems so

poised, yet full of mischief."

Gracie leaned close from Merilee's other side and snickered. "Maybe we should tell you the story about the boat she blew up on the river. One shot and kaboom. Splattered bad guys all over the rock cliff on the other side. Her husbands and sons stopped letting her go to the range, but she still sneaks in regularly. She bribes the team with food, and none of them will rat her out."

"Blew it up?" Savannah choked on the margarita she'd been nursing for the past half-hour.

"Gracie! You'd better not be telling Savannah about the river fiasco. Dammit, she'll think I'm a wild card or something." Lilly switched her attention to Savannah and smiled. "It was necessary. Those bastards were after Tobi and Gracie." Lilly tilted her chin up as if blowing up a boat was an everyday occurrence. The entire table erupted into riotous laughter, and it took Savannah a few seconds to realize they were laughing at her.

Tobi grinned at her before explaining, "We get that look a lot, Savannah…that's why they are laughing. Boy, oh boy, I thought the men were going to stroke-out. Once they knew we were all safe, they went into CYA-mode with the locals. Something about the gun Mom used not being properly registered."

"That was because I bought it at a gun show they didn't know I'd gone to. Why they thought I'd tell them I was attending an event they'd have most certainly forbidden me to go to is baffling if you ask me. Better to ask for forgiveness than permission. That's my motto."

When a woman walked up behind her, Lilly stood and turned her back on the table to greet her. The conversation returned to more sedate topics before three young women walked by their table on the way to their own at the back of the room. The first in their group stopped and looked directly at Tobi before shifting her glare to each of the others seated at the table. Pointing to Savannah and Brinn, another newbie in the group, the woman sneered, "You'd do well to steer yourselves clear of this group if you value your reputations."

Savannah blinked at the woman in surprise just as she saw Jen's hand grasp Tobi's arm, holding her in her seat. "Don't do it, Tobi. Don't let her bait you."

"By all means, Ms. McCall, keep your friend in check. After all, you wouldn't want her husbands to beat her in that perverted club of theirs. And heaven only knows what your own men would have to say." Lilly had turned around and stood silently assessing the woman as if she were little more than an unpleasant slug. When Ms. Hateful turned her attention to Lilly, her eyes narrowed in disgust. Her condescending glare reminded Savannah of the women her mother counted as friends. She'd seen that beady-eyed, vindictive glare more times than she cared to remember. Her critical gaze moved around slowly around the table...from Lilly to Regi before finally sneering down her nose at Merilee. "Well, look at this. Not a one of you seems to be satisfied with just one man to tie you up and shove sparkly doo-dads up your butts..." She didn't get the chance to finish before Lilly tossed her drink directly into the woman's face.

"Oops." Lilly didn't seem the least bit remorseful, and Savannah watched with wide eyes as everything around her erupted into complete and utter chaos. The whole scene seemed to happen into slow motion, and the one thing she saw that made perfect sense was the horrified expression on Tank's face as he stalked across the room, his phone pinned to his ear.

Between one heartbeat and the next, Jen flattened the woman on the floor when she took a swing at Lilly. Then the second woman launched herself at Tobi, and Savannah's training kicked in. Without thinking, she took the heavier woman down. The whoosh of air leaving her lungs reeked of bourbon, and Savannah wondered how much the trio had to drink before they'd arrived. The third woman in the group glared down at her friends before raising her hands and backing away. "Hey, I've got no beef with you all. They're just mad because their membership applications were rejected."

Tank plucked Tobi out of the way, setting her behind him as if she weighed nothing at all before pushing Lilly back as well. He'd just turned his attention to Jen when the door of the restaurant burst open and two men in suits ran in. Jen looked up at Tank and rolled her eyes. "Snitch." To his credit, he winced at her reprimand.

Lilly turned to the first man, flashing him a dazzling smile. "Hello, Parker. How nice to see you. Congratulations on your promotion, dear."

The corners of the second man's face twitched as he moved around the table to pull Merilee into his arms. He kissed the top of her head before setting her back and looking her over. Finding her uninjured, he shook his head and grinned. "You, sweet cousin, are in a world of trouble."

"Me? What did I do? I'm completely innocent." At his raised brow, she added, "Okay, perhaps innocent wasn't a good word choice. But I'm not guilty of any wrong doing in this case. And you can keep all those psycho looks to yourself."

"I'm a psychologist, not a psycho."

"Whatever you say."

"I swear I'd paddle you myself if you weren't a relative.

Your men are going to be pissed you were involved in this."

"I'm a victim of circumstance. They aren't completely unreasonable. I pity the woman who hooks up with you and Mr. Grumpy over there."

The man Lilly had called Parker focused on Merilee and shook his head before his gaze landed on Brinn. For a split-second, Savannah saw his eyes soften, and she wondered what the connection was between the two. Glancing at Brinn, Savannah smiled at the pink blush staining her cheeks. "Brinn, are you alright?" Tobi and Lilly hadn't missed the interplay and were watching the man with grins tugging at the corners of their mouths.

"Yes, Sir. I'm fine." She'd no sooner answered than the second man moved from Merilee's side to stand beside her. Savannah was going to make herself dizzy trying to keep up with these people. *Does everyone in this group have two husbands? Probably shouldn't be drinking the water while I'm here. Hell, I can't imagine trying to deal with two men.*

Parker turned to Tank and said, "I assume you've call Kyle?"

The other man nodded as Lilly chimed in, "Of course he's called my sons, who have no doubt already alerted their fathers. Tank dear, we really are going to have to chat about this unnatural loyalty you seem to be harboring for the overbearing men you work for." She batted her eyes at him, but the big man obviously wasn't fooled by her saccharin treatment, because he took a quick step back.

Jen and Savannah were both still on the floor with their knees pressed into the other women's backs when several uniformed officers stepped through the door. The first officer took in their similar positions and grinned up at Parker. "You sure you need us, Chief? Seems like these ladies are more than capable of handling anything that comes their way." Several of the other officers chuckled even as they stepped in and secured the women who'd gone after Lilly and Tobi.

"Take them outside while I try to figure out what the hell has gone on in here today." Savannah tried to step back, but he drilled her with a glare. "Agent North, I believe I'll begin with you." His reference to her as agent caused both women being led away to groan. Tobi's giggle broke the tension, and suddenly, Savannah wanted nothing more than to finish the margarita she'd had in her hand a few minutes earlier. When he saw her glance at it longingly, Parker shook his head. "I want you as clear-headed as possible. Just having you here would have complicated things—but having you actively involved means I'm going to be doing a mountain of damned paperwork if the Feds get wind of this. Hell, your agency thrives on in-triplicate forms. Personally, I think they're responsible for half of the South American deforestation."

Tell me about it. And you aren't the one who'll be listening to the lecture in my boss's office for hours on end.

She was just finishing her interview with Parker when the door opened to a flood of men. Two older men led the procession, and Savannah was relieved to see the slightly amused expressions on their faces. She noticed their resemblance to Kyle and Kent West as they cut a direct path to Lilly. The feisty woman's entire demeanor softened as soon as she saw them. Savannah wasn't close enough to hear the conversation, but it was clear she was telling them who'd come to hers and Tobi's rescue.

"The men have already been briefed." The information didn't surprise her, but the fact Parker had shared it with her did.

"Just for the record, I appreciate the fact you aren't lecturing me about keeping my nose out of other people's business."

"That would be my job, pet." She'd known Landon was likely on his way, but hadn't seen him walk in with the others. He turned her so she was facing him and gazed down at her in concern. "Are you okay, Princess?"

"I'm fine. It was an easy takedown. Bitch Number Two got caught up in her friend's *crazy*, but the third one was smarter, so they were easy to contain."

Parker chuckled from behind her. "Good thing the third woman backed off. I don't think Lilly and Tobi would have subdued her as cleanly as you and Jen did the first two. That could have gotten really ugly." Savannah smiled at his attempt to lighten the mood.

"If you've finished with Savannah, I'm going to settle her with something to drink and then check on Brinn." Landon's comment didn't surprise her. She'd heard Brinn mention the Ledek's club while the women had all been swapping Dom stories. "Since I'm technically still employed by Mountain Mastery, I'll make sure she gets home safely."

Parker shook his head. "No need. Dan and I will be escorting Brinn home." Landon's brow lifted, and Parker's eyes burned as his attention shifted to the woman standing to the side with her arms wrapped around herself. Savannah knew the pretty brunette had saved Koi Green's life the night she phoned in the report of his accident, but she hadn't heard the busty engineer was now working in Texas.

Brinn must have sensed the men looking at her, because she lifted her gaze, zeroing in on Parker. Even from this distance, Savannah could see the flare of heat in her eyes. A man Savannah assumed was Dan stood close by, his attention focused entirely on Brinn. When Savannah glanced at Landon, his expression held affection, but no heat, and she felt more relieved than was necessary. Reminding herself that she'd have to return to Washington as soon as Amy was safe, Savannah felt a wave of sadness wash over her.

Determined to keep her melancholy to herself, Savannah turned away from Landon and Parker to walk the few feet to the bar. Ordering a margarita, she pulled herself up onto the tall bar stool. Resting her chin in her hand, she sighed in frustration. "I'm going to muck this up before I ever start. Stop leading with your heart and begin using your head, or you're going to end up right back under Dad's and Brit's thumbs." She nodded her thanks to the bartender when he slid the salt-rimmed drink in front of her. Several large gulps later, she slumped back and waited for the brain numbing effects of the tequila to push her fears and insecurities back behind the vault door Landon kept prying open. "Frost my flakes, I've let him get to me...again. And, he's going to break my heart...*again*. I'm an idiot."

LANDON HAD BEEN half a heartbeat from pulling her from the barstool and paddling her ass for walking away from him when something stopped him. Pausing, he listened as she chastised herself and felt his heart clench at the sadness he heard in her voice, but her last comment was like a kick to the gut. He'd known his rejection had hurt her, but he hadn't realized the depth of the pain he'd caused. And hearing the resignation in her voice when she'd bemoaned being under her family's control again snapped something in him.

Sliding onto the stool next to her, he smiled and arched a brow at her half-finished drink. She shrugged. "I just needed a minute. It's been a trying couple of weeks."

He leaned his head back and laughed. "Princess, I have a feeling your whole life has been trying. Don't you think it's time you gave yourself a break?" When her eyes went wide in surprise, Landon knew for sure how badly he'd failed as her Dom. He'd always felt part of a sexual Dominant's role was empowering the submissive he was topping. It took a lot of strength to let go. Ceding power to someone else required a level of trust most people only dreamed of attaining.

"You've learned more in two weeks than many subs learn during their entire six-month training at the club." Her cheeks flushed at the compliment, and his words had been sincere. She'd done a remarkable job and under the worst possible circumstances. Landon suddenly realized how much he'd enjoyed her company. He liked spending time with her. She was smart, and her razor-sharp wit kept him on his toes. But most of all, he respected her.

"Come on, Princess. Let's get you out of here. I want you well-rested and well-fed before we go to the club later. And I want you out of here before tequila kicks in. There's no need to add indecent exposure paperwork to the mountain of bureaucratic bull shit Parker is already facing."

Chapter Twenty-One

SAVANNAH COULD TELL something was on Landon's mind before they made the short drive up to the club. But when she asked the third time what was wrong, he'd given her a warning look that caused her to cut the inquiry off mid-sentence. Stepping into the large reception area, she grinned at Tank and asked Landon if she could speak to him for a moment. He appeared puzzled but nodded his approval. Turning her attention back to the man who'd been unfailingly polite despite the mess he'd been pushed into, Savannah smiled. "Tank, I wanted to apologize for this afternoon. I hope you didn't get into any trouble."

The large man looked completely shocked for a few seconds, but then his entire expression warmed. "Miss Savannah, I appreciate your concern, but my bosses knew keeping their sweet mama and wife out of trouble was more than one man could be expected to handle. I was very grateful for your help. You and Miss Jen took care of those women before I could get there, and that was a huge help—Lilly and Tobi are more like family than...well, they're mighty special." Her heart almost burst to hear the love in his voice when he was speaking about Lilly and Tobi. What would it be like to have friendships that strong?

Landon nodded to Tank and ushered Savannah through the door. He wasn't sure what had gone through her mind when Tank spoke so fondly about the West women. But the look of sadness and longing made him want to take her right back down to the cottage and make love to her until she forgot every moment of loneliness her family had caused her. Pulling himself back from the temptation, he moved her to the side and into his arms. He was sure she was worried about doing a scene in a different club, and he'd only added to her anxiety by behaving like an ass for the past hour. And despite all that, she'd still managed to make a point to apologize to Tank. The woman was a class act.

Pulling back, he pressed a kiss to her forehead. "Just when I think I can't be more impressed with you…you shock me by setting the bar even higher, Princess." He could see the sheen of unshed tears, and he hated realizing he'd missed so many chances to tell her how impressed he'd been with her dedication. She'd gone all-in with her training; he didn't know of another agent who could have done it better.

"Thank you. Your kind words mean more than you know. I may learn more from critiques, but I'm motivated by positive reinforcement."

For a second, he thought she was going to try to retract the words, but she took a deep breath and stayed the course. This time when he pulled her close it was to seal his lips over hers. He'd planned to hold the passion in check until their scene, but the minute his lips touched hers, it was spontaneous combustion. Feeling her groan vibrate all the way up her chest threw gas on the fire, turning it into an inferno. Pushing his hands through her hair, he gripped the silken strands, tilting her head so he could deepen the kiss. His tongue explored every inch of her mouth, and she gave as good as she got.

By the time Landon broke off the kiss, he'd pushed her up against the brick wall behind her, and she was wrapped around him like a vine. She was pulling in deep breaths, and he loved seeing the glazed look of desire in her blue-green eyes.

"Wowser. That was one heck of a kiss. One Dom who walked by had to wipe the steam from his glasses." Laughter filled Tobi's voice, and Landon would have laughed with her if he hadn't been trying to remember why he wasn't hauling ass back to the cottage.

"Kitten, how many times are we going to have to punish you for speaking without permission in the club?" Kyle's tone was all business, but his eyes softened as he looked down on his scantily dressed sub. The dress Tobi was *almost* wearing was cut so low a deep breath would probably expose her breasts. And the open lace ended so high anyone sitting down would have a great view of her pussy as she walked by. If Kyle was anything like Landon, she'd also be flashing a sparkly butt plug...because, according to her Master, there was no such thing as too much bling in a kink club.

"Is that a trick question, Sir? Because it sounds a lot like one." Kyle's answering growl didn't seem to deter his wife in the least.

"Sweetness, you are pushing your luck after the fiasco you were involved in this afternoon." Landon noted the tension in Kent's voice and wondered what else Tobi had done to push her Masters' buttons.

"You're only mad at me because you can't spank me for what your mom did and you can't spank her, either." While Landon agreed with what Tobi had just said, he was gaining a new appreciation for Kent's and Kyle's frustration.

"I can tell by the expression on Master Landon's face he understands exactly how you earned your reputation as a brat, Kitten." Landon would have laughed at the astonished look on Tobi's face if it hadn't been for the fact she was setting a terrible example for Savannah. He didn't respond, but gave her a look he was certain she'd understood. As the three of them walked away, he heard Kent's promise she'd be spending time over both their knees before the night was over, but after seeing her in action, Landon wonder how much of a deterrent those paddlings were going to be.

It was time to get the evening back on track, and he wanted to reward Savannah for not speaking during the exchange they'd witnessed with the Wests. Moving her a couple of feet from the wall, he turned her so she was facing the red brick surface. "Hands on the wall, pet. Now spread your legs as far as you can." When she did as he'd instructed, he slid his hand beneath the short, pleated skirt she was wearing and groaned against her ear. His words were for her only, and he knew it would heighten her pleasure. "You are already dripping wet, Princess. I love knowing your body has prepared itself for me."

Her breathing had accelerated, and he could see her pulse pounding staccato at the base of her throat. She looked sinfully wanton with her back arched perfectly. Landon shifted so she was shielded from the view of all but a very few. This was for the two of them, an intimate moment between a Dom and his submissive that was quickly becoming a spontaneous moment of passion between a man and the woman he was falling in love with.

"Pushing through your slick folds and imagining their color changing from pink to deep scarlet makes my cock ache to replace my fingers. The flutter of your vaginal walls as they ripple around me—so fucking hot I'm afraid I might burst into flames." A surge of cream coated his fingers, and he suspected she was dripping onto the floor. Pausing, he enjoyed the way her vaginal muscles clutched him in an effort to pull him deeper. *Fucking perfect.* "Do you want to come, sweetheart?" If she noticed the shift in pet names, she didn't react, but the significance wasn't lost on him.

"Yes, Sir. Oh, God, please don't let me fall." Her words surprised him. As lost as she was in the tempest of lust, she still worried about making a scene. How programmed was her mind to adhere to the social constraints her family? He wanted to slash the tethers that kept her from fully letting go.

"Never, baby. I'll always catch you. Come for me." Her body reacted before he'd finished speaking, long before he knew her sharp mind processed the command. The arm he'd banded around her waist tightened when her knees gave out. God, it was a rush to know he'd given her so much pleasure she'd folded into his arms. She'd barely made a sound, the gasps and moans so soft they'd been for his ears only.

Ordinarily, he liked to give subs multiple orgasms during each encounter at a club, but this was going to be a one-shot deal. The scene he'd planned for tonight wasn't a big production, but he still didn't want her body completely sated in advance. There was a lot of truth in the old adage that advised *'always leave them wanting more.'*

THE TROLL SHE'D always sworn lived under the small bridge on her parents' estate had finally zapped her.

Savannah felt like a limp, well-used rag doll. That damned troll was the only possible explanation. Savannah sagged over Landon's forearm barely registering his soft mutterings of praise as he lifted her into his arms. "We'll get you some water, and you'll be back on your feet before you know it, pet."

Yes, indeed. Water...the miracle antidote for troll curses.

Closing her eyes, Savannah let the gentle swaying of being carried calm her jangled nerves. The last time she'd been carried, her brother had been home from grad-school and found her asleep on the back patio. She'd been sent home from boarding school when she contracted mono. Warm sunshine had beckoned, but she'd barely made her way outside before collapsing onto one of the loungers. She'd known her brother was livid, but it wasn't until later she realized he'd been angry with their parents, not her. God only knew how long it would have been until they or one of the staff noticed she was missing. Brit arranged round the clock nursing care for her, billed it to his parents, and left. *At least he didn't leave you on the patio.*

"Why on Earth would I leave you on the patio, Savannah?" Landon's disbelieving question could only mean one thing. Dammit, she'd spoken aloud...again. Fuck, fuck, fuckidy fuck.

"Not you, sorry. I was just remembering something from a long time ago." There hadn't been any reason to lie to him, but she didn't want to share any more than necessary, either.

"Who? Who took you in and why?" He lowered them both into a chair and opened a small bottle of water for her.

Taking several long swallows before handing the bottle back, Savannah looked at Landon and sighed. She gave him the PCBS version, but it was obvious he wasn't fooled.

"When you were carrying me, I thought about that night. I don't ever remember my parents carrying me, although I'm sure they must have." Surely her mother carried her home from the hospital? But then again, there was very little about her parents' detachment that she'd found out of the realm of imagination.

She hadn't realized she was twisting her fingers together until his large hand wrapped over them. "We're going to have a very long chat about your family sometime, Princess—but not tonight." He stood and set her on her feet but didn't release her until he was certain she wouldn't falter. When she felt confident her legs were no longer made of rubber, she gave him a quick nod. "Come. It's time for our scene, and I'm anxious to feel you wrapped around me."

He led her quickly to one of the smaller stages. It wasn't private, but it was certainly off the beaten path. She cast furtive glances around small circular platform and wanted to bolt. Most of what he planned to use was hidden from view, but the covered tray with a length of silk lying over the top looked ominous. Up until now, they'd only used a blindfold during two other scenes. He'd insisted on seeing her eyes until he was familiar enough with her body language to gauge her reactions. But the long piece of red silk told her tonight was going to be different. Savannah took several deep breaths, hoping the water she just drank stayed where it belonged.

Tobi, Gracie, and Jen all stood to the side, and she appreciated their moral support. They were each holding a small box, and Savannah wondered what part they were going to play in the scene. When her gaze returned to the padded spanking bench, her fingers involuntarily tensed in his hand. "Don't make assumptions, pet. Things are not always what they seem."

His calm was starting to seep into her, and she tried to relax as she whispered, "Yes, Sir."

She could tell her effort had fallen short when he shook his head in frustration. "It's time to give you something else to think about, Princess." She wasn't sure exactly what that meant, but she didn't have to wait long for an answer, because after a few beats, he added, "Strip."

LANDON HEARD HER suck in a breath, but she didn't say a word. Her hands were trembling as she opened the one button holding the cropped shirt closed over her pert breasts. When he held out his hand, she placed it carefully over his palm and pulled in a deep breath. "You're doing great, pet. Show the team how much you've learned." Just as he'd known it would, the small reminder was all it took to bolster her courage. The trembling abated, and she slipped the short skirt down her legs, bending at the waist to pick it up, just as he'd taught her to do. Damn, Savannah's flexibility was something to behold. Someday soon, he was going to make her do her entire yoga workout naked while he played with her.

"Kneel, pet. Hands behind your back, knees wide. I want everyone to see how beautiful you are." Her grace brought appreciative nods from those gathering around the small platform. He used the padded cuffs looped on his belt to secure her hands. He slid a finger between her wrist and the cuff's soft padding, and when he was satisfied they weren't too tight, he reached for the silk scarf. "I'm taking away your sight because I want to focus that brilliant mind of yours. I'm going to fuck your mouth, and I want you to swallow every drop of the gift I'm going to give you. My pleasure is the only thing you should be thinking about."

"Yes, Sir."

Fucking perfect. As soon as the blindfold was in place, he nodded to the Kyle, who in turn led each of the women up the short stairs. Their bare feet were silent, and Savannah had no idea her new friends were scurrying around them.

Opening his leathers, Landon heaved a relieved sigh he hoped wasn't audible, but the brief flicker of a smile lifting the corners of Savannah's pink tinted lips let him know she'd heard it. "Minx." He knew she would hear the smile in his voice. "Open for me, pet." Sliding the engorged head of his cock between her lips was equal parts heaven and hell. Pure pleasure coursed through him as the ache in his balls became a burning sensation he recognized too well. *Not fucking yet! I'm not even all the way in yet. And I'm not an inexperienced teenager, for Christ's sake.*

Gazing down on her halo of blonde waves as he slid in farther with each stroke took his breath away. She looked like an angel, but her devil-blessed mouth made him want to spend hours feeling the wet silk closing around him. When he felt his tip push into her throat, he groaned. "Fuck, pet, you undo me." She moaned around him, and the vibration snapped the last threads of his control. He stared down and wished like hell he could see her eyes. The flicker of the candles the ladies had set aflame combined with the soft scent of the rose petals now scattered over the floor painted a picture in his mind, and Landon knew he was going to remember this moment for the rest of his life.

"Swallow on me, pet, and take it all." The first flex of her throat muscles as she swallowed around him pushed him over, and his shout bounced off the wall in front of him. He'd called her name in a voice so rough and burning with passion he barely recognized it. It took him several seconds to recover enough to pull her to her feet and slam his mouth over hers. Tasting himself on her lips and letting their combined flavors burst over his buds sent a rush of blood back to his still erect cock.

Pulling back, he whispered against her ear. "You humble me, Savannah. I can't begin to tell you how amazing that was. And if I can walk, we'll step back two steps, and I'm going to return the favor." Helping her into position over the spanking bench, he smoothed his hands up and down her arms after releasing the cuffs. "I'm not binding you to the bench because this isn't a punishment. This is all about pleasure, and then I have a couple of gifts for you."

Turning to the growing crowd, Landon smiled. "I'm pleased to see so many familiar faces, and I know my lovely pet will appreciate your support after we're finished. She has only been in training as a submissive for a very short time, and as you can see, she's a very quick study." The buzz of agreement moved through the more experienced members, and he was so proud of her in that moment he wanted to burst.

"I'm going to wrap this scene up with a little remote help from Master Kent while I use my favorite paddle to remind my sweet girl why erotic spankings are something to look forward to." The first swat landed just as he'd spoken the last word. He hadn't wanted to give her any opportunity to tense, and it had worked. The broad paddle he was using distributed the force over a wide space, delivering a swat meant to warm rather than hurt. By the third stoke, he could see the glistening evidence of her arousal between her thighs.

Nodding to Kent, Landon grinned when she squealed. He'd be willing to bet she'd forgotten about the jeweled plug in her ass until it started vibrating. What she hadn't had time to process yet was that it was also expanding. Leaning down, he whispered against her ear. "I'm going to fuck that lovely ass of yours tonight, pet." She enjoyed anal play, but he'd yet to claim that part of her. Somewhere in the back of his mind, Landon knew, once he took that final step, there would be no turning back—she would be his.

He set the paddle aside for fear of hitting the enlarged plug and relished the more intimate connection of his hand connecting with her taut ass. Her cheeks were hot to the touch, and when he slid his fingers through the folds of her labia, her back bowed, pressing her juicy pussy closer into his touch, but otherwise, she maintained her position on the bench. Grateful he'd had the foresight to roll the tray he needed closer, Landon sheathed himself in a condom and cursed the fact it was necessary to comply with the club's rules. Easing the plug from her rear entrance, he set it in the small bowl and tossed a towel over the top. He'd deal with it later. Right now, his entire focus was on the pleasure of the woman bent over and waiting for him.

Smoothing the head of his straining cock through her wet folds, he was pleased she didn't require any artificial lubricant. Then positioning himself at her entrance, he smoothed his hands up and then back down the length of her spine. "Use those wonderful yoga skills of yours to relax, pet. Push back against me as I push forward." She nodded, and he heard her muted acquiescence as he slowly pushed forward. The heat from her body was melting his control. Sweat beaded on his brow as he struggled to hold back. The urge to bury himself balls deep inside her was almost overwhelming.

"Fuck me, you are so hot. You are burning a path all

the way into my soul, love. Feeling you pulling me deeper and deeper is the most erotic sensation in the world. Talk to me, pet." He could see the muscles of her lower back and ass trembling beneath her ivory skin, and his control evaporated. Thank God he'd already been close to the end, because he never would have forgiven himself if he'd hurt her. The slow pace he set wasn't going to last long, but he wanted to prolong her pleasure as much as possible.

"Oh my God, it's so good...naughty and probably addictive. More. Please. Harder. Please. Sir."

His knees almost folded in relief. "I aim to please, Princess." Quickening his pace and reaching around her to stroke her throbbing clit, he gave the command he knew she'd been waiting for just before biting down gently on the sensitive spot where her neck met her shoulder. "Come for me. Now, Savannah." Pinching her clit, he felt her stiffen beneath him as every muscle in her body seemed to tighten at the same time. Her muscles clamped him like a vice and rocketed him right over the edge with her. Brilliant lights swirled beneath his lids, and he wrapped his hands around her hips, praying his grip would hold him up without bruising her.

Surrendering to his need to feel her beneath him, Landon leaned over her. With his cheek resting against the side of her face, Landon could hear Savannah's labored breathing as she fought the aftereffects of another powerful release. Satisfaction laced with pride replaced the lethargy, and he pushed to his feet. Accepting the warm, damp cloth Kyle held out, Landon cleaned and dried her delicate tissues before pulling Savannah slowly to her feet. Gently untying the silk scarf, he kissed her closed eyes. "Open those beautiful blue eyes, pet."

Savannah blinked her eyes open, and everything in the room disappeared but the woman he'd just claimed as his own. She might not realize she was his, yet, but that didn't change the fact it was true. Her gaze moved to the edge of the stage, and her smile quickly eclipsed the candlelight bathing them. Glancing down, she sighed. "I love the smell of roses. Even though my mind was mush from…well, everything, I could still smell their sweet scent." He brushed his fingers over her blushing cheek and tried to commit everything about the moment to memory.

"I have some gifts for you, Princess. The first is a *temporary* collar because the people we'll be meeting with will be expecting it." He held the diamond choker in front of her and was pleased when her eyes widened in appreciation. Tobi stepped up behind her and lifted Savannah's hair while he latched it in place. The small gold heart at the front held a hidden tracking device—one he prayed they wouldn't need.

"It's lovely. Thank you for remembering. I should have thought to bring something."

He shook his head. "No. This is my honor and privilege. The heart has additional meaning, pet. The tracking device inside is for your safety. As long as you don't remove it, I'll always know where you are. If for some reason, we become separated, don't ever doubt I'm coming for you." Her eyes swam in unshed tears, and he used his thumb to brush away the one that eventually spilled down her cheek.

She wrapped her small hand around his wrist as she looked up at him. "I'll be waiting for you…I promise, I'll be waiting for you."

Chapter Twenty-Two

NATE GLARED AT the string of messages on his phone and cursed. God fucking dammit, he was swamped and didn't have time for this. Every lunatic this side of the Mississippi River had chosen tonight to show up at the club, and evidently, there was a new strain of crazy making the rounds. He and Taz had both been on their feet for hours putting out the fires of idiocy being lit by some pyro-demon who'd sent a veritable trail mix of fruits and nuts their way.

Sighing to himself, he wondered what was up. It was unlike his mother to send him a text during club hours and unheard of for her to be so insistent. But returning her call would have to wait until after he solved the cluster fuck playing out on the other side of the main room.

"Nate, there's trouble up on the second floor, also. Do you want me to handle it? All of the dungeon monitors are busy, and Taz is out back breaking up a scuffle."

Goddess! What the fuck? Before he muttered the blasphemous statement aloud, he nodded and thanked Mistress Anne for her help.

He was nearly to the scene area where two Doms were arguing about how to best discipline their shared sub when Kodi's hand grasped his arm. He was always amused when he glanced down to see her small hand barely spanning half the distance around his forearm. How she thought she could every hold him back was anyone's guess. "Master, I'm sorry to interrupt. I know you told me to stay upstairs, but this is really important."

Nate and Taz had both insisted she remain in their apartment upstairs because they didn't want her exposed to the insanity that had taken over tonight. As frustrated as he was by the interruption, he was sure she wouldn't have disobeyed them without a good reason. And given her close relationship with their mother, he'd bet next year's profits who was responsible for his wife's panicked expression.

Nodding to the dungeon monitor who'd just made his way through the crowd, Nate wrapped his arm around his wayward wife and led her from the room. Standing in front of the elevator, he gave her a stern look. "This better be Earth shattering, Ayasha." He saw her pale and cursed himself for the fear he saw in her eyes. Stepping into the elevator, he pulled her into his arms after pressing his palm to the reader. "I'm sorry, sweetheart. I'm not angry with you. I'm frustrated, but shouldn't have taken it out on the woman who brings nothing but joy into my life."

He felt her melt against him before he heard her soft chuckle. "I'm so going to remember you said that. I'll shamelessly use it as a Get Out of Jail Free card the next time I'm in trouble." It never ceased to amaze him how easily she could turn his entire day around. No matter what life threw his way, she always calmed the storm raging inside him.

Walking into their living room, Nate pulled out his phone and held it up for her to see the list of messages from his mother. He didn't say anything, just raised a brow in question. Her eyes went impossibly wide as she nodded.

"Yes. She was worried you weren't getting her messages. It's about your Nanna-son." His grandmother? For a moment panic flared as the thought of losing his beloved grandmother filled his mind. Kodi grabbed his arms and tried without success to shake him.

"Nate, no! Nanna-son is fine, but she's got an important message for you about Landon and Savannah's trip. You need to call your mom and get all the details." Relief washed over him, and he sagged into a chair. He knew he would eventually have to deal with losing her, but he was damned glad he didn't have to face it yet. Humbled by his emotional reaction, he gazed up into the loving eyes of his new wife and melted. The look of love and respect in her eyes made him grateful he was already sitting down.

Twenty minutes later, Nate sat at his desk, his laptop open to the video call he'd set up with Kent and Kyle West. Taz stepped into the room just as they were finalizing the change of plans. At his grandmother's insistence, they were sending a small medical team on a second aircraft. She been adamant they should not cancel the rescue mission, but she'd been equally committed to them sending another "bird."

Kyle was already typing on his keyboard before they'd even finished the call. "I've lined up a second plane, and we'll pull Ryan in if he can get away. Brandt won't go if Ry does, but we've got enough others on standby we won't have trouble filling out another small team."

"I agree. The message was very clear. We need medical back up." Nate was grateful neither Kyle nor Kent so much as blinked at the message from their grandmother. "I want you to know I appreciate the fact you're taking her warning seriously."

Kyle stopped typing and turned his entire attention to

the screen. "Don't forget we've had plenty of experience with gifted empaths. Peter Weston and your brother would make believers of even the most ardent skeptics." Nate had forgotten about Peter. He and his brothers were all gifted. Peter had been a part of the SEAL team that rescued Jen McCall several years earlier. "We never discount good intel—doesn't matter how unconventional the source." With a quick nod of his head, Kyle returned to the other screen, and Kent shook his head.

"I swear I keep thinking his people skills will improve, but so far, it's nothing but a fucking pipe dream. Please message me your grandmother's contact information. We'll send her a little something to say thanks and make a donation in her name to her favorite charity." Nate smiled, because knowing Kent West, there would be nothing *little* about their gesture.

Once they'd ended the call, Nate leaned back and stared expectantly at his brother. Taz shook his head as he started speaking. "Nanna-son never ceases to amaze me. She described Rafe's San Francisco clinic perfectly. She's never met him. We've never mentioned him. And we both know she has never visited his plastic surgery clinic."

Nate could only shake his head. "I'm not sure what to think. This is the first time she has ever given us such a clear and specific warning." Nate wished like hell they'd had this information before Savannah and Landon left Texas, but then he chastised himself for not be more grateful that they'd gotten any warning at all. Their staff had closed the club a few minutes ago, and Nate wanted to go upstairs and lose himself in Kodi's sweet body.

Taz grinned at him; his brother had heard him loud and clear. "I just sent her a text and told her the first thing I want to see when I step into the living room is her bare ass and pussy bent over the back of the sofa."

"She had a good reason for disobeying."

"Yes, she did. This isn't about punishment, although I am looking forward to seeing my hand print on her ass while I fuck her."

Nate chuckled as they made their way to the elevator. He and Taz were doing their level best to see to it she was pregnant as soon as possible. He'd be more than happy to do his part. "I'll make a snack for later while you play with her for a few minutes. Make sure she is primed and ready for both of us together."

Pressing his palm against the biometric reader, Nate looked forward to the scene that awaited them. When the doors slid open, he stepped into the room and felt his heart clench. *Perfection.* Their woman was pure perfection. She'd added black fuck-me stilettos and the clip-on clit jewelry they'd gotten her. The sparkling gem caught the light, and all of Nate's good intentions evaporated at the sight of their hot woman. "We'll eat later…" was all he managed to get out before he started shedding his clothes.

LANDON CHECKED HIS messages while Savannah was in the shower and wondered again why paranormal forces seemed to be interfering with his best laid plans. Jesus, Joseph, and Mary, he'd been worried about his mother's Voodoo buddies just a couple of days earlier. Now it was Nate's grandmother. In the great scheme of things, the additional back-up wouldn't be a problem—hell, under most circumstances, he'd say the more help, the better. But this wasn't business as usual…this was Savannah's beloved niece. And now that he'd finally pulled his head out of his ass and realized how much Savannah meant to him, he wasn't about to risk her life by having jets flying in from all over hell's half acre.

As he continued to read, Landon understood why Nate and Taz were so alarmed. Hearing that the older woman had given detailed information about Dr. Raf Newell's clinic was significant, to say the least. When the shower shut off, Landon closed out the message and set his phone aside. They would be landing in just under an hour, and he wanted to be sure Savannah was properly prepared. The slave jewelry he'd purchased for her was erotically beautiful and rife with symbolism. And even though he wouldn't ordinarily have a submissive wear these pieces for extended periods of time, he was going to enjoy putting each of them in place.

Setting the large velvet box on the bed, he leaned back to wait. With his ankles crossed and his hands behind his head, he would appear relaxed to the casual observer, but Savannah wouldn't be fooled. She would recognize a poised viper ready to strike when she saw one. Smiling to himself, he pictured her trying to contain her arousal as they made their way to the hotel. The *party* wasn't until tomorrow night, and he intended to put on a good show for the Alvarez spies he was convinced would be watching. There was a reason all invited guests were required to arrive at least twenty-four hours early and book rooms in the hotel owned by the Alvarez family.

Savannah stepped out of the small bathroom, her eyes widening in surprise to find him lounging on the bed. He shook his head when he saw the towel wrapped around her. "Drop the towel, pet. You are mine, and I like to look at what's mine." A lovely flush washed her cheeks as she loosened the knot, letting the towel pool at her feet. "Beautiful. Open for me." Her movements were slow and graceful, absolutely perfect, as she widened her stance and used her slender fingers to open the petals of her sex to his view.

"Your pussy is a lovely shade of dark pink this morning, pet. You didn't play with what's mine, did you?" He knew the answer but enjoyed very much seeing her struggle to decide how much to reveal.

"I was washing myself, and the touch reminded me of you. That made me…"

"Horney?"

"Yes." She still wasn't comfortable with the more crass words used by those in the lifestyle, and he enjoyed using them just to see her reaction.

"Show me how you touched yourself, pet. Lean against the wall behind you and show me." When she hesitated, he unbuckled his belt, the implied threat easy to read. She moved quickly into position and bent her knees, opening her folds. Seeing her fingers moving through the slick tissues made his cock swell until he finally released it from its confines.

"Sir?" Her eyes widened as he stroked his cock several times. Her pace quickened, and his gaze was riveted to the way she circled her clit with the pad of one finger. When a drop of pre-cum beaded at the tip, she moaned, "Oh, God. I want to touch you."

"And you will, but not until I am ready. You played with what belongs to me, and now you will play with it *for* me. I'm going to up the stakes, pet. We are on a short timeline so we need to finish this lesson quickly." Reaching to the side, he pressed the buzzer, knowing it would bring Carter to the bedroom. Answering the quick knock,

Landon summoned his friend into the room. He'd studied her limit list once again last night and had forgotten her interest in a ménage experience. This would be a good test of her readiness. It was entirely possible she'd be expected to allow the touch of another man during the party, and he wanted to be sure she would be able to handle it.

"Carter, my lovely slave took it upon herself to play with what is mine during her shower. Use anything but your cock to make her come. Do it in under five minutes and she will wrap those lovely lips around your cock and return the favor. If it takes over five minutes, she gets a free pass." Carter's eyes darkened, and Landon nearly laughed because there was no way she was going to last. James Carter was an experienced Dom with a penchant for eating pussy. He'd probably get her off in half the allotted time.

Kneeling in front of her, Carter moved her hands. "Lace your hands behind your back, sweetness. Perfect. Now, turn your feet out and bend your knees." Her yoga experience meant she didn't have any trouble maintaining her balance in the new position. Landon continued to stroke himself as he watched Carter do what he did best—rock a woman's world with his tongue.

"Eyes on me, pet." It was almost fun seeing her fight the losing battle to hold off her orgasm. In less than a minute, she was trembling, and Landon knew the second Carter pushed his fingers inside her juicy pussy because she fell back against the wall. Thirty seconds later, she was gasping for breath as the release she'd tried so hard to delay blew over her. It wasn't the devastating releases she'd had with him and damned if that didn't give him a ridiculous sense of pride. Her vision cleared quickly, and he smiled when she dropped to her knees.

"Thank Master Carter for the orgasm, pet. And then

show him how amazing that sweet mouth of yours feels when it's wrapped around my cock. He'll understand why I've been skipping our usual workout sessions."

After she'd thanked him, Carter held his hard cock in his hand and instructed her to place her hands on his thighs. When her hot mouth surrounded him, Carter groaned and leaned his head back, pure bliss etching his features. "Fucking hell, that feels so good. Hot, wet silk and her tongue is wicked." Landon found himself increasing the pace of his strokes as Savannah's mouth moved faster and faster over Carter's length. When she groaned around him, Carter's entire body went rigid, and Landon spilled his own seed into his hand.

Carter set his clothes right, pressed a quick kiss to Savannah's forehead, and ducked from the room. Landon cleaned himself and then helped Savannah smooth lotion over her entire body. "What's in the box?" Her question surprised him since he hadn't thought she'd even noticed it setting on the dark bed cover. Opening the oversized velvet jewelry box, he looked on as she took in the contents. She didn't say anything, but he could practically feel the questions swirling through her mind.

Taking it from her hands, he set it beside him on the bed and spread his knees apart. She didn't hesitate to move into position when his eyes flickered to the floor in front of him. Their hours of training were going to pay off, because her reactions would easily convince anyone watching that they'd spent a lot of time together. Palming what looked like small hoop earrings, Landon leaned forward and sucked her left nipple until it was drawn up into a tight bud. Slipping the first ring over the tip, he pressed the sides together until it tightened. Repeating the process, he smiled when her right nipple peaked even quicker than the left one.

"Stunning. Every time your dress moves over your pretty nipples, you're going to remember who you belong to, pet." And the sheer fabric was going to give anyone looking a peek at her luscious body. "I'd love to see your pretty nipples pierced. Decorating them would be such a pleasure." He'd had a friend fashion gem encrusted arm bracelets for her, and his cock hardened as he slid them in place. "Notice the notched area on each band, Princess? I've got lovely chains that will attach to both the nipple clamps and the bands, effectively binding your arms to your sides." He wouldn't use them when they attended the party, because he didn't want to restrict her movements.

"Foot up, pet." Setting her foot beside his hip, he leaned forward and sucked her clit into his mouth. A warm rush of her sweet cream dripped from his chin, and he groaned. "Fuck I want to spend the rest of the day playing with you, but I can feel we're already lowering in altitude." He pushed the two weighted silver balls deep inside and lowered her foot. "Turn around and bend over, Princess, I have one more piece for you before I let you get dressed."

"Oh God." Her shiver as she turned made him chuckle.

"The balls are partially filled with oil so they'll continue shifting even after you've stopped moving. Remember, you do not have permission to come."

"Are you sure you aren't a sadist?" She'd already bent at the waist in front of him, but he'd heard the whispered question anyway. He gave her a hard swat low on each ass cheek and smiled when his handprints bloomed bright crimson.

"You'd better stand up nice and straight, pet, or everyone will be able to see you've gotten a spanking." She shuddered but remained silent. "Spread your ass cheeks for me." Using the cream coating her pussy, he lubricated the small plug and fucked her tight rosette in slow strokes until she was right on the verge of coming before he pushed it fully into place. Giving her another quick swat before helping her stand, he smiled at her glazed expression.

"Your dress is hanging in the closet with the shoes I've chosen for you. I'll expect you out in the cabin in two minutes." He'd already covered the seat across from him with a soft towel. He planned to enjoy the view while they landed. He'd keep her mind occupied by updating her with the information Kyle had sent earlier, but her body wasn't going to be interested in anything but its need to come. He was going to love watching her try to reconcile two very different forms of stimulation.

Chapter Twenty-Three

SHE WAS GOING to kill him. Landon Nixon was going to die a slow, painful death, and she was going to enjoy every minute watching. *Assuming I can focus on something besides my pussy for more than thirty seconds, I'm going to find some way to make him suffer.* He'd been torturing her for the past hour, and every step she'd took along the sandy beach was winding her up tighter and tighter. He was blathering on about the remarkable sunset, and she was trying to focus long enough to plot his demise. *Can you say 'irony'?*

Landon's hand tightened around hers, and she realized he'd stopped walking. "Pet? You seem to be lost in thought. Care to share those thoughts with your Master?"

Well...actually, no. Taking a deep breath, she tried to blank her expression, but knew it was wasted energy. Lying had never been something she'd made a concerted effort to learn to do well. "If it's all the same to you, I think I'll pass."

Frown lines formed between his brows, and she knew she'd made a mistake. "I don't think so, Princess." *Holy shit.* His voice was pitched low enough no one passing by would have heard the ominous thread laced through it. She didn't ever remember seeing that particular look, and even in her highly-aroused state, she recognized how badly she'd screwed up. When she ducked her face, he tilted it back up until she was forced to meet his gaze. "Eyes on me, slave."

The significance of his change of endearment wasn't lost on her. Someone was nearby watching. That was all it took to snap here out of the emotional soup she'd been swimming in. "I was wondering why my Master is torturing me. The gifts don't actually feel like gifts now, Sir. And I'm afraid I was plotting ways to kill you...slowly." She'd whispered the last words and saw the twitch of his lips.

He used the tip of his finger to trace a line along the bottom of her collar without ever taking his eyes from hers. She recognized it for what it was...a reminder of who she belonged to. "Turn around and face the water, pet. I'm going to fuck you with my fingers, right here. There won't be a person on this beach who won't know exactly what we're doing. You want to come? I'm going to oblige."

Oh my God. She turned and sighed when he wrapped himself around her. "Seven o'clock and three o'clock, Princess. We've had company for the last ten minutes. They're reporting our every move. Open your legs for me." The seamless switch of topics surprised her, and it took her a few seconds to respond. "Now, Princess, or this is going to get a lot more public, and I don't think you want videos of me finger fucking you uploaded to every porn site on the web."

"No, my pleasure belongs to you, not every fool with a cell phone." She knew her words surprised him when he growled against her ear.

"Don't ever forget that, Princess. Come when you're ready, and then we're going back to the hotel for dinner." His fingers slid under her skirt and flicked feather light strokes over her throbbing clit. "During dinner, you'll kneel and eat from my hand. Keep your legs spread for my viewing pleasure no matter who walks up to our table."

Savannah was trying to listen to his instructions because she was certain they wouldn't be repeated, but fucking hell, it was hard to focus when her body was about to shake itself apart. "Please, Master. I'm so close." She'd turned her face so her gasped words were spoken against the side of his neck. Licking him below his ear, the salt of his skin ignited her desire, and her hips involuntarily jerked against his fingers.

"Greedy, girl. You'll get everything you're craving after dinner when you'll be coming for me alone." The message was clear. He didn't want to share their most intimate moments with the audience surrounding them. Several people had walked by and smiled when they saw Landon's hand moving under her skirt. One woman had flashed her breasts and given them a thumbs-up. But it was Carter stepping into her view that sent her reeling. His arms crossed over his chest, he looked every bit the formidable body guard he was.

Her body responded to his unspoken message. He wanted them to move it along, and Landon wasn't going anywhere until he'd proven to those watching that he was indeed her Master. Heat flashed through her like lightning, and her orgasm thundered on its heels like a herd of wild horses. Nothing could have stopped the storm, and when she felt herself soak Landon's hand, he snarled against her ear. "Fucking perfect."

SAVANNAH HAD NO idea how she'd managed to walk back to the hotel on legs that felt like they were made of rubber. *Holy crap on a cactus, Gumby has stronger legs than I do.* They made their way into the dining room, and she was relieved when they were led to a booth that was partially enclosed by a rattan screen. Kneeling on the cushion at Landon's feet had been a relief rather than a humiliation.

Landon's fingers lifted her chin. "Drink, pet." She gulped water from the glass until he pulled it out of her reach. "Not so fast, love. You'll make yourself ill." He was right, but damn, she was thirsty. When she heard the shuffle of feet nearby, she instinctively ducked her head.

"Trouble with your slave, Mr. Nixon?" A man's smooth voice filled the small space, and she fought the urge to look up to see who was speaking. Landon's fingers flexed in her hair, reminding her to maintain her position.

"Not at all, Mr. Alvarez. She is thirsty, and I'm simply reminding her that she is mine to care for." Savannah wanted to smile, but knew better. Damn, he was good. He'd taken the truth and spun it into the perfect answer. If their table was bugged, there would be no question that he'd told the truth...even though his truth sounded much better than the unedited version.

"Very well. She's lovely, and she seems to be quite well-trained. I'm surprised you are seeking a replacement. I'd be happy to help you find a new Master for her." Suddenly, his voice lost its cultured tone and became much more sleazy.

"Thank you for the offer, but I'm not looking for a replacement for my lovely pet." His fingers threaded to the ends of her unruly hair before returning to her scalp and repeating the sensuous gesture. Savannah knew it would appear as if he was petting her, but she recognized the soothing gesture for what it was...and attempted to calm her jangling nerves. "I'm looking for an additional slave. I'm demanding, and it is often too much for one." *Oh brother, he's laying it on a bit thick now.*

"Understood. She is stunning and reminds me of my own sweet sub. There is something familiar in her fragile beauty. I'll leave you to your dinner and look forward to seeing you tomorrow evening. Perhaps you'll do a scene for our guests. It's always a pleasure to see a slave's deep devotion to her Master." There was malevolence in his voice, and a dark foreboding moved through her. A scene that would showcase devotion wouldn't be anything lightweight, and she fought the shiver that vibrated just beneath the surface. She breathed a sigh of relief when he finally walked away.

Landon tipped her face up and nodded. He hadn't smiled, but his pride in her shone brightly in his eyes. "Well done, pet. Now let's eat and retire for the evening, shall we? I believe you've earned a reward."

Something tells me he isn't talking about one of those secret-spy decoder rings Cracker Jacks was always promising.

LANDON WANTED TO sling his dinner against the wall. He'd been leery when he saw Marco Alvarez walking toward him. Knowing he was going to be under surveillance was one thing. Having the target of his investigation approach him the night before the operation was entirely different. Watching Alvarez walk away, Landon let out a long breath, grateful Savannah had kept her eyes on the floor. The other man had already mentioned that she reminded him of his own submissive. He saw no reason to let him get a closer look before they had to. The team had discussed the family resemblance between Savannah and

Amaryllis, but decided to use it to their advantage. He'd need to make sure he paid particular attention to blondes at the party to lend credence to a preference for a certain *type*.

After several long minutes, Landon realized he hadn't said anything to Savannah since Alvarez's visit. He'd fed her from his hand, but had been so distracted he hadn't said a word. Fuck. This was the reason Tally often accused him of being the world's worst dinner companion. Tilting her face up to his, Landon chastised himself for her worried expression. "I'm sorry, Princess. I've completely neglected you during our dinner."

"Did I do something wrong, Sir?" Damn, he was proud of her for remembering they were still out in public. He'd been worried about her ability to maintain her cover, and she was showing him up at every turn.

"No. You've done everything right. I'm distracted by business, but I promise to reward your patience." He knew the odds of their booth being wired were astronomical, so he'd been careful with his apology, but he'd make sure she understood once they were in their suite. Playing the radio while they were in the shower would shield any conversation from any electronic monitoring the team found in their room. He wrapped his hands around her upper arms and lifted her to her feet. "It gives me a lot of pleasure to feel the slave bands around your arms, pet."

"They were a beautiful gift, Sir. I'm proud to wear them." The look in her eyes told him the words were sincere, and for the first time, he held out hope convincing her to stay after this was over might not be as daunting as he'd feared. As the elevator doors slid closed, Landon spun her into his arms and fisted her hair so her mouth was perfectly angled for his kiss. The man who'd shadowed them all day stopped the doors and slipped in as Landon lowered his mouth to hers.

Savannah kept her hands to her sides as she'd been taught, and damn if Landon wasn't anxious to help her *unlearn* that particular skill. He wanted to feel her hands on him. Although, having her small fists knotted in the front of his shirt right now would probably snap the tattered threads of his control. He had no intention of giving the man shadowing them a peep show in the elevator. He plundered her mouth, taking care to keep her face averted from the man's appraising stare.

The doors opened, and Landon held her against his side, shielding her as the stepped out. Once they were inside their room, he pressed his finger to his lips, silencing her before she'd gotten the chance to ask what had possessed him to act like a lunatic. Nodding to Carter, he noted the electronics sweep in his hands. He led Savannah into the room and looked at his friend expectantly.

"Sir, the room is wired for sight and sound. Monitor your business conversations while in this area. I wouldn't want any of your current projects compromised by the lack of security. I'd suggest you make other accommodations if you return."

"I will, and I'll spread the word to my friends. I'm disappointed to learn our host has taken upon himself to become a Peeping Tom. As a Dom, I'm disappointed I won't be able to enjoy my lovely slave in all the ways I'd hoped. And as a businessman, I'm pissed as hell that I can't make important calls due to the lack of privacy. I've half a mind to load up and move on. This isn't the only source for what I'm seeking." And truer words were never spoken. He'd gladly get right back on the jet and leave if Amaryllis Fitzgerald's safety wasn't at stake.

He stalked to the mini bar and poured a drink he had no intention of drinking. Throwing it against the wall in a show of rage, he fought back a grin at the expression on Savannah's face. She'd known it was an act, and the effort it was taking her to not smile was easy to see despite the quick step she'd taken behind Carter. To anyone watching, she'd appear to be using the other man as a human shield, but Landon knew she was hiding her amusement.

Shifting his attention to Carter, he pasted a scowl on his face. "Put a scrambler in the bathroom and get someone up here to clean that up." Turning his attention to Savannah, he held out his hand and softened his tone. "Come, pet. We're taking a shower together. I want to fuck you, and I don't need it videotaped and broadcast all over the internet." Leading her into the shower, he noted her shudder when he stopped abruptly. Fucking hell. He'd forgotten about the weighted balls in her pussy. Christ, it was a miracle she hadn't killed him.

He didn't fully trust the small device they were using to scramble the electronic monitoring equipment, so he made sure there was enough steam in the room to obscure the cameras before stripping her of the short dress he'd given her to wear so many hours earlier. With the radio playing to block any recording equipment not crippled by the scrambler, he leaned close and spoke against the warm shell of her ear. "Fucking amazing. You take my breath away."

Her hands fumbled with the buttons of his shirt before it opened and her hands slid inside. The cool touch of her fingers over his warm skin sent goose bumps racing over the surface. "I know we're supposed to be working, but my body can't take any more. Please do something."

"I fully intend to do quite a lot, but first, I want to apologize for how this day has gone. This is not at all what I had in mind. And I certainly shouldn't have left you suffering so long from the toys." He loosened the nipple clamps slowly while sucking the abused buds in soothing strokes.

Kneeling in front of her, he removed the balls and plug before pressing a soft kiss atop her swollen clit. He felt like a first-class jerk. Some Dom he was. He'd left the devices in place far longer than he should have, and through it all, she'd remained a true professional.

Moving her under the shower's warm spray, he soaped her hair and massaged her scalp until she was weaving on her feet. "Feel good, Princess?"

"Oh, so good. I'm going to melt into a pile of goo if you aren't careful."

Chuckling, he finished conditioning her long locks and then turned his attention to moving his soaped hands over every inch of her body. He brought her back up to the pinnacle, but this time, he sent her tumbling over, catching her in his arms when her legs folded out from under her. Wrapping her in a warm towel, he stepped from the shower and set her on the cool marble countertop then returned to finish his own shower.

Within minutes, he had exactly where he wanted her—naked and under him. "I've been waiting for this moment all day, love."

"I need you to fuck me, please...Sir. I'm sorry. I try to remember, but my desperation is louder than my memory." Oddly enough, he wasn't inclined to argue the point, because he was dealing with the same thing. His need to feel her clasping him, milking his cock of every drop of seed far outweighed his need for her to follow protocol.

Whispering against her ear, Landon coaxed, "Tonight, forget the rules. Forget the roles we're playing and let me make love to you, Savannah. I haven't had vanilla sex in a very long time, but I don't think I've forgotten much."

"I'll help you if you lose your way. First step, kiss me." Her airy voice made his cock jerk against her bare mound, and he heard her gasp just before he sealed his lips over hers. This kiss wasn't an out of control raging inferno. This was a slow seduction, and he wanted her to feel the difference all the way to the tips of her pretty pink toes. Without releasing her lips, Landon shifted position so the head of his cock slipped effortlessly through her drenched folds.

"So wet for me. Your honey is molten hot and twice as sweet. Let me love you, Savannah." He pushed himself in to the hilt and groaned at the heated clasp of her vaginal muscles as she stretched around him. "Fuck, love, your body was made for me."

"More. Please. If you don't move, I'm going to die."

"I aim to please, Princess." Pulling back until the rigid ring around his cockhead teased her opening, he paused for several seconds before setting a slow pace.

"Oh, yes. So...good. But too slow."

"Like it hard and fast, do you?" Her groaned agreement made him smile. "You are a greedy girl, and that makes you fucking perfect. But even though we're making love, we're still doing it on my timeline. And I want to savor you just a little longer." That wasn't entirely true. Jesus, he was dying to fuck her as hard and fast as he could.

Long minutes later, she was begging, and he couldn't hold out any longer. Her pulsing muscles were more than he could fight, pulling him deeper as she screamed his name. Nothing felt as good as this—*nothing*! And he wasn't going to give it up—not without a fight.

Chapter Twenty-Four

SAVANNAH SAGGED WITH relief when Landon announced his bag of torture devices had already been sent to the waiting jet. "No, Princess, I need your head clear tonight. We have one mission...get in, get your niece, and get out. The other officials will round up everyone else. We're only taking Amaryllis. Above all else, I'm focused on your safety." She knew he wouldn't hesitate to pull her out if things got dicey, and oddly, she wasn't angry at what could easily be considered high-handed behavior.

After leaving the hotel, they'd gotten a call informing them that other law enforcement agencies were standing by. It seemed the Alvarez family had stepped on the wrong toes, and the locals were no longer willing to ignore what was going on right under their noses.

Every nerve in her body felt like it was vibrating at a different frequency, and she was having trouble sitting still in the back of the limo. When she looked up at Carter, he lifted a brow in question. "Sorry. I'm nervous. I haven't done many field missions, and this one is so terribly important." He nodded, letting her know he understood. Savannah hadn't aspired to field work until her brother had insisted she wasn't suited for it and pressured her superiors to bench her. In her view, Brit was turning out to be every bit as overbearing as their parents. Amy had always demanded more freedom and seemed to wield much more power in her relationship with her father than Savannah had ever managed.

Driving through the estate's large gates sent a shudder through her. Landon turned her face with his warm hand, forcing her to focus on him and not their surroundings. "You'll be fine, Princess. Carter and I will not let you out of our sight. You're wearing two tracking devices, and if they insist on removing them, Carter will take you to the waiting jet, and I'll finish alone. No one is going to remove them."

Ten minutes later, Landon's resolve was tested when Marco Alvarez's staff insisted her collar and arm bracelets were removed. "No. This is not up for discussion. I do not take the safety of my slave lightly, nor do I share. I protect what I own." The guard standing in front of them appeared annoyed, but pulled a phone from his pocket and spoke in rapid-fire Spanish. He was obviously consulting someone further up the food chain, and it wasn't long before a man in a tux stepped into the reception area.

Landon reiterated his insistence she remain collared, and that the slave bracelets remain in place. "I will not risk losing an asset I've paid a lot of money to own." Turning to Carter, Landon's clipped tone made his frustration clear to the crowd surrounding them. "Take her back to the jet and secure her inside. Alvarez will just have to do without the scene he was looking forward to." The comment had the desired effect, and even with her eyes lowered, Savannah saw the men both flinch.

For a few seconds, she thought they were going to let Carter lead her from the room, but before she could cross the threshold, Marcus Alvarez's voice boomed through reception area. "Why is Mr. Nixon's slave leaving?" Landon wasted no time explaining, and Savannah felt their host's gaze move over her. His look was appreciative, but as odd as it sounded, she didn't feel as though it was sexual. She felt more a piece of art he was admiring than a woman dressed in little more than a transparent piece of gauze masquerading as a dress.

"Mr. Nixon, does your sub have any devices my staff doesn't already know about?" Savannah knew exactly what he was asking, and she held her breath hoping Landon didn't offer to prove that she didn't. But...no such luck.

"Present yourself, slave." Without hesitating, she bent at the waist and used her hands to part her ass cheeks. The position was beyond humiliating, but she was grateful he'd made her practice the move so she'd been able to block out all the people milling about. *You'll never see them again...you'll never see them again.* Savannah chanted the words in her head as Landon slipped his fingers into her empty pussy before sliding them into her ass.

When he finally pulled her back to her feet, her head spun for a few seconds. He kept a hand on her elbow until she was steady, and they moved into the main room. He leaned down and lightly bit the shell of her ear. "I'm so fucking proud of you, Princess. You were perfect." His words of praise embarrassed her more than being bared to a room full of people. But when she considered it, it made sense because he was the only one whose opinion mattered.

"Thank you, Sir." His lips slanted over hers, and she could feel his frustration. He didn't like their circumstances any more than she did and wondered if he'd ever forgive her for putting him in this position.

An hour later, they still hadn't seen Amaryllis. Savannah was beginning to worry Alvarez wasn't going to risk bringing her into the room. The slaves that were for sale were easy to spot, because they were nude and sported thick collars. Each carried a sheet of paper Savannah assumed listed their vital statistics. She'd only been able to catch fleeting glimpses of a few of them, but each one appeared to have been drugged to the gills.

"Ten o'clock, boss." Carter's voice was tight, ratcheting up her concern even as she hoped he'd spotted her niece.

"We'll wait for them to move closer. Any attempt to position ourselves will throw up red flags. Alvarez hasn't gotten where he is today by being stupid." Before she could sneak a look, Landon turned her in the opposite direction. "Don't. She is fine. The dress she's wearing is modest, and that confirms our source's suspicion Marco intends to keep her for himself." His entire body went rigid, and she wondered what had happened.

"Fuck. I was hoping his old man wouldn't be here tonight. Juan Alvarez is a paranoid bastard." Landon's words were whispered so quietly she might not have known he was speaking if she hadn't been facing him. "Doesn't matter. We'll get her out. It just isn't going to be as easy as I'd hoped."

"They're headed this way."

"Kneel, Princess. It will keep your face out of view, and the old man will assume it's a show of respect for him." He turned her a quarter turn as she dropped gracefully to the floor and spread her knees. Her hands rest atop her thighs, and Savannah breathed a sigh of relief when the dress fluttered in soft folds over her sex.

"Very nice, Mr. Nixon. Your slave is well-trained. My son told me you are hoping to add another, and I've heard you have an eye for blondes. It's unfortunate my son has decided to keep this one for himself." The minute the older man had started speaking, Savannah's stomach turned over. She recognized his voice. The name he'd given her when he'd accosted her in the elevator at the Agency wasn't Alvarez, but her mind was racing so quickly she couldn't remember what he'd told her it was. She could barely remember to breathe.

A few seconds later, her memory started to clear. He'd asked her to join him for dinner, and she'd declined despite his claim to be a longtime friend of her supervisor. *Yeah, that turned out to be a crock. Nemesis was a more accurate description of their association.*

She didn't dare move. Men like Juan Alvarez didn't forget a woman who'd turned them down. The conversation continued as the older man attempted to convince Landon to look over their available offerings and submit an early bid. "There are twice as many buyers as slaves, so they'll sell quickly."

Amy seemed to falter as Marco's warning was snarled from her side. "Father, enough. You are upsetting Amaryllis. I won't have it." Savannah's mind was filled with questions, and the urge to grab her niece and sprint to the door was almost overwhelming.

Chapter Twenty-Five

"MARCO, I'M VERY thirsty. Could we please find something to drink?" Amy's voice sounded airy, and for a minute, Savannah wondered if she'd recognized her. But when she wobbled in the stilettos she was wearing, Savannah knew she'd been drugged. Amaryllis Fitzgerald could dance backward down the steps of Lincoln Memorial in the pouring rain in those damned shoes and never miss a step. She'd been wearing sky high heels since high school. The only places she wore anything else was in the gym and on the beach.

"Are you okay, sweetness?" Carter was kneeling beside her, but he wasn't close enough for her to explain without being overheard. His warm hand cupped her shoulder, and she fought the urge to look up when he instructed her to.

"Red." The word had barely been a breath of air, but she'd felt his fingers flex. This time he leaned much closer when he repeated the question. "No. I've met the father. He will recognize me."

His muttered curses let her know he'd heard her. "Boss, your slave is ill."

"Ill?" Landon immediately knelt close, and she hoped he was blocking Alvarez's view when she used her fingers to flash 911. Thank God he hadn't questioned her. "Carter, I'll need a subbie blanket and a bottle of water." She heard

Carter's retreating steps, but the black dots dancing in her vision were making it hard to see anything. "Breath, slave. You are not allowed to damage what belongs to me."

Later...much later, they were going to have a long conversation about that damned word. Saints and sinners, she hated the word slave. But right now, she was counting the command as a blessed reminder and sucked in a deep breath.

"There is a first aid station near the entrance, Mr. Nixon. I'm afraid the local hospital will not meet your standards." Savannah bet it wouldn't. And the man standing so close she could smell his ghastly after-shave wouldn't risk being exposed. He'd make sure they went directly to the waiting jet. What the old man didn't know was the local authorities were already focused on uncovering the truth about the Alvarez mansion.

Landon wrapped the blanket around her shoulders. "Up you go, pet. I'm going to ask Carter to accompany you back to the jet." She kept her chin against her chest and fought back tears. *Fucking hell, how has this happened?* She'd seen a picture of Juan Alvarez, but it had been so old she hadn't recognized him as the sleazeball who'd crowded her into the corner of the elevator.

Carter clutched her arm so tightly she'd likely have bruises...*assuming you get out of this place alive.* They'd only covered half the distance to the door when a woman bumped in to her, and Savannah instinctively looked up to apologize. That one microsecond slip was all it took to bring the house of cards tumbling down around her.

"Savannah?" Amy's voice sounded from several feet away. She and Marco were standing between them and the door.

"How do you know Miss North, *mi pequeño la flor?*"

Amaryllis must not have heard the hard edge in his voice, because she didn't hesitate. "She is my aunt." Turning back to Savannah, Amy flashed her the same goofy smile she always had when she'd been drinking. Two steps, that was all Amy took when the entire world slowed, and Savannah looked on in horror as pandemonium broke out.

Someone behind her shouted her name, but she didn't have time to react before Juan Alvarez's voice thundered around her. "Marco, let me introduce you to Special Agent Savannah North *Fitzgerald*." The emphasis he put on the last word made the younger man blanche.

"Marco, I'd like to introduce you to Savannah. Oh my God, I'm so happy to see you." Amy started toward her again, but screams filled Savannah's ears just as her niece's eyes went wide with fear. Savannah looked to the side for Carter, but he was being pulled away by several men she assumed were Alvarez's goons. Marco launched himself in front of Amaryllis at the same moment Savannah was stuck from behind by what must have been a runaway truck. As she flew to the floor, the crack of gunfire sounded from a few behind her, and a man's grunt of pain in her ear made her heart clench.

Several shots rang out, and she watched in revulsion as red bloomed over Marco Alvarez's white shirt and he fell to the floor. Amy was bent over him, crying hysterically and clutching his limp body against her own. Savannah pushed the heavy weight off her and turned to find Landon lying in a growing pool of blood. Yanking the blanket from around her, she pressed it against the wound in his shoulder and nearly fainted when she saw the slice that started near his left cheek and continued over his ear.

The gaping cut fell open as he turned to call out to

Carter, and the sight of his skull between the edges made her gag. "Get her out of here. Fucking get her out *now*."

What? No! She wasn't leaving him bleeding on the floor. He could just forget that right now.

"No. I'm not leaving you. Carter can take Amy out. I'll leave with you." She'd no more than spoken than a muscled arm wrapped around her waist and she was lifted into the air. She screamed at the man sprinting toward the door, rage replacing the fear she'd felt a few seconds earlier. Carter never paused as he plucked Amaryllis off the floor, unceremoniously throwing her over his shoulder and running out the door.

"Put me down. Marco! Oh God, I'm so sorry. I didn't know she was coming. Let me go, you big oaf. Marco! Please don't die."

"If he's not already dead, he will be soon. He caught one right over his heart. Nothing you can do. Now stop fighting me before I tranq you."

"She's already been drugged. Don't give her anything." Savannah wasn't sure what they'd given her, and any mix of meds could be deadly. Carter tossed them both into the back of the nearest car, shoved the chauffer out of the way, and roared down the drive.

Amy threw herself into Savannah's arms, sobbing so hard she worried the younger woman would be ill before they reached the airport. She could hear Carter talking on the phone and knew both planes were waiting with medical personnel, and Savannah hoped they had something to numb the pain squeezing her chest.

The car bounced over the rutted highway, and Savannah reached over to latch Amy's safety belt. Not bothering with her own, she stared out the window and let the tears flow unchecked down her face. One mistake…less than a blink in time was all the inattention needed to cost one man his life and seriously injure another. How could she have been so stupid?

The car slid to a stop, and both rear doors were pulled open before it finished rocking. Carter pulled Amy into his arms and moved to the Nixon's large jet. "Come on, sweetheart. You'll feel better as soon as we get you cleaned up." Savannah was surprised at the soft tone of his voice and wondered if he realized how sweet his words sounded.

"Agent North?" She glanced up into the concerned eyes of a man who looked a lot like Jen McCall's husband. "I can tell by your expression you've met my brother, Sam. I'm Sage McCall, Special Agent. Let's get you on board, and then we'll make sure none of this blood is yours."

The entire flight home was filled with questions and debriefings. She'd finally been allowed to clean up just before they landed. Watching Landon's blood swirl down the drain of the marble shower set off a tsunami of tears. She had no idea how long she'd knelt on the floor, but the water was ice cold when she heard Carter's curse.

"Jesus fucking hell. Come on, sweetness, you're going to catch your death of pneumonia. Landon will kick my ass if he finds out I left you in here alone." He turned off the water and wrapped her in a bath sheet before pulling her to her feet. Picking her brush from the counter before leading her into the bedroom, he ordered her to sit and then moved behind her. He patiently detangled her long hair and laughed. "I'm getting really good at this. I just did the same thing for Amy. She's scared of Sage, called him a giant, and wouldn't let him near her. I think she must be the only woman in the world who didn't immediately fall at his feet. Damn, I think I'm in love with her."

Savannah appreciated his attempt to lighten the mood,

but the emotional edge she was riding was too sharp to risk lessening the tight grip she had on her restraint. When the floodgate finally opened, she was going to cry until she collapsed...and she didn't want anyone to witness her breakdown.

Her brother met them at the small airfield when they'd landed to avoid the press. Brit thanked her for bringing his daughter home and then lifted her sleeping form from Carter and walked away. He'd gotten in his car and driven away without so much as asking how she was or how she would get home. *Typical.*

Sage McCall looked at her with sympathy in his eyes. "Damn, sugar. You brother is a real dick." His blunt words and spot-on assessment of her brother were the straws that snapped her restraint, but it was hysterical laughter that bubbled up, not tears.

She heard Carter asking her if she was okay, but she couldn't answer. Sage shook his head at the other man. "I've seen this with Jen. Get her home ASAP. She's going to crash, and she needs to be in her own space when that happens."

The ride home was short, and before she realized it, she was standing alone in her living room. Leaning with her back against the door, she slid to the floor and let the flood of emotions overtake her. Sobbing into her hands, all she could think about was how hard it had been to leave the man she loved. *Loved? Oh hell. I've fallen in love with Landon Nixon.* How had she let herself do something so foolish?

Running her fingers over the diamond choker she still wore, she remembered his promise to find her...his reminder that he'd always come for her. That small comfort was all she'd needed to let go. Curling into a tight ball, fatigue battering her from all sides, she let his words play through her mind until the darkness of sleep pushed everything from her mind.

Don't ever doubt I'm coming for you

Epilogue

Six weeks later

WIPING THE SWEAT from her eyes, Savannah executed another round house kick before dropping to the mat. She'd been taking her frustration out on the bag hanging in the corner of her gym for the past two hours, and she still hadn't found the relief she was looking for. "Fuck a waddler. It's supposed to numb my brain. What the hell is wrong with me today?" She'd been working out every day since Carter left her on the doorstep of her living quarters and walked away without a word. He hadn't even told her whether or not Landon had made it safely to San Francisco. Nope. Nada. Not a damned word, and she'd been going insane ever since.

She'd been called in to the Agency's DC headquarters, questioned for hours, and then summarily fired. Outrage had filled her, and without even asking, she knew her brother had been to blame. It had taken her almost an hour of browbeating her boss, but he'd finally admitted her brother's influence was behind her release.

Jumping to her feet, Savannah kicked the bag with enough force to send it swinging into the wall. Just thinking about what Brit had done made her madder than hell. And, of course, her cowardly brother had been too busy to meet with her for the past five frick-fracking weeks. But his time was running out. She planned to attend his annual charity gala in a few days. If he wouldn't talk to her in private, he could face her in front of his stick-up-the-ass friends. "You can't hide forever, big brother. I will hunt you down like the dog you are...even if you seem more like a shivering Chihuahua than an overly protective German Shepherd."

"Princess, I'm not sure what you've got planned, but I'm certain he has it coming." Landon's voice sounded from behind her, and she spun so quickly she stumbled into his arms. He didn't seem put off by the fact she was soaked in sweat...his arms wrapped around her, and for a few sweet seconds, Savannah forgot she was pissed at him, too. He must have felt the shift in her emotions, because he set her back and smiled. "Let's have it, pet. All of it. Right here. Right now. We need to get this over with so we can move on to something more pleasant."

When she didn't answer, he ran his fingers along the collar he'd given her...the one she hadn't been able to bring herself to remove. The reminder was clear; she belonged to him as long as she wore the beautiful gift he'd given her. It didn't matter it was supposed to be for show, and they both knew it.

His eyes flickered to her upper arms, and he frowned. Wrapping his large hand around her bicep, he looked at her with his brow raised in question. "They won't stay on when I'm working out." She silently cursed herself for answering...after all, she was still madder than a hornet about being whisked off to the east coast while he'd gone the opposite direction. No need to point out how much weight she'd lost. He wouldn't have missed the way her workout clothing bagged around her.

"They'll be fine soon enough. Now, spit it out. All of

it." The command clear...he knew she was angry, and he wanted it all out in the open.

Fine. She'd be happy to accommodate him. "You let Carter drag me away from you. I begged him to let me stay, but he wouldn't listen." She stomped her foot in frustration when she felt tears welling in her eyes. Dammit, she'd promised herself she would tell him exactly what she thought of him if she ever saw him again.

"I did. Continue." To his credit, his expression hadn't changed...if he'd so much as smiled, she swore she'd shoot him herself.

"You didn't call me." And there it was. The very bottom line. "I've been so worried. And so very lonely. And you just abandoned me." Tears streamed down her cheeks, and she cursed her emotional reaction.

He frowned and nodded once and then pulled her into his arms. "Finish it, Princess. If you're angry, you must learn to say so. Be honest with me...be honest with yourself."

"How could you leave me so easily? I thought we had something special. You broke my heart...*again*." Her words were muffled by his crisp, white linen shirt, but she was sure he'd be able to hear her. "I felt rejected...tossed aside. You promised you'd come for me"

Firm hands gripped her shoulders and pushed her back so he could look in her eyes. "And I have." His thumbs brushed the tears aside, and he gave her a sad smile. "I've been calling you since the moment I got out of surgery. I knew you'd left your cell phone in Montana, but it wasn't until yesterday I discovered your family wasn't relaying my messages."

"Messages?"

"Oh yes, my sweet girl. Messages, flowers, and an unused plane ticket." He'd finally gotten Karl to call and find out what the fuck was going on. The household staff had been much more reluctant to lie to a United States Senator. His friend had volunteered to drive out to the Fitzgerald's and talk to Savannah, but Landon had already sent a message to his pilot. He was in the air in less than two hours.

"I don't understand. Why? Why didn't I know?"

"That's a question only your parents can answer."

She went from confused to furious between one heartbeat and the next. "I made the mistake of answering the door the morning after I was unceremoniously dumped on my front porch. My mother took one look at me and told me I belonged on the K Street sidewalk." He didn't have to ask. He already knew the woman who'd given birth to her had called Savannah a whore, and his blood boiled.

Taking a deep breath, he stepped back and took her hand. "I've come to bring you home, Princess. Let's go." He started leading her to the door, and she seemed to finally realize what she was wearing and stopped. Shaking his head, he picked her up and continued walking to the door. "You can shower after we take off. And Carter and Ellen have already packed your clothes and personal effects." When she blinked at him in surprise, he laughed. "We arrived just as you started your work out. Fuck, I didn't think you were ever going to wear yourself out, Princess."

When she sagged in his arms, Landon was flooded by relief. For the first time in six weeks, he felt content. The days he'd spent in Rafe's clinic after the surgery to repair the damage to his face and shoulder were some of the longest of his life. Letting Carter drag her away from him as she cried and begged to stay was the hardest thing he'd done in his entire life. For the first week, he'd assumed she was simply angry and refusing his calls. Once he learned she didn't have a phone, he'd begun calling her parents' home and gotten one excuse after another. When the ticket he sent her went unused, he'd been discouraged and close to giving up.

It had been Nate who'd suggested he ask Karl to call. Ten minutes later, he had his answer and was on his way to Washington. They'd arrived early this morning, and Carter had shaken his head when he discovered she'd left the front door of her small apartment open. Smiling to himself as he climbed into the back of the limo with Savannah cradled in his arms, Landon found himself looking forward to watching her pay for that mistake.

The End

Books by Avery Gale

The ShadowDance Club
Katarina's Return – Book One
Jenna's Submission – Book Two
Rissa's Recovery – Book Three
Trace & Tori – Book Four
Reborn as Bree – Book Five
Red Clouds Dancing – Book Six
Perfect Picture – Book Seven

Club Isola
Capturing Callie – Book One
Healing Holly – Book Two
Claiming Abby – Book Three

Masters of the Prairie Winds Club
Out of the Storm
Saving Grace
Jen's Journey
Bound Treasure
Punishing for Pleasure
Accidental Trifecta
Missionary Position

The Wolf Pack Series
Mated – Book One
Fated Magic – Book Two
Tempted by Darkness – Book Three

The Knights of the Boardroom
Book One
Book Two
Book Three

The Morgan Brothers of Montana
Coral Hearts – Book One
Dancing with Deception – Book Two
Caged Songbird – Book Three
Game On – Book Four
Well Bred – Book Five

Mountain Mastery
Well Written
Savannah's Sentinel

I would love to hear from you!

Website:
www.averygalebooks.com/index.html

Facebook:
facebook.com/avery.gale.3

Twitter:
@avery_gale

Made in the USA
San Bernardino, CA
22 November 2017